HOLLYHOOD

"*Hollyhood* is a masterfully told story about Hollywood
from a unique African-American perspective.
Valerie Joyner takes you into the world
of being a sitcom writer with an unforgiving honesty
and truth-filled memorable characters.
I dig it!"
—Devon K. Shepard
Writer/Producer, *Weeds, Everybody Hates Chris*

"In *Hollyhood*, Valerie Joyner delivers
all the juice that's fit to print.
She craftily untangles the lives
of Hollywood's rich and so-so famous
with enough sass, smarts and savvy
to make you care for these sometimes twisted souls
from beginning to end."
—Cori Murray
Entertainment Director, *Essence*

By Valerie Joyner

HOLLYHOOD

HOLLYHOOD

VALERIE JOYNER

AVON

An Imprint of HarperCollins*Publishers*

FIRST AVON PAPERBACK EDITION PUBLISHED 2009.

Designed by Diahann Sturge

Library of Congress Cataloging-in-Publication Data
Joyner, Valerie.
    Hollyhood / Valerie Joyner.—1st ed.
        p. cm.
    ISBN 978-0-06-166244-7
    1. Television programs—Fiction.   2. Television actors and actresses—Fiction.
    3. African Americans—Fiction.   4. Hollywood (Los Angeles, Calif.)—Fiction.
    I. Title.
    PS3610.O98H65   2009
    813'.6—dc22
                                                                        2008043381

09 10 11 12   OV/RRD   10 9 8 7 6 5 4 3 2 1

For Mel Wayne Joyner
I can still hear you laugh

Acknowledgments

I am not a writer who works alone. Many have assisted me on this journey. Thank you Eric Felder and Judy Dent for always listening and letting me talk it out. Thank you Carol Passariello, Dr. Yoland Sealy-Ruiz and Eisa Ulen for critiquing my work with kindness and respect for the craft. Thank you Nichelle Tramble, Mondella Jones and Michele Rubin for guiding me through the business of publishing. Thanks to my early fans. My friends who liked *Hollyhood* before it was even finished: Susan Boyd, Anietie Antia-Obong, Erin Robinson, Jennifer Bartok and Rachel St. Leger. Thanks to Lisa Simunovic for having my back between the hours of nine and five. Thanks to Devon Shepard, my muse. You influenced me far more than you ever imagined. Thanks to my loyal and faithful friends who were always there reminding me how much they believed in me and my writing: Valari Adams, Jennifer Jones, Claudette Best, Jamie Stewart, Janice Johnson and Chris Leonard. Thanks to Tillie's of Brooklyn for providing a space for me to write. Thanks to Frederick Douglas's Creative

Arts Center for providing a place for me to learn. Thanks to my editor, Esi Sogah, for your wit, your guidance and your gift for words. You make me look good. Thanks to all of my friends who have supported me over the years. Thank you to ALL of my family. It is because of you that I am.

HOLLYHOOD

1

Ty lowered the volume of his CD player and braced himself for an interrogation as his Range Rover slowly rolled toward the security gate.

Rojas, the security guard, poked his head out of the glass booth and started his usual battery of questions. "How are you today? How's the show coming? I sent my headshot over to your office, did you get it? What roles are you casting for this week? You think I could get an audition? Yeah, I've been talking with the casting director but I'm not getting anywhere with her." The buttons of his gray uniform shirt threatened to expose the beer belly that rested a good three inches beyond his belt buckle. In his mind, even in Hollywood, his gut was an asset, affording him opportunities to play character roles skinny guys would never land. After all, who ever heard of a slim plumber?

Ty slid his hand over his shimmering, bald head to cue Rojas that thirty seconds had passed and his patience was coming to an abrupt close. One thing he admired about the security guard/wannabe actor, he was persistent and never wavered. Once a week he could count on Rojas detaining him at the studio gates like a suspect. Ty would have had him fired had his ego not savored the attention. As an executive producer of a sitcom for two years, his days of begging someone to read his scripts were firmly imbedded in his memory, and he still possessed an ounce of compassion for the struggling artist.

"Send your headshot over to my assistant and follow up with her," he offered.

Rojas gave a satisfying grin. "All right, Ty. I will. Have a good one, man."

Ty accelerated past the security booth onto the Rex Studio Lot. It resembled a huge university campus. He'd spent countless days and nights dreaming of working in a big studio like this one, of having his name painted on the curb of his personal parking space. But now that the dream was a daily reality, he no longer noticed the vast, green manicured lawns that looked like expensive carpet, the meticulous layout of the colorful flowers and the lofty pine and palm trees that strategically lined the buildings. It was just another sunny day in Southern California, and he couldn't have cared less whether his designated parking space had his name on it as long as it was in front of the production office. The only thing that mattered now was the prominence, the power and the paycheck.

Checking the time, Ty jumped out of his truck and walked briskly. Like every Monday morning of a tape week, there was the compulsory table read. The entire cast, along with the guest cast for the week, read through the script to give it a test run, to see how the words on paper translated onto the characters' lips. It was a private rehearsal for the show staff and executives. Anyone worth his or her weight was required to attend. Ty moved briskly through the glass doors of Building 33 and headed upstairs with his blond Timberlands pounding the steps and balancing his six-foot-one frame. The table reads never started on time, but he always arrived at least fifteen minutes early. As the only black executive producer at Rex, he figured the network was waiting for him to stumble a bit and that was the last thing he intended on doing.

Aside from others expecting him to fail, Ty himself worried his power might be slipping. The show was in its second season and the ratings had dropped by three points. Television was nothing more than a numbers racket; the number of episodes, the number of advertising dollars. And without a consistent ratings figure, the sum of all figures equaled zero.

Low ratings were every producer's nightmare and the prerequisite for a show cancellation. And once your show was cancelled, there was no telling when you might work again, especially if you were black. There were only two African-American sitcoms on the air at present, and the other was produced by white guys.

So the situation was precarious for Ty, even if he did have the highest-rated show among blacks. The entertainment industry was so iffy, so insecure, so contingent upon people's moods and the positioning of the planets. There was just no way of knowing what would happen next in your career. Whether you were a production assistant or the star of the show, it didn't matter. Tyrone was one of the best and on top of his game, yet he had to hustle every day, like a hooker working a corner.

He trekked down the long halls lined with large-as-life cast photos of shows produced by Rex over the last twenty years. He made a right turn by *The Wonder Years* and entered the conference room. Using his index finger, he slid his Gucci sunglasses closer to his face. The smell of coffee and fresh baked goods floated through the room along with the sound of chitchat and laughter. All of his writing staff was present, including his co-executive producer, Maxwell. He pounded fists, handed out half smiles and wassups to everyone in his path as he made his way to the craft services table that was loaded with bagels, croissants, donuts and cereal. He gazed at the food in search of something to tempt his taste buds.

"Mornin', Boss," Venus, his assistant, said.

He looked around. "Hey, Venus. You got the ratings from last night?"

"Yep," she answered and handed him a single sheet of paper.

He glanced at it. "Send someone out to get me some Starbucks. Caffè Americano, two shots espresso, low-fat milk."

"Sure."

"Where is Leede?"

"I don't know. I haven't seen him." *And it's not my day to watch him.* Venus turned to walk away, twisting her lips.

Ty's eyebrows furrowed. The star of his show was close to being late again. How many times had he told him how important it was for him to be prompt? That it was too early in the Hollywood game to get comfortable? He made a mental note to speak to him about it again. This is why he hadn't wanted him for the show in the first place. Leede had a reputation around town for getting high and closing down joints every night of the week. Yeah, he was funny and talented, but who needed the headache of having to clock a star? The network executives had chosen him, but what did they really care? They wouldn't blink about firing him or cancelling the show. They'd tell the NAACP's president, "We tried having black shows but they just don't work out."

While maneuvering his way to the conference table, Ty spotted Sid Porter, one of the studio execs. A buppie by anyone's description, Sid had graduated from Harvard cum laude. Trained and educated to use his left brain, he'd failed to have any success using his right brain. Frustrated, he found himself behind a desk working in Current Programming, overseeing shows and throwing in his two cents' worth of creativity when possible. What he really wanted to do was produce. But for some reason that didn't come as easily to him as number crunching and analyzing ratings did. He was nice enough, but Ty didn't trust him to take his rottweilers out for a piss. Most of the other studio and network execs were white or Jewish men who were part of the old-boy network. They had their own interests to protect.

"Hey, buddy. Did you see the Lakers this weekend?" Sid patted Ty on the back, imposing on his personal space. Ty's body stiffened in response. He never liked the way Sid violated his personal space, standing so close one could question whether he meant harm or good. A move like this could get Sid seriously injured where Ty came from. Ty took a deep breath and relaxed. "Yeah, man. I've been telling you, the

Lakers are going all the way again this year. Nobody in the east or west can stop Kobe. Nobody."

He spoke with the authority of an NBA coach. A season ticket holder for three years now, it was against his religion to miss a home game. He loved the game as much as he loved rubbing elbows with the who's who in Hollywood. All the heavyweights and half of the welterweights in the entertainment industry held season passes at the Staples Center. The closer you were to the purple and gold paint, the more clout you had and the deeper your pockets. At present, Ty held eighteen-thousand-dollar seats in the lower stands, but he had every intention of working his way down to the floor alongside Jack Nicholson, Dyan Cannon and Denzel Washington.

Sid, a pessimistic fan, rebutted. "They played a good game against Philly, but you give them more credit than they deserve. They've had their slump and they're likely to choke and have another. I wouldn't bet too much money on 'em if I were you."

"I'll bet my life savings in this lifetime and the next. And if I find out you bet on 'em, I want ten percent for the tip." Ty gave a friendly chuckle and walked away.

Before seating himself at the table, he slipped through the crowd to greet the guest star of this week's show, Cell Block. His hair was cornrowed from the temple back, revealing a sharp widow's peak and a face so hard he looked like he'd spent three consecutive decades in the pen. His jeans hung from his narrow ass like a pair of hand-me-downs and his blue Sean John sweatshirt fell like a sack over his slim frame. With the exception of the gold chain and diamond-laced charm

around his neck, Cell Block could have been cast as a slave in
Roots in his oversized, secondhand-looking clothes.

Ty extended his fist toward Cell Block. "What's up, man?
Glad to have you on the show."

Cell Block lifted his chin and pounded Ty's fist. "I'm aight.
I dig the show, man. The shit is funny."

"Thanks. It should be a fun week."

"I'm lookin' forward to it."

"I know this is your acting debut, but you're used to the
cameras. Try to relax and enjoy it."

Cell nodded.

"If you need anything, just holla. We'll get started in a few
minutes."

"Cool."

Cell Block was the hottest gangster lyricist, getting twenty-
four-hour rotation on MTV with his hit album, *Serving Double
Life*, which was number one on the Billboard Chart. His first
CD, *Testimonies from the Cell Block*, with the hot single, "No
Longer Dreamin' About Parole," had sold more than two mil-
lion copies.

Ty silently prayed Cell Block and his crackhead-looking cro-
nies in the corner would not cause any headaches during the
week. Rappers, like rock stars, had the tendency to be trouble-
some artists. Most were unaccustomed to following any rules
except their own, the ones declared in the street. Well, at least
he was on time, which was more than could be said of some
others. Ty glanced at the door, on the lookout for Leede.

Ty sat at the head of the large conference table and exam-
ined the ratings. The show had only rated a five point nine on
the previous night. A five point nine wasn't bad, but he had

an ego and wanted more. At its peak the show was getting a seven-point-five share, which was uncommonly high for a black sitcom. They weren't exactly *The Cosby Show* numbers, but no other black show had come so close. Ty removed his sunglasses and scanned the script in front of him. The drop in ratings made every episode a personal challenge. The network wasn't applying any pressure yet, but he could smell it coming.

He glanced up from his script to check out the new arrivals. Seated at the table to his far left was Naja Starr, the female co-star of the show. Her stage name was just par for the course. She sat perched on her seat, sipping Evian water like she was the star, when actually this was her first real acting role. She was a beautiful girl with a body that curved everywhere it counted. Her long, sexy legs supported her forty-inch bust and lioness-brown hair. Carrying more density on her upper body than the bottom, she kind of looked like a lollipop. Men saw her on TV and drooled, while women envied her. Neither was aware that her voluptuous bust was as artificial as her wild cascading hair. Fake or not, any man in the room and even a few women would gladly lick that lollipop any day of the week.

She'd started out as a dancer, performing in numerous videos before she took up acting classes and landed herself an agent. She had a better chance at hitting the lottery than winning an award for her acting. She was far from the best, but she was smart and used other skills to create opportunities for herself. For instance, once the table read started she'd scoot her chair up real close and spread her D-cups all over the conference table.

Ty usually enjoyed her creative performances offstage. It was a reminder of why he'd cast her in the first place. Every sitcom needed a bombshell to capture the attention of the male audience. When she glanced over at him his ego whispered, "She wants you." From his point of view, every woman in the room wanted him because he was rich and the HNIC, Head Nigger In Charge. A man with power, capable of launching careers with a single phone call. And like any man with power and pussy at his fingertips, in due time he'd explore all of his "fucking possibilities."

But Naja was no cheap possibility. After only one successful season on the show her ego had been altered. She'd come back from a three-month hiatus high on some type of diva amphetamines, demanding special provisions when renegotiating her contract. The studio had already upped her ante by seven thousand dollars per episode, but she demanded more. Her wish list included a personal assistant, organic fruit in her dressing room and more story lines centered on her character. Ty had mulled over her list for all of thirty seconds before telling her agent, "No." Had she been an established TV star, he and the studio would have jumped through flames to appease her. But for an up-and-coming actress to make such requests was ludicrous. She would have to spread more than her D-cups to convince them.

Ty carefully scanned the room, noting the executives taking their seats. There was Gary Ackerman, the network executive, David Levine, also from the network, and Stacey Morris, from the studio, who worked along with Sid. As they made small talk amongst themselves, they caught Ty's roaming eyes, waving their watches as if to say, "It's time to get

started." For the second year in a row, they had all been as-
signed to oversee his show. It was their job to make sure *Same
Day Service* was on track. That's how they would have ex-
plained it anyway. Ty would say they were paid to make his
ass ache. They were nitpicking people who understood very
little about story development and even less about his black
characters.

Ty felt a vibration in his pocket. He pulled his cellular
phone from his velour sweat jacket and examined the caller
id. It was Leede. Without any change in his facial expression
he answered, "Where you at?"

"I'm pulling onto the lot now."

"Peace."

Leede's mother should have named him "Late." He'd prob-
ably call the undertaker from his casket on the day of his
funeral, reporting delays. He was earning eighty thousand
a week and he still couldn't arrive on time. What more in-
centive did he need? Ty made another mental note: suggest
Leede hire a driver. He underlined the word "suggest." That's
all he could do. As the star of the show, Leede basically did
whatever he wanted to because it was *he* who Americans in-
vited into their homes every Sunday night. This alone gave
him power above all else.

Those standing closest to the door got a good whiff of
Leede before he actually reached the conference room. The
aroma of seventeen various plant blossoms from his Aveda
cologne filled whatever space he didn't. It always preceded
him and announced his arrival.

"What's up, people!" He strutted in with his chest out, loud
and late. He smiled, handed out handshakes and pounded

fists like a politician campaigning for office. He'd have kissed babies had there been any present. Leede loved attention and being late put him at center stage.

He wore a bright red, yellow and white leather racing jacket with black stripes running from the tunic collar down to the sleeve. Underneath, he had donned a white T-shirt made from Egyptian cotton, boots from Brazil and tailor-made black leather pants. The ensemble had worked for him last night at the Sunset Room, but in the light of day he was overdressed, no matter which way you looked at him.

Underneath the jovial entrance Ty saw the fatigue weighing down Leede's eyelids, could see last night's booze on his face.

Leede took his seat at the conference table. The sound of paper shuffling filled the room as everyone opened their scripts to page one and the table read began.

There was a natural chemistry between Leede and Naja that enabled the show to work. Her lack of experience was overshadowed by his impeccable comedic timing and his exceptional acting skills. Though he played a funny guy on the show, his acting range was so broad, he could have played any role he wanted, comedic, dramatic or anything in between. When he hit his comedic groove onstage, he could make Naja look like a novice. Combined, they constructed the blueprint for a conventional comedy team. He was Laurel and she was Hardy in a dress.

During the read Leede delivered his lines with vitality, though he was sleepy and hungover. The other cast members did likewise. His energy was always high and he forced others to elevate their performances.

Cell Block was clearly nervous, though he wore a hard gangster mask on his face. His delivery was stiff and flat. Ty had the good sense not to give him too many lines in the script. Though it was a growing trend, Ty never liked the idea of casting rappers or any other music talents. Making a video was one thing. Shooting a television show was another. Limiting his lines had been paramount. Still, it was only his first day. Ty hoped he just needed time to warm up his acting chops.

There was phony, raucous laughter around the conference table as the writers laughed at their own jokes. It was a self-patronizing act, but they had to. If they didn't think the script was funny, who would? The network execs would have blasted them all for writing a bullshit script that even they didn't think was funny. So they busted their guts to pump up their egos, to support the actors and to prove to the suits they were worth their ten-thousand-dollar-a-week salaries.

It was in the middle of a big hee-haw that a panting young production assistant hustled in and handed Ty his Caffè Americano, two shots espresso, low-fat milk.

2

The lively read turned into a serious conference once the stage managers ushered the writers and cast members out of the room a half hour later. The only people left at the big table now were Ty, Maxwell, Leede, Gary Ackerman, Sid Porter, David Levine, Stacey Morris and Venus, who was taking notes. It was time for the network and studio suits to throw their two cents in the pot. Ty resented the input of four people who wrote nothing more than emails most days. People who held business degrees and knew nothing more about story development than what they'd learned taking crash weekend courses from Robert McKee, books they'd purchased from Samuel A. French, or a class at UCLA Extension Center. And thanks to preferential hiring, here they were serving as judge and jury of his show, when he'd spent eight years writing on various sitcoms, honing his skills. He could piss better ideas than they could think of collectively.

The story outline had been submitted to the network weeks earlier for approval and now they'd smile and rip every line apart. Ty leaned back in his chair, raised his chin slightly and stroked his goatee like an old man.

"I like the story, but I'm not feeling Cell Block," Gary said.

Ty didn't flinch. "His delivery wasn't what one would call smooth, but it was his first day."

Stacey chimed in. "It's not his performance per se. It's just I don't think he projects the right image for the show. I mean, think about it . . . would Naja's character really fall for a street thug?"

David agreed. "Yeah, he's very angry-looking."

"Many young white girls between the ages of fifteen and twenty-five have not only fallen for Cell Block, but they've also paid his rent by purchasing his CDs," said Ty. He was always prepared to defend his choices.

"Yeah, but it's the whole jail image that bothers me. I don't know if it works for the show," David said.

"Is he going to wear his hair braided when we tape?" Gary asked.

"Have you seen MTV lately? Everybody is wearing corn-rows except Eminem. And he wishes he could," Maxwell laughed.

"He'd be perfect if we were filming Oz. But this isn't HBO."

"And I wouldn't fall for him and I don't think the audience will either. His clothes, his hair, his image—he's just too . . ." Stacey's voice trailed off.

"Too what?" Ty calmly asked. He loved putting them on the spot. Making them verbally express their suppressed racist thoughts.

She paused, searching for a nice way to say *too black*. ". . . Too ethnic."

"I don't think Cell Block is going to shoot or cut anybody this week, if that's what you're worried about," Ty replied.

Sid made light of it. "Of course not. But he should have his arms covered during taping. There should be no visible tattoos."

"So, let me get this straight. Cell Block is too ethnic for a black sitcom. That doesn't make sense," Ty argued.

"I just don't think he's going to help ratings," David said.

"You guys approved of the casting," Ty replied.

"Yeah, but that was before we saw him. Maybe wardrobe and hair can clean him up a bit," Gary said.

Venus fanned the pages of her pad as the conversation heated up.

Ty smirked. "I don't think that's going to fly with Cell."

"As much as we're paying him, he should be able to fly." Cell Block was being paid far more than scale for a guest star. He was getting what his face was worth.

Maxwell jumped in. "Do ya'll know who Cell Block is?"

"Of course I know who he is," said David.

There was silence. Ty had a feeling the suits weren't at all familiar with Cell Block.

"Does this mean you're against getting rid of him?" David asked.

"Absolutely. What other notes you got?" Ty said.

The suits read from their list of notes, which covered everything from the use of curse words to changing the B story.

"Naja's character doesn't have many lines this week," Sid said.

Leede interjected, "It's not Naja's show."

Ty silently looked on. Every week Sid was at the table fighting for Naja. She must have been swallowing his dick whole.

"I think Leede should have more jokes. He's acting too serious in scene two," Gary said.

Ty said, "Nobody walks around making jokes all day. His character is not one dimensional. I never intended for his character to be a replica of George Jefferson."

There was more silence. It was clear the suits thought the audience would only accept these black characters if they were constantly funny—shuckin' and jivin'.

"That's all I've got," Gary announced, bringing the meeting to a close.

"Me too," David said.

"It should be a great show this week. Good work, guys," Sid threw in.

Stacey smiled and started packing up her briefcase.

The guys all walked out the door making small talk and chuckling like old friends. The disputes were a routine part of a workday. It was the same as the senators and congressmen debating on Capitol Hill, then toasting to each other at happy hour. It wasn't personal. It was business and all in a day's work. Ty and Maxwell walked out, while Stacey and Leede lingered behind, chatting.

Ty and Maxwell walked across the sidewalks lined by the green carpet of grass on the lot as they made their way back to the office. Maxwell's shoulder-length locks swayed back and forth as his long, gangly body sauntered along. Standing at six one, weighing in at one hundred and sixty pounds, he could have posed as a weeping willow tree on the lot. He maintained his slim stature by keeping a strict diet. He consumed no meat, no fish, no poultry, no cheese, no milk and no butter—the only animal derivative he ate was pussy. Originally from Oakland, Maxwell thought of himself as down to earth and spiritual. The Asian girls he dated would say he was nothing more than a spiritual hustler dressed in chic, hippie clothing.

Ty had put up a big fight with the network to get Maxwell hired. They'd tried to shove a white boy down his throat as co-executive producer. Somebody to oversee Ty and report back to the suits, but he wanted a strong writer at his side. One he totally trusted, someone to watch his back when and if he wasn't looking. In general, he never discriminated any more than the world around him forced him to. With the studio fanning its big, white hand so much, he'd become a Nat Turner, always planning a revolt. He didn't have a problem hiring white writers provided they were good. He had two, but he didn't need one standing over his shoulder, overseeing his show.

Ty realized his success was part talent, part timing. Prior to Spike Lee and John Singleton, it was rare to find young men like him or Maxwell writing for sitcoms, regardless of talent. But he, along with many other boys from America's hoods, came up after the success of *Jungle Fever* and *Boyz in the Hood*. Now he and Maxwell were two of the many influencing the art of television and film and changing Hollywood into Hollyhood.

As Ty and Maxwell continued their walk to the office, Leede caught up with them. Though he was five eight, he looked like a midget standing between the two long-legged men. "That Stacey Morris is fine. I'd love to get my mouth on them big titties!"

Ty and Maxwell gave him a you-can't-be-serious look and laughed aloud.

"Get outta here," Ty said.

"You wouldn't have half a chance in hell with that girl." Maxwell mocked her voice. "I wouldn't fall for a black sitcom star. Oh, how repulsive."

They all laughed.

"That's why she needs some good lovin'. One night with me and next Monday she'll be singing the title song."

Ty and Maxwell had to stop and laugh again at that one.

"I know y'all thinking she's a stuck-up, preppy chick. But I see a woman who needs to be unleashed. She's probably buck wild under the sheets. Hell, she probably doesn't bother with sheets. Just a beast."

Ty shook his head. "I don't see it."

"See, you don't have the X-ray vision I have. Cell was checking her out too."

"Cell can definitely forget it," Ty said.

"Don't sleep. Jermaine Dupri got Janet Jackson. I rest my case," Leede said.

"Pu-leaze. She wouldn't give you the chance to smell her pussy," Maxwell said.

"That's where you're wrong, dawg. And I'm going to prove it to you."

"Aw, hell no! That's all I need, you pissing her off," Ty said.

"It'll be smooth. She won't even know what hit her."

"You won't know what hit your ass when the studio hits

you with a sexual harassment case and makes you remember your color!" Ty said.

"For real," Maxwell agreed, still laughing.

"I was just kiddin', dawg. I'm going over to the stage and crash in my dressing room. I'm tired as hell. Last night I got some stage time at the Comedy Store, then . . ."

Ty interrupted him. "Leede, you gotta do better getting to the table reads on time."

A frown easily formed on Leede's tired face. "What? I was there. I'm here. What are you talking about?"

"Come on, man. You called at five after. Why don't you get a driver?"

"'Cause I ain't P. Diddy. I don't need a driver. You know I don't like all that formal bull. I keep a low profile." Leede didn't like the extra people tagging along behind him everywhere he went, at least not for the sake of protecting and clocking him.

His entourage was made up of flunkies who did what he told them to do. Not people who told him what to do and where to be and at what time. On rare occasions, he preferred to be alone. During the first season, he'd been threatened by a crazed fan who constantly called the show. Even then, he settled for carrying a .38 in the glove compartment of his car rather than hiring a bodyguard.

"You keep being late and we'll all have lower paychecks. You feel me? It's only season two." Ty held up two fingers.

Leede shrugged, annoyed, then hitched a ride with a passing PA over to Stage Six. Ty and Maxwell headed toward their offices.

When Ty entered his office, the phones were ringing off the

hook, as usual. There was always someone on the line trying to get a piece of him. His agent called about the screenplay he was trying to sell. Other people's agents called to see if he was looking for new writers. Struggling writers called to see if he'd read their scripts. Actors and actresses called to see if he'd received their headshots or to invite him to a play they were in. Publicity called to ask him to do interviews. Charities called for contributions. Producers called about doing lunch. His mama called to ask Venus if he was eating properly. His cousin called to borrow more money. One of his brothers called from the dealership to ask if he'd co-sign on a car again. His father called from time to time when he'd had a drink or two. His old friends called asking him to invest in business ventures. His childhood friend, Boogaloo, called collect from jail, hoping Ty could help free him. His girlfriend, Sasha, called to check up on him. Ty was a wanted man in LA County and the San Fernando Valley.

He picked up a stack of messages from Venus's desk and ran off a list of things for her to do. "Call and see if Donna can come over and give me a manicure today. And see if you can't get Kiko to come and give me a massage. Wednesday would be good. Maybe after the casting session." He paused, thinking. "See if you can get me two comp tickets for the House of Blues next week. RSVP me for Al's birthday party." He dug in his jeans pocket and pulled out a receipt. "And pick up my dry cleaning when you get a chance." He paused, remembering his manners. "How was your weekend?"

"It was good."

"Oh, and drive my car over here. I left it parked at the other building." He dropped his keys on her desk.

"Okay."

He fanned through his messages as if they were a deck of cards. "Anybody I need to call back?"

Yeah, all of them! Ty was notorious for not returning calls. And every call he didn't return meant a headache for Venus. Did you give him my message? Why hasn't he called me back? Just let me hold. Yes, I can hold all day if that's what it takes. Do you know this is the third message I've left for him? Did he get my script? Did he read it? What did he say? Is he interested? *Interested? Did he call you back?*

Venus knew more about Ty's business dealings, personal and otherwise, than he did. By default he left it up to her to determine what was most important, who he should get back with and when. Sometimes she minded. Most times she didn't. Just twenty-five, she was only two years into the entertainment business. Every Hollywood day was still exciting, even if her boss was a pain in the ass sometimes. Chatting with celebrities, sitting in on the network meetings, hanging out on the stage during rehearsal, overhearing gossip about folks in the business. She would have gladly come in every day on time and done the job for free.

The position as his assistant had basically been about getting her baby toe in the door. She stayed for the promise of things to come. Venus wanted to be a writer. She'd been taking weekend writing workshops, reading up on the subject and had two spec scripts under her belt that she'd slaved over. All she needed was a break and she hoped Ty would be the compassionate soul to give her one. She was just waiting for things to simmer down over the ratings.

When she'd interviewed for the job, she sat nervously, running her fingers down the nape of her neck. Ty's confident and commanding presence caused her to doubt herself and she struggled to spit out the lie she'd conjured in response to his question, "Where do you see yourself five years from now?" *In your job*, she thought. But her friend, Melody, had advised her, "Don't tell him you want to be a writer. These producers like complacent assistants who won't pester them about getting ahead. Of course it's ridiculous, but they are ridiculous people." Melody had been an agent trainee at William Morris for two years. So, Venus had refrained from spilling her dreams of being a writer/producer like Ty and made herself out to be a non-ambitious country bumpkin. As their relationship graduated from co-workers to semi-friends, she had dropped hints, here and there, of her goals. Whether he paid her any mind, she wasn't exactly sure. One could rarely guess what thoughts were running through Ty's bald head.

But she wasn't putting all her hopes in him. She developed her own contacts in Hollywood, sitting in Ty's office each day, answering his phones. If he didn't hook her up, it's likely one of his contacts would. It was her second season with him and she already knew fifteen people in Tinseltown: agents, writers, struggling writers, actors and directors. No matter where she went, shopping on Melrose, brunch on Sunset, rollerblading in Santa Monica, she bumped into someone she'd met through *Same Day Service*. Not bad for a country girl from Houston, Texas. She'd already sent her spec scripts to two agents who called the office incessantly. Who knows? If she landed representation, she might tell Ty to pick up his own damn dry cleaning and move *her* Honda!

She jotted down Ty's instructions and made a few notes to herself, like follow up with potential agents.

"You should call your agent. He's trying to set up a meeting with Paramount."

"Call the stage and cancel rehearsal for today. We've got rewriting to do."

Ty grabbed the *Hollywood Reporter* and *Variety* and headed into his office.

Maxwell sat in his blandly decorated office, tapping a number-two pencil on a pad, waiting for his agent, Barry Rueben at Creative Talents, to jump on the line. Barry had been representing him for two years and thus far had done next to nothing to advance his career. Seeing as he was pocketing ten percent of his salary each week, Barry should have been the one sitting on hold. Maxwell resented his agent collecting a portion of his income when he didn't even have to sell him for this job. Ty requested him. Had he been thinking, he'd have simply hired an attorney to negotiate his deal. But it was too late for all that. He was stuck with Barry until his contract ended. Until then, he'd pester him like a fly at a picnic.

The hold music ended as Barry picked up the line. "Hey, Max. How's it going?"

"It's going, Barry. Just not fast enough."

"Your script went over well, I presume."

"Ya know, the regular notes from the network. Not too much rewriting to do. So what up with my pilot script? Have you heard anything from CBS yet?"

"They passed."

"How about Warner Brothers?"

"They passed too. Just keep your panties on. Your day is coming."

"I thought we had a pitch meeting set up with Rex this week?"

"We still might. Don't worry, Max. You'll know when I do."

"All right."

"You take it easy, buddy."

"Yeah. You too."

Disappointment covered his face as he placed the receiver on the cradle. His career was too important for him to be overly concerned about the ratings on the show. Sure, he loved working with Ty, but he was anxious to step out of Ty's shadow and have direct light shine on his face. Maxwell and Ty had worked and written together for several years but Ty was always the front man receiving the accolades. Maxwell desperately wanted his own show. He wanted the credit of "created by" and the hefty check that accompanied it. He longed for a large office with designer furniture and a view. Not the small, glorified closet filled with studio furniture that had been passed down from one show to another. The dilapidated upholstery had an energy no amount of feng shui could clear.

Ty and Maxwell met ten years ago working as production assistants, their first gig in the business. As PAs, their responsibilities began and ended with whatever anybody ranking higher than them wanted. And that meant everyone. The lowest on the totem poll, they worked the longest hours for the least amount of pay. Something about copying, making coffee and running errands for eighteen hours a day bonded people. Working side by side in the trenches, the two shared their hopes and aspirations to make their stamp on Hollywood. They worked as a writing team for years, working up the ranks from writer trainees to producer status before breaking off and working independently. Now here they were, Ty, a showrunner, with Maxwell as his right-hand man.

Ty had written his one contractual script at the beginning of the season, but it was Maxwell who was in the writers' room beating out script ideas, day in and day out. It was Maxwell who kept the jokes coming while Ty lived his Hollywood life, getting manicures and massages. Ty didn't spend nearly as much time in the writers' room as Maxwell, and resentment had taken root and started to blossom.

He had two brilliant pilot scripts floating around Tinseltown. Two, and no one was calling his agent anxious to strike a development deal. He'd meditated about it, had one of his spiritual teachers from church bless the pages, burned candles and gotten on his knees and begged the universe for divine guidance and favor. And still nothing.

He was blankly staring at the Zen book on the corner of his desk when he heard a tap on his door. "Come in."

"Wassup, Buddha," Zack, a PA, said. He slipped through the door and shut it. He noted the serious look on Maxwell's face. "You in here meditating? What's that incense you burning? It smells good."

"Nag champa."

Zack shrugged. "Okay. I'll take your word on it. Looks like you could use this little gift I got for ya," Zack announced as he made himself comfortable in the chair across from Maxwell's desk. Zack dug into the pocket of his baggy jeans and pulled out a white piece of paper carefully folded into a small square. He tossed it across the desk and flipped the bill of his Yankees baseball cap. "That's for you, my man."

Maxwell snatched the folded paper. He stood up and shoved it in his pants pocket. "So what's going on?" he asked as he sat back down.

Zach slouched with his legs spread open. Zack was a white boy of the hip-hop generation, with his extra-large T-shirt and double-X basketball jersey layered over it. "Yo, I can't believe Cell Block is on the show this week. I delivered his script to his crib. Maaaan, you should see how he's living."

"His crib is phat?"

"Hell, yeah. What did he sell? Like two million CDs or some shit like that. He's paid."

"Hopefully, his fan base will mean a boost in the rating. That's the plan."

"His latest CD is off the meter. I'm not one for autographs and corny shit like that, but I might have to ask. He might put me in his next video. Wouldn't that be a trip?"

"Just don't get in his way. It's not cool for the crew to be all over the guest."

"Chill out, Buddha. It's just an autograph."

"I'm just saying."

"Okay, man. I hear you."

"How's it going? The job going okay?"

"No major mistakes, if that's what you want to know."

"Good, 'cause if you want to get into the guild and become a stage manager you're going to have to keep a clean record," said Maxwell, dangling a carrot in front of Zack.

"Why are you always sweating me? I know that. And you know you can't keep these pompous people happy. Okay, so a brother was late delivering lunch once."

"I'm just trying to keep you straight. I want to see you get ahead."

"Yeah, whatever man. I have to go."

Zack was up and out within seconds.

N aja's small dressing room was like any other on Stage Six. They were all standard hotel-like rooms filled with furniture that looked rented and used. There was a beige sofa, a dated coffee table with a partial glass top, cheaply upholstered chairs, a mirrored vanity and a small white refrigerator. She'd given her room some personal touches, with scented candles, two ficus plants and the fresh flowers she had delivered each week. One week, white or yellow roses. The next week, stargazer lilies or gardenias. She'd specifically asked for one of the four flowers, though she never knew which would be delivered. She'd given the florist special instructions to surprise her. It made her feel special, as if someone had sent them to her. During the second month of production the florist did just that, by overlooking her request for roses and stargazer lilies *only* and sending her a vase of calla lilies instead. She phoned at once and gave the owner a performance from her Brooklyn days, cursing him out like he'd pickpocketed her purse on the A train. The Asian owner apologized over and over again, but it didn't matter. His accent only served to piss her off more. When Naja got revved up, she was slow to cool down.

She reached into a cabinet, pulled out three jars of baby food and a spoon, then sat on the sofa. She shoved spoonfuls of the slime down her throat. She was starving. Everything on the craft services table at the reading was far too fattening for her restricted diet. What would be the point in spending all that money on a personal trainer if she was going to blow it on bagels and croissants? If she blew it on anything, it would be some mouthwatering homemade biscuits, not bagels. Baby food was better, easy to digest and easy on the waist and hips. And definitely better than being bulimic, she reasoned. She was making a healthy choice; baby carrots, baby spinach and baby peaches for dessert.

She meticulously counted the fat content of everything she ate, and avoided carbohydrates as if they caused cancer. Her mother and all three of her aunties had been lean, curvaceous women in their twenties but had eventually expanded to full-figured women, wearing clothing sizes that started with the letter X. There was little doubt in Naja's mind that the fat gene was swimming in her DNA, and temporarily dormant. She feared one day it would awake from years of slumber, yawn, and blow her rear end up to the size of a 747 aircraft.

The camera added ten pounds to her lean frame. That was the one disadvantage of her job. Who wanted to look ten pounds heavier than they actually were? If she added more to that, her career would equal a zero. And that just wasn't going to happen before she got a chance at being the star of her own show. That's what she wanted, what she dreamed of day and night. Why not? She was good enough and popular enough.

She screwed the tops on the empty baby food jars, placed them in a plastic bag and deposited them in her purse to be discarded later. She couldn't run the risk of someone finding her empty jars. She picked up the phone and dialed Sid's cell.

Sid was zooming down Wilshire Boulevard in his blue convertible Beamer, headed toward Beverly Hills for lunch. "Hey, what's up?" he answered.

"How'd the notes go today?"

"The usual. Nothing special."

"I was just going over the script again. I swear, Anita has more lines than I do." Anita played her best friend on the show, and Naja counted and compared her lines with the other actors each week like a statistician.

"I mentioned the lack of lines in the meeting."

"And?"

"They've got some rewriting to do and they said they'd work on it," he lied. Sid appeased her any way he could in order to get what he wanted.

"They'd better. There are two stars on this show."

"I agree, honey. I really do. But my hands are tied."

"How are we going to sell the idea of me having my own show if I can't carry an episode on this one?" she complained.

"Don't bitch at me. I'm on your team."

She sighed. "I'm sorry." She wasn't sorry. She was hungry. No matter how nutritious Gerber's was for infants, it did little to settle the growling stomach of a grown woman. And she was always cranky and impatient when she was hungry. She gathered herself. "Well, how about the kiss? Did you mention the kiss with Cell Block?"

"No, I didn't get around to it. Cell Block was getting enough heat."

"He didn't give the best performance."

"He's Cell Block. He doesn't have to. Listen, I've got a lunch meeting. I'll talk with you later, honey."

"Of course." She hung up the phone and went for another jar of food. She could hardly wait for dinner so she could fill herself with some fish and foliage without guilt.

Love had absolutely nothing to do with her relationship with Sid, though she liked him a lot. He was a gentleman, treated her nicely and supported her dreams. He wasn't like the other men she'd met in Tinseltown, who'd promised her stardom before she slept with them, then kicked her to the curb within minutes of having an orgasm. From them she'd learned how to get what she wanted first, and she delivered what they wanted second. It was basically an even trade with Sid, because they were both pimps pandering to each other. He didn't mind giving her what she wanted as long as he got what he wanted in return. If he was able to use her name to get a show, then it would be he who would become an executive producer. Aligning himself with an up-and-coming star and throwing her name around town gave him added leverage in landing his dream job of producer. They were a perfect team, for now. They had a plan, a scam, for now.

In one year she'd soared from virtual anonymity to being recognized in malls and airports. She'd graced the cover of *Black Hair* magazine, *Essence*, and had even made *People*'s sexiest celebrity list. Waiters in restaurants asked for her autograph. Fans honked at her on the street. She received VIP privileges most places she went. Perhaps there would be a spin-off of *Same Day Service*. That's what she and Sid had discussed over dinner at Koi a few weeks ago. It had actually been his idea and she loved it. "See, that way," he'd explained, "you'd start out with a built-in audience and you'd have every advantage over a newcomer." She'd smiled and fucked him silly that night.

Sid had better get something brewing for her soon, because she was aging by the minute. She'd be twenty-eight in just a few months. Once she hit thirty her chances for stardom were cut in half unless she was a character actor, ready to go on camera looking like somebody's mother. That's not who she was and she had sense enough to know this town would never accept her as a serious actor. Her hair was too big, her breasts too full. She was simply too beautiful for that. Time was precious and the clock ticked louder and louder whenever she was alone. Just because she was a late bloomer didn't mean she couldn't skyrocket to the top. Since her childhood, she'd dreamed of becoming a star. *Same Day Service* was only a launching pad for where she wanted to go. First, she'd get her own sitcom, then a clothing line and, hopefully, her own perfume one day.

There was a knock on her dressing room door. It was Bernie, the stage manager.

"The cast is being released for the day. Your call time for tomorrow is at ten."

She smiled. "Thanks, Bernie."

She gathered her things. It was only twelve o'clock. If she were lucky, maybe she'd be able to get a facial today.

When Russ Tobin's assistant placed the Nielsen reports on his desk, Russ rolled up the sleeves on his Lorenzini shirt and put his reading glasses on in preparation of his morning ritual of reviewing the ratings. It was the most important part of his workday and he could barely hold down his breakfast until he'd seen them. The ratings would dictate the decisions he'd make that day and determine his job security as the president of Rex Network. It was like getting a performance review Monday through Friday. Well, actually more than that, since he had them faxed to his home on the weekends. But during those two days there was little he could do, and his wife, Annie, was grateful for that. She loved the lifestyle her husband's job afforded her, but his demanding position left her lonely. Basically, he'd left her ten years ago when he entered into holy matrimony with Rex. All Annie was now was his escort when he attended the Emmys, the Golden Globes, fund-raisers or network functions.

Under his leadership, Rex had escalated from the number-four network in the country to the second-highest-rated network in a matter of ten years. It was a great feat and it had taken sacrifice of home and health for such an accomplishment. Russ had the ulcers to prove it. He'd used his intuition, taken a few risks that paid off, suffered the loss of others that didn't and made far more good decisions than bad. He'd been the first to air a reality show. He'd brought the Masters and the NFL to Rex. And he'd lost hair contemplating a talk show that would compete with Oprah—and he was still trying. But he had taken on another talk-show format with four women that had worked out quite well. If Russ knew nothing else at all in life, he damn sure knew TV.

He reclined in his high-back leather chair, held the spreadsheets back a ways and peered over his glasses, studying the list of show names and the numbers beside them. With the aid of his magnified frames, he zoomed in on *Same Day Service*. He ran his fingers through his layered brown hair and bit his bottom lip. For the third week in a row, the numbers had dropped. Damn. He sat up and rifled through the papers on his desk for the advertising reports. The advertising dollars had been stable. That was a temporary relief. He still had time to do something about the ratings. Still had the opportunity to get the show back on track, though he wouldn't make much effort in doing so. Hell, he had an entire network to run and bigger issues awaited his presidential attention. He wasn't crazy about the show anyway, never had been. The story was average and though Leede was a very talented kid with great comedic timing, he was not a mainstream comic. Nothing personal, just business.

Russ had been a skeptic from the very beginning, only ordering six episodes of the show in the first season, unsure of the show's ability to grasp an audience and keep it. Yet the show had caught the attention of viewers all over the country like wildfire and only then did he dole out the network's money and order a full season of twenty-two episodes.

Had he not been so tired of the NAACP president calling his office, he'd have never given the show a time slot in the first place. The Beverly Hills chapter had picketed in front of his building for two weeks in a row like he was the Grand Wizard of the Ku Klux Klan, threatening to boycott his network. Every morning show had invited him to come on and defend his network and explain why Rex had no black shows on the air. It pissed him off. They carried on like sitcoms were free. Were they insane? One sitcom cost his budget at least a million a week. The cast alone had price tags on their butts that Neiman *and* Marcus would stutter at. Then there were the other one hundred and ninety people, all of whom belonged to one union or another with a million rules, eager to hammer him with fines. He couldn't afford to just hand out shows.

To maintain the network's image during the picketing, he'd accepted every invitation, appearing on *Good Morning America*, *The Today Show*, *The Early Show* and *Larry King Live*. On camera he imitated sincere concern and responded to all questions with left wing, liberal language. After two months of having a match lit under his network ass, he melted from the heat. He summed it up one night after two shots of scotch at an intimate party with his colleagues: "Those people punked me into a show."

He pushed the inter-office intercom button and instructed Betty, his assistant of ten years, to get Gary Ackerman on the line. Gary was a vice president of Programming and Development, and *Same Day Service* fell under his supervision. Two minutes later she buzzed him back.

He pressed another button on his phone console and put Gary on speaker. He removed his glasses and reared back in his chair again.

"Gary?"

"Hey, Russ. How's it going?"

"So far, so good. Listen, I was just looking at the numbers for *Same Day Service*. Tell me I have nothing to worry about."

"Russ, you have nothing to worry about. And I'm not just saying that. *American Icon* has snatched some of our audience. There's been a slump but I'm convinced it's temporary."

"You think so, huh? What are you doing to assure me of that?"

"All I can, Russ. All I can. They've got a rap sensation on the show this week and Ty thinks he'll help pull in ratings."

"And what do you think?"

"I hope he's right."

"I didn't ask about your hopes and dreams. I asked what you thought. Who's the rapper?"

"Cell Block. He's huge. Humongous."

Russ leaned forward. "And what do you think?"

Gary paused. "I think a better choice could have been made. I think he's a risk and could possibly turn away advertisers. But Ty thinks otherwise."

"Did you tell him that?"

"Sure, I did. But you know him. The minute you say something about a character, he plays the race card."

"I hate that. But never mind all that. I've got a network to run. It's my show, not his." He paused. "How about putting a white guy on the show?"

"If that's what you think is best."

Russ pondered the thought. "Maybe. I suspect we're losing the crossover audience. It's worth a try."

"I'll have a meeting."

"And keep me posted."

"Okay, Russ."

Russ hung up and went back to the business of ratings. Damned if that freakin' cable wasn't trying to take over with all their uncensored programming.

Gary sat behind his desk with petrifying thoughts swarming his head. The last time he'd spoken with Russ Tobin was at the company Christmas party. So when the Big Kahuna himself dialed him directly to discuss business, it was a big deal. It meant Russ had his nose to the ground, sniffing. But was Russ watching *Same Day Service* or was he watching Gary's performance?

4

Venus was on hold, waiting for a potential agent to jump on the line, when a groggy Leede appeared at the entrance of her office looking like he was walking in his sleep.

Venus paused, dumbstruck. *Oh, my God*. It was Leede staring at her with those seductive brown eyes, waiting on *her* attention. He generally had this paralyzing affect on women. Back in Pittsburgh he'd been just another kinda cute brother, but now that he had enough money to treat himself like a king, he looked like one. His two inches of dusty-brown hair was twisted into a stylish mess. His caramel skin had a hint of red, like he had some Cherokee down his bloodline somewhere. And based on his lean thighs and tight ass, Venus suspected he was packing *The Titanic*. Oh, how she'd fantasized about the tricks he could do with those full lips he constantly licked with his tongue. She wouldn't change a thing on him but his height. At five eight he was shorter than she liked her men, but the cameras gave him all the length he didn't have. One flaw. What the hell? She bought irregular items at Marshall's all the time. She'd take him.

She disconnected the line and stopped breathing, gladly giving him all the oxygen in the room. She couldn't be bothered with anyone at the moment. Leede was beckoning her.

"Hi, Leede." She greeted him as if she hadn't seen him all day.

"What's up, Big City? You're looking sexy today. I like that hairdo." He winked.

She blushed all over herself. "Thanks." The compliment, she loved. The nickname, she wasn't sure about. One of the PAs had coined her Big City because she was a country girl who'd come to Hollywood in absolute wonderment. She'd run halfway across the studio lot her second week on the job, filled with excitement because she'd seen the singer Brian McKnight. It had taken her heart an entire hour to return to its regular beat.

"How was your weekend?"

"It was cool. Nothing special."

"You should come over to the crib sometime, play video games and chill by the pool."

"Chill by the pool? How about swimming *in* the pool?"

"You know you black girls don't swim. It's a hair thing."

They laughed.

"Seriously. You should come over to the crib sometime."

"Can I bring a buddy?"

"Of course." He smiled. *But I'd prefer you come alone.* "I'm getting hungry. Can you have someone get me lunch?"

"We're ordering from California Pizza Kitchen. You want that?" Venus asked.

"Nah, I don't want any California food today. I want some grease. Some place like Roscoe's."

"I'll get a PA to go. Just tell me what you want."

"I'll take a number nine, country boy. A breast and waffle." Leede watched her from the corner of his eye, taking in her short French manicured nails, her unblemished skin, her simple jewelry and her natural clean scent as she wrote on a yellow Post-it note. There was an innocence about her that gave him a rise. Untainted by the glitter, glamour and scandal that surrounded her, she was a fragrant flower among Chanel-scented thorns.

Venus found it almost impossible to write with Leede hovering over her. Under his glare she was powerless, down to the pen in her hand. All she could do was daydream about lying in the sun on a blow-up chair, floating in the deep end of Leede's pool. She tried to snap out of it by saying, "Uh, huh," as he spoke, but it was useless. Gravity couldn't hold her down. She was caught up in the vision playing in her head. She pressed the rewind button and floated around the pool some more.

The video in her head abruptly stopped. *Is he fucking with me?* She knew she shouldn't get excited over a playboy like Leede, since he invited folks to his house all the time. That was no secret. Neither was the fact that he was a womanizer. She'd heard all about his triple-X pool parties, where women stripped off their swimsuits, swam topless, while the men got drunk and gawked and did whatever else she didn't hear about.

But the personal invite to the pool sounded different. His tone had intention behind it. *Damn, damn, damn! What if this guy really likes me?* It was really too much for her to fathom and continue breathing all at the same time. So she just breathed, if only to save herself the embarrassment of passing out in front of him.

With the largest space in the production office, approximately one thousand square feet, Ty didn't have the ordinary hand-me-down studio furniture. He'd taken the time and expense to hire an interior designer to attain fine contemporary furniture from Europe. There was a large butter-soft chocolate sofa on one side of the rectangular room and two high-back matching chairs across from it, propped between three floor-to-ceiling windows. To the far right of his office sat a bathroom complete with two vanities, a shower and a changing room. On the walls hung framed vintage movie posters from *Superfly*, starring Ron O'Neal, and *The Mack*, starring Max Julian. Closer to his desk was his wall of fame: a picture of him with Russ Tobin and his parents taken at the Emmy Awards, a picture of Sasha and their one-year-old daughter, Taylor, and framed photos from when he'd graced the covers of *Ebony*, *Entertainment Weekly* and GQ magazines. There were framed articles about *Same Day Service* from the *New York Times*, the *Los Angeles Times* and the *Washington Post*.

He sat alone in his office, conversing with his mother, Daisy, via his speakerphone.

"Ty, baby. Your brother just called me. He's at the dealership trying to get a new truck."

"Why'd he call you?"

"Because he couldn't get ahold of you. You know he needs a new car. Can't you help him out this one time?"

"One time? I helped him get his last car. And the one before that."

"That's your brother, Tyrone. He's blood and you should help him any way you can."

"I'm hindering him more than I'm helping him."

"Nonsense. He's family. You can't ever do too much for family."

Ty didn't respond. His mother was in deep denial about his older brother, Craig, who was a pothead and quit every job he had when the spirit hit him.

She continued. "It wouldn't kill you to sign for him."

"Look, the last time I co-signed for him, I ended up paying for the car myself. Why? Because he'd gambled the car away in a bet, then refused to pay the note, saying he wasn't paying for something he didn't have."

"You know how he can be sometimes. We all make mistakes. Don't make me remind you of some of yours."

It was clear to Ty that Craig was using Daisy to lobby for him. He'd called and given her some bogus story about what Ty wouldn't do for him, knowing she'd jump in and plead his case.

"I'll sign only if he promises to keep his job." It would be a promise that would never be kept. Last season Ty had hired him as his driver. That was a joke. Craig was quite content riding through life, hanging on to the coattails of his younger brother.

"Well, call him and tell him that. You know the Lord has really blessed you and you've got to share your blessings."

"I know, Mama. Where's Pop?"

"Damned if I know. Probably somewhere with a bottle up to his lips. Last night he came in here looking like I don't know what. Come asking me, 'Daisy, why don't you fix me something to eat?' So I told him, 'No. The kitchen closed at eight o'clock.' Then he poked his drunk lips out and says, 'Pretty, pretty please with whip cream on top.' " Ty snickered. His parents had been married for thirty-five years and they were one of the best comedy teams he'd ever seen. Retired and financially secure with his aid, they had all day to get in each other's way.

"But you fixed him something, didn't you?"

"I made his ass a *ham* sandwich and went on about my business. I declare, he gets on my nerves. Humph. You know me and Ernestine are going to Vegas this weekend."

"How about Pop? He's not going?"

"Not with me, he ain't!"

He smiled. "I've got to go, Ma." If he didn't get Daisy off the line, she'd talk all day.

"Okay. But listen, when am I going to see my grandbaby? It's been at least two weeks. Maybe more."

"Call Sasha."

"I'm calling you."

"I've been working a lot."

"I know. I've got to call your assistant to see how you're doing."

"I'll talk to you later, Mama."

"Okay. And Ty?"

"Yes?"

"Call your brother. He really needs your help."

"I said I would, okay?"

"Bye, son."

"Bye."

Ty's mother, Daisy, used to say, "That one right there. My middle chile', Ty. He's going places. Uh, huh. 'Cause he don't think his shit stinks." Ty always knew he'd be successful at whatever he chose, even if it was drug dealing. He'd begun to dabble in that field while attending UDC (University of the District of Columbia), lining his pockets with fat and fast cash. It was a lucrative and addictive line of work. While he said no to drugs, he said yes to the money. The more he made, the more he yearned for it.

But all that changed in one night. He'd watched his older brother shot dead, falling to his knees and then flatout on his chest over a drug deal gone bad. For months Ty kept envisioning himself lying on the street, lifeless. Courtney had been the brother he was closest to and without him, Ty himself was only half alive. He blamed himself. He should have been there for Courtney, should have been able to save him. That's when he gave up the drug game. There would be no revenge, only refuge in California. His Aunt Ernestine told his father,

Lynwood, "Send the boy out here. I'll keep him so busy he won't have time to jerk off." Lynwood obliged, determined not to lose another child in the streets of DC, the murder capital. Hell, when he got enough money, they'd all come.

Ty's eyes sparkled like fireworks as he gawked, taking in the mansions and luxury cars that lined every street in Beverly Hills. "It's more money than you can count out here." He knew then and there, he wanted to stay out west and be a cowboy. He enrolled at Cal State and worked part-time at UPS. During his weekly visit to Skillz, a barbershop in Compton, he'd talk shit and cut the fool, and befriended an older gentleman named Al West. Ty would shoot the breeze with the patrons, using his wit and youthful wisdom to entertain them. Al, an up-and-coming producer himself, was impressed by Ty and always told him, "When I get my show, I'm gonna hook you up." Al kept his word. When his show got the green light, he hired Ty as a PA and mentored him like a father as he worked his way up the ranks. Al had hired him as a writer trainee in the second season and within five years, Ty had graduated from staff writer to producer, writing for various shows. Ty would always be grateful to Al for giving him his start. Always.

Now, Ty made more money than Wookie and Fray, who were the most profitable drug dealers in his neighborhood back in the day. But that illegitimate, underground world was far behind him.

When Leede entered Ty's office, he was on the phone again, this time with Sasha, his girlfriend and mother of his firstborn. Leede sank into one of the down leather chairs and waited patiently, resting his eyes.

He opened his eyes when Ty disconnected. "Did I hear baby-mama drama?" he teased.

"Man, you know how women are. She's on the 'let's live together' campaign."

Leede smirked. "You are in troooooouble."

"No, I'm not. I know the deal. All it took was one conversation with my attorney to set the record straight. He told me if I moved in with her in the state of California, she'd be recognized as my common-law wife and would be entitled to half of everything I've got. So, remember that, okay? It might sober you up when you're drunk with love."

He raised his brows. "She probably knows that."

"Good, then she should understand when I say no. I don't see what the big deal is. I've put her up in that house. I'm paying for the nanny and everything else. She's got everything I've got and she didn't even write a script."

"I don't blame you. Ain't no chick taking half of my money! I don't know what I fear more."

"Me either, man. And if it's not broke, why bother trying to fix it."

"Yeah, 'cause if you move in, then it will be 'when we getting married?'"

"That's way down the road, and not without a prenuptial."

"You keep holding out on her and she might leave you, dawg."

"And go where? I've been taking care of her for three years. She'd have one helluva time trying to get a job."

"Another man might be her job."

"And she can move out of my house and give me back the keys to my Benz."

Over the past month Sasha had been riding Ty bareback about getting hitched. Every other conversation was about the future, their future. Ty would do anything for her except marry her. He could give some of himself, but not all. He loved his child with all his heart and he loved Sasha as he had loved no other woman, but a husband he was not ready to be. He was only thirty-four. She was twenty-three. 'Til death do us part was a long time off. What if it didn't work? There were no guarantees. It was as risky as investing his life savings in the stock market. He could wake up one day and be half broke in less time than it took him to say I do.

"Yeah, well. I'm never getting married. When I meet someone with a good job and good credit, I *might* consider it," Leede said.

Having big bank accounts had been the dream of both men. They'd interpreted the abundance of monetary possession in terms of power and invincibility, not weakness; but that's where wealth had placed them—in a vulnerable position. Almost any and everyone was a threat because they were open and accessible to be legally robbed. If they treated someone rudely in a store, they were more likely than the average person to be sued. If a girl mistook their advances negatively, it could mean a sexual harassment case. Loving the wrong woman could cost them half of their assets, in addition to heartache. The world around them was on twenty-four-hour duty, ready to snatch a huge portion of their dream.

Leede continued. "I wanted to talk to you about Naja."

Ty stretched out his long legs under his desk. "Oh, yeah? What about her?"

"You need to talk to her. She's been trying to make small waves since the beginning of the season. First it was her contract. Then it was her hair. Now it's the lines. This is not her show and she needs to be put in check."

"I wouldn't worry about Naja. I've got her under control."

"Then you need to get Sid under control. I'm tired of him grumbling over how many lines she has like he's her damn agent."

"Who cares what he says? He's a two-bit programming manager. The scripts and her lines are at my discretion. And I don't tell my writers what to write for her. They write what is required for the story."

"I'm simply expressing my concern," Leede stated.

"I'm surprised to see you trip about Naja. It's not like you to trip over a chick."

"I'm not trippin'. I like Naja. Remember, I was the one who shagged her first." Leede needed to address his suspicions about Ty and Naja. Maybe she'd been seducing him, distorting his view and decisions. Perhaps she'd sexed Ty in her dressing room just like she'd done him during the first season. He wasn't sure if anything had happened between them, but Ty never responded aggressively enough to Sid's comments, and it annoyed the hell out of him.

"And your point would be?"

Leede shook his head. "I'm just saying."

"Are you happy with your character? That's all you need to worry about."

Leede shrugged. "I guess so."

"Then that should be your focus. The ratings are down and you're the one carrying the show. It's your reputation on the line, not hers."

"Maybe yours is on the line. You're the creator. This is your baby."

"Perhaps. But we're not talking about me and what I do."

Leede backed down. "I'm not trying to tell you how to do your job."

"Good. I'm glad we have that understanding because I *am* the one running this show." With that, Ty ended the conversation.

Venus tapped on Ty's door, which sat ajar. They both looked up. The smell of food shifted their attention. "Ty, your lunch is here." She walked in balancing a china plate upright on her palm like a waitress, made her way around his desk and placed it in front of him. She'd discarded the Styrofoam containers the pasta and salad had been delivered in. Ty never ate from paper plates if he or Venus could help it.

Venus stood ill at ease. The thick air in the room raised the hairs on her arms. She'd overheard nearly every word between the two. Well, as much as humanly possible between the ringing phones. When Ty's conversations got too juicy to ignore, she let the calls go straight to voice mail, at the risk of losing her job. Some things were worth the gamble.

She gave Leede a shy smile. "Your food should be here shortly."

"Thanks, V."

Leede watched lasciviously as she exited the office.

Ty leaned forward and looked Leede straight in the eye. "Don't even think about it."

"What?" Leede exclaimed.

Ty replied softly, enunciating every word as though Leede was deaf and could only read lips. "Fucking my assistant."

Leede waved his hand. "Man, that's the furthest thing from my mind."

Ty smirked. "You lying S-O-B. It's the *only* thing on your mind."

5

There was no memorable time and date when Leede realized he'd been blessed with a talent, but at an early age he knew he'd make people laugh for a living someday. Raised in foster homes in Pittsburgh, Leede had grown up poor. His relationship with his mother was more of a friendship than a kinship. She'd walked away from her motherly responsibilities when he was six years old, leaving him in the care of strangers who were posing as family. With his security blanket ripped from him, he was never quite as secure as the next kid, and this gave him a different perception of the world. More important, it gave him a funny one. He did impressions of his foster mother when she was in church: her gestures, her shouting steps and her hallelujah tones. He could imitate his junior high school principal, Mr. Shaffer, from his beard scratching right down to his limp.

At nineteen he started hanging out at an open-mike night at Mr. Henry's. During his first performance, a thick fog hit his brain and nervousness dominated him. Perspiration trickled from his pores. He stumbled over his words and forgot half his lines. He pressed on, corrected his wrongs and was successful in attaining a few laughs. The culmination of so many emotions within ten minutes gave him a rush he'd never felt before, and a comedian was born. On-stage he found the love and security he'd missed as a child. He became a stage junkie looking for his next fix. He honed his skills, studying the tapes of Richard Pryor and Eddie Murphy. He noted their posture, their timing and every other nuance of their comedic delivery. He watched hours and hours of television studying celebrities to impersonate, and he spent even more hours in front of the mirror working on his act. Within three years he'd become a celebrity at Mr. Henry's and other clubs around town, but longed for the big time. His appetite for the spotlight had grown and he desired to be more than a local comic. With nothing more than blind ambition and a prayer, he headed for Los Angeles, the home of every super comic.

During his stay in LA, he'd done some acting on television shows, a few national commercials and was a regular on the LA comedy circuit. His income was decent enough to keep him current on the rent for his Silver Lake apartment and the note on his Lexus. But to date, no gig had grossed him the one-point-five million-dollar paycheck he would earn for one full season on *Same Day Service*. He didn't care that Uncle Sam would be poking his long, white index finger in his face, demanding a cut. He'd been scratching his itchy palms since signing the contract with Rex, and celebrating his financial blessing in unholy ways until 4 and 6 A.M., the devil's happy hours.

Two weeks after Leede had been cast in *Same Day Service*, he met Ty at Mr. Chow's for lunch. When he entered the swanky restaurant, snooty patrons suspiciously glanced in his direction. Any black man lunching in Beverly Hills had to be a celebrity, an athlete or a drug dealer. At present, he was none of the above, but that would soon change. If the show were as nearly as successful as he anxiously anticipated, he'd soon be a celebrity and his life would be a series of colorful photos, strategically laid out on the pages of tabloids.

As the waiter led him to his table, Leede nervously swiped his tongue over his bottom lip every so often. His big Hollywood opportunity had rushed in like a twelve-foot tide and though he'd been practicing, waiting for a gigantic wave to ride, its magnitude terrified and excited him at once. As the star, the success of the sitcom rested firmly on his shoulders, and his confidence buckled from the weight.

Ty greeted him wearing extra-dark jeans that weren't too baggy, with his white shirttail hanging out. His demeanor, cool as ice. His smile, easy and welcoming.

Leede's lips curled into a smile as he gave Ty a pound. Upon their first meeting, Leede had felt an instant connection with Ty. He'd shrugged it off as street instinct, hood recognizing hood. "What's up?" Leede said.

"Hey, man. What's going on? I hope you like Chinese food.

This place is highly rated—or maybe overrated. I thought we'd rank the joint for ourselves," Ty replied.

"Maaan, the only Chinese food I've had came in a white box. This will be more like an experiment for me," Leede joked.

Ty gave a lighthearted chuckle. "How you feeling?"

"Never been better."

"Good. I want you to be comfortable. This is your first show and I'm going to do all I can to make sure this is a good experience for you."

"I appreciate that."

"Hey, we're partners in this. My office is an open door. You got a problem? I'm your man. I want to keep the communication flowing."

Leede nodded, enjoying the verbal massage.

Ty continued, "Preproduction starts in a few weeks. Between now and then, I'd like to check out your stand-up. You know, see what I can use to enhance your character on the show."

"Yeah, man. That would be cool. I'm at the Improv on Tuesdays and the Comedy Store on Thursdays."

"If I can incorporate your strengths, I think it increases our chances of success. As a black show on a major network, we're only going to get one chance to get this right."

"Let's make it happen and do it right."

After they ordered, Ty conveyed his goals for the show and the direction. "I don't want to reinforce any negative stereotypes. I want the show to be funny without the characters acting like buffoons."

Leede nodded. Ty was much more serious-minded than

he'd thought him to be. "You mean I can't bust a move and dance like George Jefferson?" he teased.

Ty smiled. "Well, if there's a party, yes." He paused. "When I wrote the script, I was trying to reflect the life of real people making it. There will be no episodes about your character scrambling for rent money like on *Good Times*. You feel me?"

"I feel you."

Ty picked up his glass and took a sip of water. "I think you're talented and I'm looking forward to working with you."

"Thanks, man. You too."

Ty smirked. "Then, let's have fun and make a lot of fucking money."

With Leede's acting insecurities temporarily at peace, he moved on to another concern. "The next time you wanna take me to lunch," Leede said, "let's travel toward Crenshaw and avoid Beverly Hills. The BHPD have nothing better to do than stop my black ass any chance they get. I don't come this way, if I can help it."

Ty rubbed the three-day-old stub on his face. "My bad, man. I wasn't even thinking like that. I guess I've been de-sensitized."

"It's okay," Leede said.

"Naw, man. I've been stopped several times myself. But now that I'm older they don't fuck with me like they used to." He smiled faintly. Four years back, Ty was accosted on Maple Drive, hurled to the ground by Beverly Hills' finest and frisked like a cold-blooded criminal. Ty didn't like discussing his brush with the law, didn't like reliving the agonizing humiliation of white motorists glaring down at him like he was nothing more than toxic waste. He never allowed the incident to deter him from traveling through and to Beverly Hills as he pleased. It was a free country and he'd exercise his rights as an American citizen, no matter what.

"Don't worry about it." Leede's eyes panned the room. "You know, I used to play basketball at this gym in West LA and I'd take Robertson to get there. It was a shortcut and less congested than Wilshire." Leede exhaled. "Man, the cops stopped me every other week. Once a cop asked me, Why was I coming that way?" Leede frowned. "I was too angry to answer, so I didn't." Leede shrugged. "What is this, Apartheid? I have to show a pass? And explain where I'm going?" He shook his head, sickened by the memory.

"I'm sorry, man. It won't happen again." Ty paused. "Are you any good on the basketball court?"

Leede smiled again. "Of course, I've got game. As a matter of fact, I've got plenty. We should play sometime."

Their meeting lasted two hours. The two disclosed information about their pasts, where they'd been and where they were headed, and forged a friendship based on common ground: growing up in the hood, their love of basketball and a desire to conquer Hollywood despite the color of their skin. In the weeks that followed, Ty shadowed Leede around to the comedy clubs on Sunset, noting aspects of his routine that would enhance Leede's character on the show. Soon they were shooting hoops together on Saturday mornings, randomly calling each other when an idea came to mind and partying together. He'd been thrilled to be cast on a show with a black executive producer. He'd assumed there would be more understanding of his character, his language, his personality and his talent. Over time, Leede had grown to respect Ty as a producer and looked up to him like an older brother. Little did he know that two years later, no one would be looking out for Leede but Leede.

6

Sid pulled up in front of the Grill on the Alley and handed his Beamer over to the valet attendant. Upon entering the Beverly Hills restaurant, he was surrounded by the buzz of chatting all over the room. He scanned the not-so-special-looking place, spotting a lot of very important people. Steven Spielberg was at a booth talking with two men he didn't recognize. Berry Meyer, the CEO of Warner Brothers, sat at another. Clive Davis, the biggest man in music, was dining with a young man, probably a music talent on his way up the charts. Nick Stevens, agent to Jim Carrey, sat at a table with another gentleman who looked like an agent. Then he spotted his date, Barry Rueben from Creative Talents. Barry closed his cellular phone and motioned to him as he made his way over.

Sid was already on a high, getting an added surge of oxygen as he strutted across the room, packed wall-to-wall with Hollywood's most powerful people. This is where he wanted to be, where he belonged. One day he'd walk through the doors of this same restaurant and everyone in the place would look around and know who *he* was.

Barry stood up and offered Sid his chubby hand. The excess weight he carried was from having too much of everything. Too many clients, too much pressure to sell their work, too many hours at the office, too many lunches and dinners out on the town and too much drinking. The lifestyle of a seasoned, successful agent had gradually inflated him to the size of a submarine.

Sid placed his slender hand in Barry's and shook. "I hope I didn't keep you waiting."

Barry squeezed his heavy frame back into the leather booth. "No, not at all. I was just making a few calls. It's a pleasure to finally meet you."

"Likewise. Needless to say, your reputation precedes you."

"I hope that's a good thing," Barry joked.

Sid offered no response. He'd done a background check on Barry and he couldn't find a single soul within twenty miles who didn't like the fat guy. Yet no one loved him either. He was known for his mafia-style negotiating, and all proclaimed Barry knew the art of the deal, which is what made him successful. So Sid fully expected Barry to serve him some bullshit along with his lunch.

The waitress came over and took their drink orders, then Sid got right down to business, ready to prove himself. "I read the script. As a matter of fact, I read it twice. It's good. The premise is solid. It's got drama, comedy and lots of action. All of my personal favorites."

Barry smiled. Of course he liked the script. Poor material was never sent out of his office. He wasn't two hundred and seventy pounds for nothing. "Maxwell is a strong, solid writer. He's going to be my biggest client one day."

"That's good to hear. It makes me feel like I'm getting in on something early."

"You certainly are, my friend."

The waitress delivered the drinks. Barry gulped his martini.

"Now, I see Naja playing one of the lead characters," Sid said. "Who do you have in mind to co-star?"

There were three main characters in the sitcom Maxwell had written. Two females working as a detective team and one male with whom one of the female characters falls in love. However, there were several smaller roles for newer talent like Naja to take on. Barry wasn't sure she was ready to carry a show. Not unless she had a strong co-star beside her.

"I've got a few people in mind. Gabrielle Union or Sanaa Lathan for starters," he lied.

Sid got an instant hard-on. With the right celebrity, he and Naja would become overnight sensations. But he had even bigger, whiter ideas in mind. "I thought an interracial team would be good. Like Naja and Courtney Cox."

"I thought you read the script twice?" Barry said.

"I did. But characters can be changed. Think about the crossover possibilities," Sid said.

"I'll let the studio that buys the damn thing change it, if the price is right. I'm just interested in attaching names and landing a development deal. That's my job."

"I'm surprised Maxwell didn't think of it," Sid said.

"He's too hungry to sell it."

"Have you had any bites from the studios?"

"Yeah, a few. But I'm just playing one card at a time," Barry lied.

Barry had Sid's nose on a hook as he poured on the lies. He could smell the rookie's extreme zeal to strike a deal. He didn't have one studio committed to making the pilot, but if he could attach that one magical name to the project, he knew it would go. Rex's interest would soar. In the event that Maxwell agreed to cast Naja, the rookie would damn near owe his career to him. He was getting older and pushing maximum density by the milli-second. He'd need favors from the next big producer down the stretch when his client list was on the decline. Might as well start lining up the debts now.

After lunch, they got back to the business at hand.

Barry started twisting the knife. He needed Sid to believe he was doing him a huge favor so he'd feel indebted. "Now I have to be honest with you," he started, wiping his greasy fingers on a cloth napkin, "I had a smaller part in mind for Naja."

"I'm not looking to cast Naja in any small roles. Her role on *Same Day Service* is as small as it will get."

Barry raised his eyebrows, impressed by the rookie's tenacity. "Naja is not carrying that show. She's merely a co-star and she doesn't have any other major experience. Besides videos."

"That's all she needs."

"I don't know," Barry faked. "Maybe I'll have her read for the part."

Sid tried desperately to remain calm. Without a starring role for Naja, he'd never be able to negotiate a producer credit for himself. "I suggest you take another look at the show tapes. Naja is delivering comedy and drama every week. That's the only reading you'll get from her."

"You sound sure of her."

"Of course, I am. I wouldn't waste your time, and hope you aren't wasting mine."

Barry smiled in admiration of the rookie wearing a crisp shirt and khakis. "I'll run it by Maxwell and we'll go from there."

Lunch for Maxwell was a veggie burger and fries. For dessert he inhaled two slender lines of cocaine in a bathroom stall. With his brain numbed to cruise control, he was ready to glide through the rest of his day. He walked down the hall into the writers' room.

The writers' room was merely another conference room housing a large round table, chairs and a computer desk for the writers' assistants. As co-executive producer, it was his job to run the room by directing the stories, keeping the writers on track and making sure deadlines were met. Today they'd rewrite this week's scripts according to the network notes. To-morrow they'd move on to tightening up next week's script.

The table before him was littered with coffee cups, soda cans, candy wrappers and empty food containers. Three of the writers sat casually around the table. The others were goofing off and wouldn't come into the room until they were summoned.

"What did the network have to say?" Sampson, who'd written the first draft, asked.

"The usual bullshit. And they think Cell Block is too gangster for the show."

"I read an article on him in *Vibe*. The guy is just a kid. He's like twenty-one or twenty-two," Monique said.

"Every time we cast someone who doesn't look like a punk, they trip," Sampson said.

"Yep, how many black guys on TV have facial hair? Oooohh. Too scary for white America, you know," Monique said.

"Barely even a mustache. Even Wesley Snipes, my personal favorite, shaves his face all the time now. You think he succumbed to the pressure?" Leslie said.

"Denzel rarely has a mustache unless he's playing the bad guy," Maxwell said.

"In real life, brothers wear facial hair. You see these cats when they are not working and there's a beard. Trust," Sampson said.

"What's the big deal about Cell Block? I think he's sexy as hell, in a roughneck sort of way," Leslie said.

"I think he's a bit young for you."

"Right, his age falls within the demographics of our show."

"So, what's the verdict? Is he in or out?" Sampson asked.

"He's in," Maxwell said.

"I sure hope they don't yank him later in the week or we'll be pulling all-nighters."

"Ty was pretty straightforward about what he wanted. Other than that, just tightening the screws. Maybe some punch-up on the jokes. After listening to the cast read this morning, I can see where we could make a few adjustments," Maxwell said.

The other writers filed in one by one and took their usual seat formation as if in school, wearing casual clothing, mostly sportswear.

From an outsider's perspective the room appeared to be full of love. A place where work meant creating jokes, having food fights, playing video games and fraternizing. But there was always underlying tension because of jealousy and deceit. They all kissed Ty's butt to secure their jobs but were quick to blow the whistle and scream foul play on anyone else. Behind the backs of their colleagues they gossiped about who turned in a bad script, who thought they were funny when they weren't, who sold a film script undeservingly and who slept with whom. There was enough gossip floating around to print their very own *Enquirer*, a *Same Day Service* special edition.

No matter how important Maxwell's job description sounded, at the end of the day he felt like a schoolteacher for *Romper Room*. How many times a day did he have to say, "No talking," "Let's get focused," "No, we can't leave yet"? It wasn't easy dealing with eleven personalities closed off in one room all day.

By two o'clock Leede's stomach was growling like an angry dog. As time progressed, he longed to feed the mild hang-over threatening to give him a day-long headache. As he tramped down the hall in search of the PA who was picking up his lunch, his cell phone rang. It was Steve Van Arden, his manager.

"Leede, what's going on?"

"You tell me," Leede replied.

"I've got good news. Joel Schumacher wants you for his next film. He's offering a half a million for two weeks of work."

"That's not starring-role money."

"Colin Farrell has the lead. It's a nice part, though. You get to play a real character role and show the world your skills, baby. The character is not only funny, but witty and intelligent."

"What will I be, a bank robber giving comic relief?"

"Nooooo. You'll play the bus driver who takes Colin Farrell's kid to school and discovers the detonator in the parking lot. And get this, you have a West-Indian accent."

"I wouldn't play a bus driver if they were filming *Speed 3* and offering me ten million bucks!"

"I thought you'd be excited. You're always talking about taking it to the next level, moving toward film and staying busy."

"Right. I want a leading role saving the world from weapons of mass destruction, or leaping from tall buildings in a single bound or robbing the rich to give to the poor. You feelin' me?"

"Yeah. You want a Will Smith role."

"You damn right. And you should want fifteen percent of Will Smith's money. What's he getting? Twenty million a film?"

"Around that, yeah. But he didn't start out making that. In his first film he kissed a man and was paid nothing."

"I'd kiss a monkey's butt on screen if it's a leading role and the price is right. How about this, Van Arden? I'd even settle for a stand-up movie. I thought that's why I was on the road this summer."

When the ratings on *Same Day Service* shot through the roof, Van Arden had immediately started collaborating with a promotions company to organize a comedy tour. He booked Leede, along with two other lesser known comedians he managed, at a venue in every major city. The tour grossed a truckload of money in a short period of time. With a hit show on the air, Leede was on fire. His name was on the lips and tongues of America. It would have been easy to get caught up in the flames, but Van Arden held out under the national heat of fame, making only well thought out moves when it came to Leede's career path. His goal was to expand Leede's audience, but the roles for black actors in big-budget films were extremely limited.

"Come on. A stand-up movie is such a risk. Only Richard Pryor and Eddie Murphy have been able to make a box-office hit out of a stand-up performance. I've tried but it's too risky. Nobody will invest."

"What do you mean? It's a low-budget project and you didn't say that shit when you had me on the road for three months."

"I know. I know. I'm just telling you what I'm hearing."

"So, what? Should I get another manager? I know what your client roster looks like. Chris Rock, Martin Lawrence. If you can't handle having another star, then let's move on. I need to be a priority."

"I devote just as much energy to your career as I do my

other clients. And remember, Chris and Martin are not locked down on TV shows. Your schedule is limited."

"Now it is. But my four-month hiatus will be here before you know it. And if I'm sitting at home chillin' by the pool unemployed, you're going to catch almighty hell."

"Honestly, I think you should take the part. You can do this and something bigger on hiatus when you have more time. This small part would be good exposure."

"I get exposure every Sunday night at eight thirty," Leede argued.

"All right, all right. But don't expect any miracles."

"With all the clout you have in this town, I'm not expecting anything less."

Leede closed his phone, fuming from head to toe. Van Arden was dishing out bullshit by the mouthful. The last three times Leede had called his office to ask a question, he'd spoken with Van Arden's assistant. A goddamn assistant managing his career. What an insult. Van Arden had too many high-profile clients and was too greedy to admit it. And he was making Leede fight for attention like a child with ten siblings.

If *Same Day Service* lasted through one hundred episodes and sold in syndication, he'd still need to prepare for the next phase of his career. There was pressure to strike while the iron was hot. He was determined not to fall into the abyss of forgotten stars. He could envision it now. A VH1 special, *Where Are They Now?* Whatever happened to JJ on *Good Times*? And whatever happened to Leede from *Same Day*

Service? Then they'd show footage of him wiping down cars as they rolled out of the car wash. The thought was frightening. He wanted his career to end with big movies and big bucks like Steve Martin and Eddie Murphy. He needed a manager who'd deliver on his promises to make him a bona fide movie star.

Leede entered the production playroom, an extra office designated for housing the production junk food and drinks, a TV, an Xbox, a stereo and two sofas. With Snapple stacked up to the ceiling on one side of the room, Arrowhead water on another and enough chips, cookies and candy to celebrate Halloween every night for three months, the office space looked like a bomb shelter designed by a bunch of ten-year-olds.

Totally engrossed in Xbox, Danny and Zack shouted, "What's up," to Leede without ever taking their eyes from the screen.

"Hey, what's going on? Who went to get my lunch?"

"I think Kevin did," Danny answered, his fingers moving faster than the speed of sound.

"What did he do, walk? It's been over an hour."

"Let me just finish kicking Zack's ass and I'll beep him."

Kevin walked into the room damp with perspiration. He'd been sitting in the 101-degree heat in his old Toyota that was threatening to overheat, stuck in midday traffic. Beads of sweat peppered his forehead as he proudly handed Leede his lunch order in a big plastic Roscoe's bag. Another Hollywood task completed.

"Thanks," Leede mumbled as he sat down and tore open the bag and Styrofoam. Using the tips of his fingers, he felt for the temperature of the food. "Got dammit," he mumbled. "This food is cold. You had me wait half the damn day for a cold waffle? Roscoe's is ten minutes from here." Kevin stood dumbfounded as more sweat trickled down his forehead. He was a PA. He couldn't argue with the star of the show, he'd be fired for sure. Zack and Danny stopped playing as Leede stormed out of the room like a seven-year-old brat born with a silver spoon in his mouth.

While most of the world left their homes to go to the club, Hugh Hefner built the club in his house to avoid traffic. His Beverly Hills estate was party central, equipped with a dance floor, three long bars, a fancy pool encircled by tropical plants, a bath house, a game room, a theater and an honest-to-goodness zoo with snakes, exotic birds, monkeys and alligators. Hugh had constructed the first *Neverland Ranch* when Michael Jackson was still a pup, singing about his ABC's. Except his was an X-rated playground for adults only.

Ty didn't frequent the Playboy Mansion, but tonight was a special occasion. Al West, his good friend and mentor, was celebrating his fifty-fourth birthday. Al had lived a thousand lives over the span of one lifetime. A pioneer in black Hollywood, he had produced and written for the early shows, like *Good Times* and *What's Happening*. He'd been on and off the

wagon enough times to lose count. He'd done pot in the six-
ties, coke in the seventies, crack in the eighties, and still lived
to tell about it in his NA meetings. He'd gambled away ev-
erything but his drawers in Vegas, lost half his money to his
two ex-wives and watched what was left burn up in smoke
as he got high and partied. It had been his sheer talent that
gained him respect in the industry and enabled him to keep
coming back from the dead. As for why his stormy life had
not left him looking weathered? Nothing more than DNA.
The only obvious characteristic that dated him was the thou-
sands of gray hairs scattered throughout his head and beard.
No doubt he'd earned each and every one of them and de-
served a lot more.

Al was standing on the pool patio near the bar when he
saw Ty. He pulled a Cohiba cigar from his mouth and flashed
a welcoming smile. "Hey, Youngblood," he greeted. They
slapped palms and embraced.

"Happy Birthday, playa!"

"Thank you, man." Al stood back a ways, examining Ty
with fatherly pride in his eyes. "Look at Youngblood. You're
looking good. It's hard to believe I found you in a South Cen-
tral barbershop."

Ty ran his palm over his head. "That was before the good
Lord became my barber."

Al chuckled. "The Lord giveth and the Lord taketh away."

"He hasn't taken nothin' from you. You look well."

"So do you."

"I'm just trying to keep up with you, Al. Always have."

"I don't know if that's a good thing or not. So, how's life as
a showrunner?"

"You know the drill. Dealing with drama queens, better known as actors. And fighting censorship over curse words."

"Too bad it has to be that way, but a black man gets few breaks no matter what line of business he's in."

"You're right."

"Damn right I'm right. It's just we don't know Colin Powell well enough to get the real scoop on the shit he's dealing with. Jesse Jackson never mumbled a word about how many death threats he had while running for president. Hell, Youngblood, it ain't much prettier on top than it is at the bottom. People think it is, but it ain't."

"Yeah, man. I see that now. Everything anyone on the show does affects me."

"That's why you get paid the big bucks," Al teased.

Ty shrugged. "I guess."

"How's the family doing? And how is my girl, Daisy? She left your old man yet?"

Ty laughed. "Everyone is doing good. You know, my daughter is a year now."

"Time flies. Where's Sasha?"

"She's around here somewhere. I'm sure you'll see her before the party ends."

"This is the Playboy Mansion. The party never ends. Hey listen, I'mma go shout at my guests. I'll catch up with you later."

"All right, man."

"And let's do lunch real soon. Have your girl call my girl." And Al was off to the game room.

* * *

Sasha was fluffing her poodle tresses in the mirror of the ladies' room when a fair-skinned woman with almond-shaped green eyes stepped out of a bathroom stall and stood at the sink next to her. Sasha stole as good a look as her peripheral vision would allow. The woman had sharp features and curly, dark brown hair that was cropped close to her head. She wore Yves Saint Laurent trousers, halter and diamond earrings large enough to give sight to the blind. Her attire was not ostentatious, but clearly couture. Whatever neck of the woods this woman was from, she was definitely running with a pack of rich wolves. Not just any poor, lone wolf could gain entry into the mansion of the most famous playboy in America.

"How are you?" Sasha asked as she dabbed her forehead with Mac foundation she didn't need. Between tanning at her beach house in Malibu, weekly steams at Burke Williams Spa and monthly facials, her cocoa skin was airbrush perfect, along with the rest of her body.

The woman smiled slightly. "I'm good."

"Cute outfit. The halter is nice."

"Thanks."

"I hope you don't take this the wrong way, but you are really pretty."

She smiled. "There's only one way to take that. Thanks."

"Do you know Al?"

"Not really. He's a friend of a friend."

"Oh, I see. I'm Sasha, by the way."

"Pleased to meet you. I'm Dominique."

Sasha placed her compact on the vanity counter. She

wanted to reach out and touch the woman but resisted, since Dominique's hands were wet. Her skin was creamy like butter, and inviting. Her breasts round and mouthwatering.

"You look so familiar. Are you an actress?" Dominique asked.

Sasha heard this line all the time. "No."

"I know you from somewhere," Dominique toyed, faking as if they'd met before.

Sasha shrugged. "This town is small. Perhaps we've met. So, Dominique, I'm here with my boyfriend, Ty. Maybe you could join us for a drink?"

"Sure, I'd like that." She pulled two bucks out of her purse for the bathroom attendant. "Let me find my friend and I'll look for you."

"Okay. We'll be in the lounge area. My boyfriend is tall, dark and bald."

"Lucky you," she teased before dropping two bucks in the bathroom attendant's basket and grabbing a piece of spearmint gum.

Sasha smiled and looked on approvingly at Dominique's slender hips as she walked away. Sasha guessed she was in her late twenties and had less than eighteen percent body fat. Given Dominique's soft-spoken voice and humble vibration, Sasha presumed she had no idea how gorgeous she was. That turned her on even more. Damn, she'd love to get Dominique between her silky sheets. She hoped like hell she'd keep her word and have a drink with them. She jammed her makeup into her bag, threw a few dollars in the basket and rushed out of the bathroom. She couldn't wait to tell Ty about the gem she'd found in the ladies' room.

* * *

Six months after she and Ty had started dating he'd invited her over to his house for an intimate dinner. When she arrived the place was lit with candles and had more flowers in the dining room than a funeral home. He'd ordered shrimp with pasta from Spago and as the grand surprise of the evening after dinner, a female exotic dancer just for her pleasure.

Their sex life was passionate, fulfilling and experimental, from positions, oils and costumes to massages, blindfolds and videotapes. So, adding a third party to their dynamic duo was a natural progression. Ty had mentioned on several occasions how much it would excite him to see her making love to another woman. Initially she was apprehensive yet still eager to please him, growing progressively more open to the experience with each mention. Though eleven years his junior, she was no fool. Half the women in Tinseltown would do another woman and another man at the same time for him. In Tinseltown orgies were a hobby and there were more swingers than Lakers fans. If she didn't comply, he'd simply go behind her back. At least this way she'd be in the know. There would be no secrets between them and they'd have a completely open relationship. Besides, how bad could it be? She looked at women all the time, admiring one thing or another about them. Whether it was their hair, clothing or figures. And she definitely had a fascination with breasts, having secretly fantasized about playing with some bigger and fuller than her own. She'd done it once back in high school with her best friend, Tamara, who was a cheerleader. Even then, the thought of going down on a woman was repulsive. But if Ty wanted her to try, she would. It wouldn't be life threatening. She'd never heard of anyone dying because they ate a bad piece of pussy.

The exotic dancer, Loyda, had an incredible body. She curved like an hourglass and her C-cups were full and round. After seven minutes of prancing around the living room in black, sheer chiffon, Loyda came over to Sasha and tongue kissed her like a dude: strong, deep and hard. Once Sasha squeezed her breast between her fingers and sucked on her nipples, she'd grown slippery with excitement. Sailing down south might not make her seasick after all.

The party moved to the bedroom upstairs, where Ty had even more candles lit and his bed smothered in rose pedals. He sat in the chaise lounge across from the bed gawking, totally engrossed, like he was watching the last five minutes of the seventh game of the NBA Conference Finals and the score was tied. He wouldn't have left the room if a smoke detector had sounded off. As long as Sasha was freakin' this dancer, the entire first floor could have burned down for all he cared. Once the two women had had their fun and he couldn't resist any longer, he stripped, dived on top of Sasha and screamed like a bitch when he came.

Sasha embraced her new sexuality with fervor. With female lovers she discovered a tenderness she'd never experienced with a man. She liked the feel of soft, supple skin against her own. She enjoyed their warm, gentle palms that stroked her breasts, never groping them as men did. In women she found a kindred spirit that understood the magical energy of being connected, touched and cuddled. Many nights she lay entangled in the arms of her female lovers, talking late into the night long after Ty had *come* and gone to sleep.

Three and half years and a baby later, Sasha was a self-proclaimed bisexual, picking up women at the grocery store, movie premieres, the mall and tonight at the Playboy Mansion, a very likely place. Though she'd never utter the words aloud, Ty would definitely be her last brother. After him, only sisters would follow.

Everyone who had ever worked or gotten high with Al West was at the party. Old cats he'd known from back in the day and young cats he worked with now. There were a few has-been models he'd had orgies with and younger ones he was sleeping with now. Regardless of their age, they all had bleached poodle ringlets or Pocahontas weaves and clothes plastered to their slim bodies, with only a few ounces dividing the slim and healthy from the thin and sickly. And though they were all there to celebrate Al's big day, they all went out of their way to schmooze with Ty, the black producer of the year. He was the hottest male in the room, attracting nothing but red-hot flames. Women came on to him in front of Sasha and even more behind her back. The smart ones came on to them both.

Seated in a coveted corner in the lounge, Ty relaxed on a red velvet pimp sofa. Sasha moved toward him, surprised the barracudas had not surrounded him, sniffing his money.

"I made a friend in the ladies' room," she said as she sat down next to him.

"Oh, yeah. What's she like?"

"Beautiful. Puerto Rican, I think. You'll see. I invited her over."

"What does she do? Where's she from?"

She shrugged innocently. "I don't know. I just met her."

Though he had turned her on to women, or "enlightened" her as he liked to say, her passion for women deeply disturbed him now. Every time he turned around, she was dragging someone new through the door, picking up chicks at any opportunity, never asking his opinion. It had gone much further than he'd anticipated. Sure, she had great taste in women. Never once had she brought home an off-brand mutt, but the scenario he'd created was chipping away at his ego, causing him to question his sexual prowess as never before. *Maybe he hadn't been pleasing her before all the women came into the picture? Maybe she'd been faking orgasms all this time? Maybe she was using him to procreate?* All she talked about was how many kids she wanted and the only job she ever wanted in life was to be a mother.

Ty threw his head back and swallowed half of his champagne in one big gulp. The negative whispers of his alter ego were momentarily silenced when he leaned forward and laid eyes on Dominique. Those emerald-green eyes intrigued and enticed him at once. Damned if Sasha couldn't pick them better than he could. The girl was drop-dead gorgeous. He wished he'd crossed her path while he was alone. Now here was a woman worth cheating with. Who knows? Sasha had guessed wrong once or twice before. Maybe Dominique wasn't into cunt. Maybe, just maybe, she was an old-fashioned girl who was still down for the conventional missionary fuck.

Jay-Z was spitting out lyrics over a deep bass beat in the background. A few people sitting in the semi-dark room got up and danced right in front of their seats.

"Dominique, I'm so glad you could join us. This is my boyfriend, Ty."

Dominique nodded and smiled. "This place is so crowded I was beginning to think I wouldn't find you."

"That's what happens when Hugh Hefner and Al West have a party in the same place. We probably couldn't count how many people have come and gone in their lives."

"I don't know Al personally. Just know of him. And based on that, I guess you're right."

"Have a seat," Ty offered. "What are you drinking? We're having champagne."

"Champagne is fine."

Ty headed for the bar.

"Have you been here before?" Sasha asked.

"No, it's my first time."

"What do you think?"

"I think I wore too many clothes," Dominique joked, looking around at the scantily dressed Bunnies and other women. "And I'm amazed that this is someone's home."

"It's wild, isn't it?"

"In more ways than one." Dominique had her radar up, trying to size up the couple and their intentions. She already knew hers. Sasha was attractive, but it was Ty whom she wanted to get close to. It was Ty who could accelerate her budding acting career, put money in her pockets and make her a star. Since Dominique landed at LAX from Chicago five years ago, she'd done extensive research, rummaging through the *Hollywood Reporter*, *People* magazine and *Entertainment Weekly*, accumulating bios, film and television credits and photos of Hollywood's who's who. Those with big bucks, those with almighty power and those she wanted to know. She'd spent days carefully cutting and pasting her hit list. The scrapbook comprised of mostly men; studio heads, a few producers and directors; faces she wanted to recognize if she by chance bumped into them in the frozen-food section at Ralphs Supermarket, the West LA Gym or the Playboy Mansion in Beverly Hills. As a fairly new producer, Ty was near the back of her book, number thirty-four. On his page she'd pasted a few articles along with a picture of him at the last year's Emmys and another she'd torn out of *Jet* magazine's Photo of the Week of him and Sasha walking the red carpet at a movie premiere. She knew exactly who Ty was, right down to his murderous hometown. Actually, she found out about the incident from a friend. Ty refused to discuss his brother's death or any of his family with reporters. The death of his brother was insider's scoop.

Her friends thought she was a certifiable nut case, but she considered herself a genius for thinking up the scrapbook idea. After her third audition, she realized she'd need a different approach to stand out from the crowd of all the pretty actresses. And she didn't believe in coincidences. If she ran into someone who could help her career or give her an advantage, she'd have to seize the moment. Make the most of an opportunity. And tonight had presented a damn good opportunity. The rumor mill had brought the news to her ears that Ty and Sasha had an open relationship. Sasha had flirted with her and saved Dominique the trouble. She had figured Sasha to be soft, docile and passive, but Sasha was much more aggressive than she appeared to be in her innocent-looking photos. Dominique wasn't easily intimidated. If she saw a hole for stealing Sasha's man, she would. Whether big enough for a truck or tiny enough for a fly, she'd sliver her self through it. Dominique could feel excitement boiling up within her. Being so close to Ty made her tingle all over. He had presence, charisma, gentlemanly grace, good looks and lots and lots of money. And most importantly, he had the power to change her fate.

"You and your boyfriend make a cute couple." She pondered how tight Ty and Sasha really were. She planned to push and pull until she found a weak link or created one, whichever came first.

"Thanks, but he's not my boyfriend. He's my life partner." Sasha lowered her eyes. "He just doesn't know it yet," she joked.

Dominique laughed aloud as she stored this bit of information in her memory bank.

"Have you seen Hugh walking around?" Dominique asked.

"No, but I'm dying to see if he looks older in person. See if he wears makeup or something strange like that," Sasha said.

They giggled. "Surely makeup doesn't help him when he's on camera 'cause he still looks old as dirt. He's older than my grandfather. Can you imagine?" Dominique asked.

"Imagine what? Hugh can't do anything for me at his age. As Moms Mabley said, an old man can't do nothin' for me but bring me a message from a young one," Sasha said.

The two women giggled.

"Who is Moms Mabley? I'd like to meet her," Dominique said.

"A comedian from back in the day. You know, Viagra has probably changed Hugh's life," Sasha said.

"Literally brought a wrinkled pimp back from the dead," Dominique said.

They laughed again.

Ty returned with two nearly naked Bunnies hustling behind him, one carrying glasses, another toting a bucket of ice filled with a bottle of Cristal champagne. After the flutes were passed and filled, they smirked and toasted to health and happiness out loud. Secretly they all toasted to a good night of sex. The energy of the Playboy Mansion was overwhelming and inescapable.

The deejay decided to give everyone a free Concord ride back into the nineties with the Notorious B.I.G. Tingling from the champagne, Sasha got up from her seat and started dancing. She beckoned Dominique to join her. They moved toward the dance floor, where Sasha, facing Dominique, took her by both hands and swung her hips left to right. Dominique picked up the rhythm and moved with it. Sasha smiled flirtatiously, losing herself in the alto voice of the rapper and Dominique's green eyes as they danced. Dominique did likewise, before freeing her hands and turning her back to Sasha, giving her a rear view. Sasha swayed left to right as she held on to Dominique's small waist, before dropping her hands to her hips and eventually her outer thighs. Beneath her palms she felt firm, hot flesh.

Dominique moved her hips and thighs like a ballerina, skillfully, taking the time to feel every beat of the music. She zeroed in on Ty, and watched as his eyes sucked in the show. She squinted her eyes for clarity. She could have sworn he was foaming at the mouth. She winked and ran her pink tongue across her glossy lips, then gave a devilish grin. That's when his dick woke up and he started mentally undressing her, one designer garment at a time.

An hour and a half later Ty and Sasha sped along the Pacific Coast Highway toward Sasha's house in Malibu with Dominique following close behind in her Mercedes.

Before Ty opened his eyes to greet the new day he felt a shadow, a weight between him and the morning sun. When his eyes opened, Sasha was breathing over him in her skimpy silk kimono, looking like the Wicked Witch of the West. Her golden ringlets tousled into a mess. Her eyebrows so furrowed they connected as one. "You humped Dominique too long and too hard."

He shut his eyes and flipped his six-foot-one frame over like a fish. "What are you talking about?"

She shoved him a bit on the shoulder. "Don't play dumb. You humped that girl as if I wasn't even here."

He rolled over and gazed at her, knowing she wasn't going to let him rest for the remainder of the day. "We had the type of party we always have, Sasha. Two girls and one man, me."

"No, no, no. This was different."

He sneaked a peek at the clock and decided to get up. He was due at the studio in an hour and Sasha wasn't about to let him snooze. He stepped into his boxers for cover. His nakedness made him feel too vulnerable to put up a good fight. He rummaged through the plethora of sweatsuits and jeans he housed at her place. "Did you have a nightmare?"

"Damn right, I had a nightmare. I saw my man humping another girl."

"Why are you trying to ruin my day from jump?"

"I'm serious, Ty. Don't ever embarrass me like that again."

"Embarrass you? How did I embarrass you?"

"By acting as though you enjoyed her more than me. You would murder the man who screwed me in front of your face."

"Damn right."

"Right now, Dominique is driving down the PCH thinking she's got you. Thinking she could probably take my man from me."

"By the sound of your temper over this, apparently you're thinking the same thing. But you need not worry about that."

"Yeah, yeah, yeah. I know. I am yours and you are mine," she mocked the words he'd told her a million times as they made love. "Maybe it's time we define the swinging rules, 'cause this isn't working for me."

"I wasn't the only one who enjoyed Dominique. You were eating her out last night."

"I don't care. No more penetrating the third person. You can watch us get it on and that's it. Only watch."

"Fine." He had no objections. Watching worked for him. Always had.

She plopped down on the side of the bed, too angry to appreciate the ocean view in front of her. "I knew this would happen one day. I knew it," she said, damning herself.

"The only problem last night was the champagne. You had too much," Ty said.

"Is that why you were fucking her as if I wasn't here?"

"No, that's why you are tripping. Every time you have more than two glasses, you start hallucinating. I knew where you were. You're putting too much on this."

Sasha folded her arms and poked out her lips as Ty stood over her.

"Now, who picked her out for us?" he asked.

"I did."

"Who always picks our partners?"

"I do."

"I rest my case." He turned and headed off to the bathroom. The marble floor felt slightly cool on the bottoms of his feet.

Sasha followed him, both of them facing the long rectangular mirror as he turned on the faucet. "But I thought she was a straight lesbian."

He smirked at himself in the mirror, savoring Sasha's jealousy. A tinge of guilt lay seated in his subconscious.

"Your bad. Not mine. And I'm not taking the blame," Ty said.

"How was I supposed to know?"

"How about asking?" he said smugly.

The regular routine was she and the other girl would have sex and Ty watched. He knew the deal and she knew the deal, but Dominique didn't. She'd wanted him, not Sasha. He'd seen it in her eyes as she danced at the club. He knew it when she sat beside him and gently stroked his thigh. In bed she kept reaching out for him, touching him, exciting him. So he stopped resisting the overwhelming feeling in his groin and entered her. It was for physical relief as well as mental. He was paying Sasha back for enjoying the women more than him, consciously breaking the rules out of pure spite. And it worked. He tried desperately not to smirk as she ranted about him enjoying Dominique. Revenge was sweet. And so was Dominique.

Sasha leaned against the tiled wall, staring at Ty's reflection in the mirror. "We wouldn't be having this conversation if we were married."

Before Ty could respond the baby started crying over the intercom and Sasha raced to her rescue.

After Ty dressed, he came into the kitchen where Sasha fed Taylor, and Maria, the Mexican housekeeper, was busy cooking eggs and toast.

"*Buenas días*, Señor Ty."

"*Qué pasa*, Maria."

"You like breakfast? I make you some."

"No thanks, Maria."

Ty grabbed Taylor from a still pouting Sasha and held her up in the air. "How's my queen?"

She kicked her chunky legs and reached for his face. Taylor had fat, chubby cheeks to match her legs. Her face was a perfect combination of Ty and Sasha. His cheekbones and eyes. Her nose and chin. With an inch of hair to call her own, Taylor was an adorable, jovial child. "Daddy. Daddy."

His smile spread from ear to ear. Taylor was his heartbeat. He'd never truly breathed and loved before she appeared in the world. Work kept him away from her most of the time, but he was able to give her anything money could buy. His dream was to provide a better life for her than he'd had. He hoped drugs and the streets never played a role in her life. He wanted Taylor to have the best education and see the world. He planned to spoil her irreversibly with money, and Sasha would spoil her with time and attention. One day his schedule would allow him to do the same. At least that's what he told himself.

After a half hour of quality "daddy time," he was on his way. He opened the double maple doors at the front of Sasha's house. An ocean wind grabbed him by his sagging jeans, sending a chill through his legs. He could never figure out why she wanted to live in Malibu. Black people rarely went to the beach, let alone lived on one. On the brick front stoop lay the revised script. One was always delivered to his home as well as Sasha's. He picked up the envelope, jumped in his truck and jetted down the PCH toward the 10 freeway.

The sun was warm against Venus's back as she lay on her belly by the pool at Leede's home in the hills of Hollywood. She was wearing a white bikini. Leede's hands were even warmer than the sun as his palms methodically massaged her calves with oil. She giggled. Teasing her with every stroke of the hand and fingers, he slid upward to her thighs. She exhaled with pleasure. His touch could not have been more satisfying if Jesus himself was massaging her. Suddenly a sound disturbed her supreme peace. She frowned. It was Leede's cell phone, ringing and ringing and ringing. Why didn't he answer it? Wait. She was the assistant. Was she supposed to get it? That's when Venus cracked open her eyelids and realized she wasn't lying by a pool. She was lying in her bed, *dreaming*. And the phone that kept ringing and ringing was *hers*. Like a vampire threatened by the daylight that seeped through her windows, she quickly shut her eyes, trying to leap back into her divine dream, but it was useless. She was already lucid.

Her eyes shot over to the clock on her nightstand. It was 8 A.M. She didn't have to show her face at work until 10. Who was calling at this hour? Probably someone in her family back in Texas, maybe one of her aunts, calling to tell her about who was, or more important wasn't, in church on Sunday. She just couldn't appreciate gossip in the morning. But they didn't care. It was already 10 A.M. where her aunts lived and the hungry, the homeless and the unemployed should be out of the bed by now. Even though she'd been living in Los Angeles for over a year, they still didn't care about the difference in the time zones. She reluctantly reached for the receiver to see which member of the clan was cutting in on her steamy fantasy.

"Hello." Her voice was fuzzy. She cleared her throat.

"Venus, this is Kurt. Sorry to wake you." Kurt was the line producer. There was urgency in his voice. She braced herself.

"Sid's script didn't get delivered last night." Sid had no doubt phoned Kurt this morning and had a conniption fit over the matter.

What am I supposed to do, call LAPD and report forty-four pages of dialogue missing? "I'll make sure Ty knows," she replied.

"Yeah, I want him to be prepared when Sid brings it up. He might have a temper tantrum over this."

"Okay, bye."

She rolled over. Hollywood people could make a feature film out of anything. Everyday life was acted out as if it were a drama on a fifteen-foot screen, making the least little thing larger than life. And just like a movie, it would take the staff two hours to resolve this one little mishap. Like there was some complicated mystery. It was as simple as the time zones, as far as she was concerned.

First of all, the writers didn't complete the script until midnight. They could have finished before then had they not spent half the evening deciding on dinner and critiquing videos. By the time the production assistants made all the script copies and bratted enough for the cast and crew, it had to be around three. And that was if the copier didn't break down. So the scripts probably didn't reach the doorsteps of producers until three thirty or four in the morning. Was he planning on getting out of his bed to peruse it then? He was probably lying up with Naja, feigning like a junkie for a second hit at that hour. Uh, huh. She'd heard the rumors floating around the production office about Ol' Sid and his addiction to Hershey's Kisses. He always did strike her as a freak trying to pass himself off as a nerd with those wire-frame glasses and crew-cut hair, scanning chocolate-coated ass each time one passed.

As the assistant to the executive producer it was her duty to pass this information on to her boss. Had Sid been a cast member, there would have been reason to be alarmed. But crying over scripts was just part of the game. No one wanted to be excluded or overlooked. Everybody wanted to be a player and receive their due attention to reaffirm his or her importance. Nevertheless, a PA had screwed up royally for not having delivered that script, and somebody's head was going to roll off the studio lot, straight into the unemployment office as a result.

She sat up on the side of her bed, gathering herself. She didn't dare call Ty at this hour about something as frivolous as a script. No telling what time he went to sleep. She knew he'd gone to the Playboy Mansion last night. She'd RSVP'd for him. Then again, he might fuss because she'd waited to tell him. This was the hardest part of her job, gauging his frame of mind and anticipating his reactions. As a mere mortal with no psychic abilities, she was left to use deductive reasoning. Concluding Sid wasn't important enough, she made the executive decision to wait. No need to rush the day's drama and raise the body count of fired employees. She and everyone else in the office had heard about Leede flipping out over a warm waffle he thought should have been hot. Surely that issue would come up today as well. She folded her arms, contemplating. *I wonder if he'd pull that childish stunt on me.* Dreaming about Leede might actually be better than living with him. Using the remote control, she turned on the television and took a trip around the world in three minutes with CNN.

After she leisurely showered and dressed, she called Ty on his cell phone.

"Hey, Venus. What's up?"

She was happy to hear him in a good mood and happier that he was out and about. Traffic boomed in the background. "Kurt called me this morning. It seems Sid didn't get a script delivered to his home last night."

"He barely reads the damn things." Ty sighed. "But that's beside the point. This is the second time this season a script wasn't delivered." Ty took all of these things as a reflection of his show, considering his production the black sheep of

Rex. "Next time it could be someone who really is important. What time did he call?"

"At eight."

"Who was supposed to deliver the script?"

"He didn't say."

"If it's the same PA who screwed up Leede's lunch yesterday, he's fired." He paused, thinking. "Find out and set up a meeting with Kurt and Maxwell first thing this morning. We need to get to the bottom of this script situation."

"Okay."

"I'll see you later."

She hung up hoping poor Kevin was not the culprit behind the missing script. As a PA he made slightly above minimum wage, yet was expected to perform miracles daily.

"Someone should be fired for this," Naja had whined when she awoke at Sid's house and waltzed to the front door in a hot-pink silk robe she'd taken home from the show and found no script at his doorstep.

Standing at the kitchen island Sid advised, "Take it easy, babe. Don't whip yourself into a frenzy over this."

She smacked her lips as she watched him measure ground coffee. Sid was ignorant of the pressures of acting. She needed her script like a builder needed his tools. "I cannot do my job properly when others aren't doing theirs," she huffed. As a routine, she reviewed her script, coffee in hand, lying in bed. During the first few hours of the day she found it much easier to commit words to memory.

"You need to call and complain. You need the script too.

Isn't that part of your job?" she said, her arms folded tightly across her chest.

Sid hit the ON button on the coffee machine. With crust still caked in the corners of his eyes, he reluctantly picked up the phone and voiced an official complaint, knowing he'd be the one labeled "asshole."

Ty sat behind his desk with the *Hollywood Reporter*, skimming the headlines. Maxwell was seated to his left in a chocolate chair, his long legs stretched out in front of him. Kurt rushed in with a voluminous vanilla folder under his arm.

"Hey guys."

Both men greeted him as he took a seat on the sofa, setting his folder on the coffee table. Kurt was one of Ty's favorite white people. They'd met three years prior while working on another production. As the line producer, Kurt handled everything from hiring the crew to balancing the budget. He knew all the ins and outs of creative accounting. Had he been willing to wear anything other than jeans and a sweatshirt every day, he'd have made one hell of a tax attorney.

"So what's this about Sid not getting a script?" Ty asked.

"He phoned my assistant at the crack of dawn, apparently furious about his script not being at his front door."

"And who was supposed to deliver it?"

"Zack," Kurt answered.

"Then fire him," Ty commanded.

"Come on. Give the kid a chance. It's his first time. He's only been here a few months."

Ty looked to Kurt for answers. He didn't keep up with PAs.

"He's just okay. And it's not his first mistake. Two weeks ago he was late bringing lunch for the office."

"What are we going to do? Fire someone every time something goes wrong?"

Ty turned to him curiously. "Why not?"

"It's called human error. A PA messed up Leede's lunch order yesterday and he's still here."

"That's because he didn't mess up my order. Otherwise, he'd be fired too."

"I say give the kid a chance. It was only Sid Porter. What's the big deal?"

"Next time it will be Russ Tobin."

"He doesn't get the scripts."

"But what if he did? Look, I'm trying to run a tight ship here. There is no room for errors."

"This happens all the time. You know how those execs are. They can be fussy about the least little thing," Maxwell argued.

"PAs are a dime a dozen. There are a million kids out here trying to get their foot in the door. Why are you holding on to him?" asked Ty.

Maxwell shrugged. "I see potential in him."

"From what I hear, Zack comes from old money. He doesn't need you to see his potential. His rich daddy can hook him up without any potential whatsoever."

Maxwell was silent.

Kurt jumped in, anxious for a conclusion so he could plan his day. If he had to hire another PA by tomorrow, he needed time to line up some candidates. He didn't care one way or another. He generally steered clear of office politics and focused on kissing Ty's butt, which is why Ty liked him so much. He never spoke the one word Ty hated most: no. "So what's the verdict, gentlemen? Is he in or out?"

"He's in," Ty answered, his eyes resting on Maxwell. "And you take full responsibility for his actions. You got that?"

"All right."

"I'm serious. If he screws up again it's on you. And you are going to fire him."

"Okay. No problem. I'll keep him in check."

"I'm serious. I've got better things to do with my day."

"Don't worry. I got this," said Maxwell.

Kurt picked up his folder. "Ty, I've got some credits for you to sign and I need you to approve the budget for next week's show."

Maxwell excused himself from the office and entered the anteroom where Venus sat behind her desk manning the lines.

Rojas called asking if she'd received his headshot and resume. According to him, Ty gave him special instructions to follow up with her. As if she had the power to cast him or anyone else for that matter. Craig, Ty's brother, called from the gate in his new truck requesting a drive-on pass. Venus had spent the previous afternoon on the phone with the dealership, conveying all of Ty's credit information so he could get the vehicle. Gary Ackerman's assistant called barking demands. The more powerful the boss they assisted, the more pompous the assistant. "Gary has to meet with Ty today," she commanded before Venus had the chance to glance at his schedule.

Leaning against her desk, Maxwell saw the frustration on

her face. "This is one hell of a morning, huh?" he said, speaking for himself and her.

"You just said a mouthful. And it all started at eight o'clock this morning. Before I even got here."

"I was meditating at eight, and it's a good thing I did."

"Really? You meditate every day?"

"I try to. It really makes a difference. It helps you to remain calm when everything around you is blowing up."

"Like my phones," she joked. "But it really helps, huh?"

"It does. Helps get you focused on what's important in life, which is life itself. This plastic world we work in isn't important in the big picture of things."

"All these pain-in-the-butt people. It sure feels like the real thing to me," she joked.

Maxwell was always around the office preaching what he professed to practice. He could hold court for hours discussing everything from astrology to metaphysical theories. With his thoughts thirty-five thousand feet above sea level, it's a wonder he was able to work a mundane job, punching a clock each day.

"You should try it. Imagine this, V. You close your eyes and there's nothing but darkness." The excitement in his voice escalated. "Then, you stay in the darkness meditating until you see light."

Her eyes widened. "Wow. That's deep. You take that journey every day?"

"No. That would take routine practice. I'm also in a meditation group and we're having a special one tonight. One of my spiritual teachers, Paulo, is in from Brazil and he's leading it. You should come check it out."

"Maybe I will." Venus had been raised in a conventional Baptist church. Since coming to California she'd learned about other spiritual practices. She'd even had a tarot reading from a tanned middle-aged woman, wearing rings from her nose down to her toes, who told her she'd make a lot of money from a stack of papers. Venus prayed they were script pages. Venus had tasted just enough of the California spiritual world to be even more curious about it. The spirituality rather than religion attracted her.

"I'll get you the address. Look, I gotta go do some work before I get fired." He lowered his voice, "You know your boy is on a roll." They both snickered.

As Maxwell exited, Craig walked in, the hem of his blue jeans sweeping the floor. A smile slowly crept across his mouth, flashing four fourteen-karat-gold-trimmed teeth.

"What's up, Big Tittie?"

Venus glanced up at him, disgusted by the name and his gold. "It's 'Big City.'" She emphasized the C.

He chuckled, grabbing the crotch of his pants. "That's what I meant. Big City. You know I was just playing with you, girl." He laughed with a grunt. "How you doing?"

"I'm okay. How are you?"

"I'm all right, now that I'm here. This joint got more security than the FBI Headquarters."

"What do you know about the FBI Headquarters? I know you wouldn't go there."

"Hell no. They'd have to come after me with a notarized warrant." He sucked his gold teeth. "So what y'all servin' up in here for lunch?"

Great! Now, not only would she have to get Ty's lunch,

she'd have to fetch some for his knucklehead brother. Then he'd want her to write and type a letter to his probation officer. After that, he'd want to use her computer to surf porn websites. Then she'd have to call IT to unscramble her hard drive. She wondered if Steven Spielberg had a special-ed brother who harassed his assistant. Probably. President Clinton suffered his brother Roger. Every family had at least one fool.

Craig spent more time fooling himself than others. Working two days a week as an extra on the show, he deemed himself an actor. His acting gig earned him just enough money to supply himself with Newports and fill up the tank on the truck Ty bought for him. The other three days of the week he worked his second job, which was hanging around the office being a nuisance.

Zack timidly rapped on Maxwell's door before entering.

Maxwell looked up from his computer. "Come on in."

Zack removed his Yankees cap and sank down in a chair, prepared to catch hell. Danny, a PA, had been the first to phone him about the missing script. Kurt had been the second, but was less kind about it. He only imagined how much less Maxwell would be, especially if he hadn't had his fix this morning. Either way, he was expecting a pink slip and his last paycheck.

"So what's going on, man? What happened last night?"

"Nothing happened. I delivered papers and I got home at three o'clock this morning."

"Well you overlooked a spot, because Sid didn't get his papers." Maxwell stressed the word "papers," mocking Zack's slang.

"You think I haven't heard? Maaan, you know this type of thing happens all the time. People walk out and forget them. A neighbor ends up picking it up. Or they miss it in a corner."

"I know how it can all go down. But how did it go down last night?

"I delivered a script to Sid's house. He's been on my route all season. I can get to his crib with my eyes closed. It's always midnight or after when I go. Tell him to check behind all those bushes around his yard."

"I'm not telling him nothin'. But I am telling you. No more fuck-ups. I can't keep sticking my neck out for you. Next time you're out of here."

"Thanks, Buddha." Zack reached in his pocket and pulled out a paper neatly folded into a square. He extended his arm out. "Here. This is on me."

Maxwell reached out, accepting the package.

"This is some good shit," said Zack. "Cell Block would probably like this. He definitely looks like he gets down."

"Look, I've told you. Don't be trying to sell this stuff to nobody up here. Nobody! I just saved your ass. I'm not doing it again."

"Calm down, Buddha. I was just kidding. You know I ain't no drug dealer, for real. I'm just hooking you up. And if you want me to stop, I can."

Maxwell held his tongue, remembering they needed each other. "I don't want people to get suspicious."

Zack was the only person who knew about his cocaine habit and Maxwell planned on keeping it that way.

It was Maxwell who'd helped Zack secure a gig on the

show. He was a friend of a friend Maxwell had met during his stay at the Betty Ford Clinic. He'd told everyone he had spent a month of his hiatus in the Palm Springs area. No one had suspected he was in a rehab airing out. For one month he laid poolside in a luxury rehab, tanning next to America's elite.

Zack had started hooking him up at the beginning of the season. It was high-quality snow he couldn't get from just anybody. So, while Maxwell claimed to have saved Zack's job, the only thing he was worried about saving was his drug connection.

N aja circled her dressing room like a caged puppy in a shelter. She flipped through the revised blue pages, counting her lines before she forced them to memory. She twisted her lips, annoyed. She had no more lines than in the first draft. That damn Sid. He'd said there would be more lines. She sauntered back and forth along the small floor, mouthing the words until the stage manager summoned her down for rehearsal.

Everyone, with the exception of Leede, was onstage when she arrived wearing a hooded baby-blue terry cloth sweatsuit. Her jacket hung open, revealing the white tube top she wore underneath. After greeting the other cast members she turned her attention to Cell Block. "We haven't officially met. I'm Naja." She extended her soft, slender hand.

He took her right hand and kissed the back of it like a fine gentleman. "I know exactly who you are."

She blushed, savoring the accolade. "Really?"

"Word. I'm a fan of the show."

"I'm glad you like my work."

"And I always know who the beautiful ladies are." Cell licked his lips with admiration.

"Have you done any acting?"

"Nope. This is my first shot at it. And I'm glad it's with you." He paused, taking a good, long look at her from breast to thigh like she was something to eat. "You are fine."

"Uuhh, thanks," she said, uncertain if she liked the compliment or not.

"You were in that John Legend video, weren't you?"

"Yes. That was me."

"Uh, huh. I'd like to put you in one of my videos."

"Oh, my video career is over. I don't do videos anymore."

"Really? That's too bad. Then maybe we could have dinner or something?"

She smiled. "I don't think so."

"Why not? You don't like rap music or somethin'?"

When Leede finally showed up twenty minutes late for rehearsal, the director started guiding the actors through the script, line by line, step by step. While Leede and Naja took center stage on the set Cell Block sat off in the bleachers with his eyes glued to Naja.

The only thing Cell Block could think about was having sex with Naja. His lascivious thoughts were a subconscious distraction, keeping his fears of acting at a manageable distance. So, rather than focusing on fear, he focused on Naja.

When the cast broke for lunch, Naja stood over the craft service table nibbling on carrot sticks and taking inventory of the fattening foods. She gazed longingly at the cinnamon buns. She couldn't remember the last time she'd tasted one. Her eyes roamed over the chocolate candy. As she dreamed of what she'd dare not eat, she felt a body beside her. It was "Block-head," looking at her like she was a chocolate morsel ready to be eaten. Naja twisted her lips in annoyance and pretended he was invisible. This young hoodlum was coming on to her like she was a video ho. She knew what that world was like. He probably banged, literally banged, every chick in his videos and the groupies at his concerts. He was kind of cute, even if he did have a big head and neck like Shrek. She'd give him that much credit. But that was it. She was far above him in every way. He was a child and she was a grown-ass woman. He must have been high if he thought his designer thug-wear and diamonds would impress her.

He stood over her right shoulder. "I was checking you out onstage. Maybe you could give me some acting lessons?"

She smiled and sidestepped away from him, never taking her eyes from the table. "I think a professional would be better."

"Umph, umph, umph. Girl, you got skills onstage."

"You think so, huh?"

"I'd love to work with a beautiful woman like you every day," he said, inching closer to her.

"Thanks," she said flatly.

"Maybe you could give me a few pointers?"

"I don't give acting pointers. I'm still taking them and learning myself."

"Don't worry. I catch on quick." He paused, looking for her reaction. "And who knows? A young brother like myself might teach you a few things."

"Is that so?"

"You never know. I've been around."

You've been in jail. "I'm sure you have."

"I see you can't find anything you want. Let me take you out to lunch," he said, moving in even closer, invading her personal space.

"I'm fine right here, thanks. And I need to go over my lines."

He stepped closer. "Why don't I come in your dressing room and we can rehearse that kiss in the script?"

She took one step away from him, creating space. "Why don't you back off, Block-Head? I mean, Cell Block. I'm not interested."

He smirked, taking pleasure in her challenge. "You don't know about what you've never had."

"I can assure you, I know more than enough."

He bent down and whispered in her ear, the heat of his breath tickling her ear. "I can tell you like it hard and fast. I'll make you scream louder than my fans at a concert," he said while sliding his left paw ever so lightly over her ass.

She turned to him, disgusted and appalled, giving him a deadly stare. Her lips tightened as she spoke in the same soft whisper as he had. "Listen, I'm sure you're probably used to having your way with the little groupies and all, but I'm not interested. You got that? And if you ever touch this high-priced ass again, you're going to have some new testimonies to write from the cellblock."

Cell Block's ego was deflated before her eyes. A laugh

came out of his mouth to hide his embarrassment. Naja would bet he wanted to curse her, but refrained. "Girl, you can't take a joke or a compliment," he said before walking away.

Same Day Service was the story of a couple who'd married right out of college and had a dream of becoming the Jeffersons. They'd both worked hard and saved enough money to open a dry cleaning business. Four years later when the business was off the ground and they were out of the red, their marriage had ended. Having invested everything they had in the cleaners, neither was willing to give up their share of the business. Still good friends, they held on to their entrepreneurial dreams. Both refused to walk away and so they struggled to make the business work as they skirted the fact they were still in love with each other.

During the first season, the scripts revolved around them pulling antics on each other, each trying to make the other give up and leave. This season the focus was on each of them dating—supposedly trying to move on with their lives, but really attempting to make each other jealous.

There were regular characters on the show, like Johnny Mack, best man at their wedding and confidant to Leede's character. Johnny was a cab driver who always needed to hold a few dollars. Leede's ongoing joke on the show was that Johnny Mack passed ten potential passengers on his way over to borrow twenty dollars. Then there was Anita, who was Naja's character's best friend. She never liked Leede and he never really liked her. So, they were always throwing insults at each other, like Fred Sanford and Aunt Esther. From time to time the couples' parents made appearances, when the writers ran out of ideas for Leede and Naja and wrote in-law episodes.

This week Cell Block would walk into the cleaners and offer Naja tickets to his concert after she pretends to be a fan to make Leede jealous. And it works. Leede's character would try to sabotage the date by not cleaning Cell Block's clothes in time for the show. The credits would roll while Cell Block closed the show with a performance as Leede and Naja stood in the audience, friends again.

When the cast returned from lunch, it was Cell Block's turn to rehearse. Standing in front of Naja with his script in hand, Cell's confidence quickly vanished as he painfully struggled to keep up with his lines. His hardcore face turned blank. When Naja delivered a line, he was confused over what his line was in response to hers. His lines had not changed at all, but hers had and he couldn't keep up since he read on a third grade level. He stood paralyzed until the director fed him his line. He stiffly repeated it.

"Try to relax, Cell," the director instructed him from his tall folding chair. "Act like you're onstage rapping. Let the words just roll off your lips."

Cell Block nodded. Acting did not compare to rapping. He never had to read or play against anyone else. At his concerts it was just him and the rhymes in his head. The very first one he'd ever created was safely tucked away in his memory bank.

Having skipped the audition process because he'd been hired based on the weight of his image and record sales, he simply had not thought about the fact that he would be required to read. On the previous Saturday night, Cell had hung out all night with his cronies and returned home high as Halley's comet at six o'clock Sunday morning to find a script at his front door. Glancing down at it, he sobered instantly. He picked up the pages, went in the house and called his momma, Diane. She knew his secret and would keep it as long as her name was on his payroll. With her hanging on the speakerphone, he skimmed through the pages searching for his name. Then he faxed them to Diane and called her later that evening after he'd slept all day. He could have sounded them out, but success had spoiled him and so had his momma. She'd gone over the script with him like a dialogue coach until he'd committed his scenes to memory.

Now standing in front of Naja, who stared at him as if he was a retard, his heart raced and he flashed back to Jesse LaSalle Junior High School. In his third-period geography class, the teacher, Mrs. Wright, had called on him to read. When his eyes fell on the page, the letters melted into one another, making one big blur, and he had to use his index finger to follow. He stumbled and stuttered through the paragraph with soggy palms and a rapidly palpitating heart. And to make matters worse, Tameeka Monroe, the biggest crush of his entire seventh grade year, was sitting right beside him looking annoyed, the way Naja was looking at him now. He ranked that day in Mrs. Wright's class as the most embarrassing moment of his life and the one good reason he had for dropping out of school by tenth grade. When one teacher mentioned dyslexia his ego folded. He simply couldn't admit the problem.

"My bad. Maybe I need some time to go over my script," Cell Block said. What he really needed was time to call his momma.

"We're close to the end. Just go with it. We've got all week to get it right," the director said.

Naja said her last line before Cell was to kiss her. Holding her script in hand she leaned up toward him for a quick peck. There was no need to really kiss now. Yet, Cell bent down, licked his lips, then sucked her mouth and slid his tongue down her throat. It was a weak attempt to regain his confidence, to salvage what was left of his ego. Naja jerked her head back abruptly and pulled away against the suction of his lips. Then she tramped off the stage, her D-cups bouncing, and slammed her dressing room door.

Naja removed her sweat jacket and tossed it on the back of the vanity chair. Then she plopped down on the sofa, seething, eyes narrowed, lips tightened. She wasn't going to be sexually harassed by a stupid convict who'd gone platinum. When she was struggling to make it as an actress, there were several instances when she'd been physically violated by producers demanding sex in exchange for jobs. Yet she had remained mum. But now, she had transcended from being a nobody. She was Naja Starr, god damn it. She had some weight to throw around and she'd sling it like a penis if she had to.

She picked up the phone and called Ty's office.

"He's in a meeting. I'll have him call you, Naja," Venus said.

"Have him come over to the stage. I'll be in my dressing room. And I'm not going back into rehearsal until I see him."

Venus's eyes widened with excitement. She recognized drama when she heard it. The director had called for Ty only moments earlier. "You got it. He should be back soon."

Naja hung up and dialed her good-for-nothing agent, Lars Howerton, who never returned her calls on the day she called and never sent her out on enough film auditions.

"He's out of the office," Lars's assistant said.

"Then call him on his cell and tell him I need to talk to him today! Not tomorrow. Not the day after tomorrow. But today."

"Is there something I can help you with?" the assistant asked.

"Yes, you can have him call me today. It's important," Naja said before slamming down the phone.

She thought of calling Sid, but this would only piss him off. Besides, there was really nothing he could do to help her in this situation. She exhaled, glancing at her watch. It was about time she put something in her stomach. She got up and went for her stash of baby food in the closet. Perhaps a meal would help calm her down.

There was a knock at the door.

"Who is it?" she asked, hiding the Gerber jars.

It was Bernie, the stage manager. "Are you okay?"

She cracked the door three inches. "I'm okay. I just need to talk to Ty."

"We're still rehearsing. You want to talk with the director?"

"No."

Bernie looked confused. He'd missed the slip of Cell's tongue.

"I'm okay, Bernie. Really."

"What should I tell everyone? They're all asking about you."

"I don't care." She paused. "Tell them I'm sick," she offered before shutting the door in his face.

Building 130 was the administrative office for every division of the television department. As Ty entered, he could almost smell the starched shirts of the employees as he walked down the quiet hallways. His meeting with the network suits was scheduled for two o'clock. Gary Ackerman had requested the last minute meeting that very morning. Ty had been anticipating it for a few weeks, ever since the ratings had taken a small dive. As he stood at the desk of Gary's pretentious assistant, Cheryl, he hoped that was the only matter up for discussion. Still, he was unsure of how they'd handle it. What solutions they'd offer to abate the problem. He shoved his hands into his pants pockets, faking cool when he was anything but. Sure, he was a big-time executive producer and creator of his show, but ultimately he was an employee of the network, a subordinate. And the network could snatch away his power and his paycheck at any time.

Cheryl smiled, her dimples sinking into her round cheeks. "Go right on in, Ty." She examined him carefully as he turned away. She found him sexy as hell, in a Michael Jordan sort of way.

Gary's sunny office was filled with mid-grade contemporary furniture that was one step above what was in the production offices. His credenza held framed photos of his wife and kids. The shelves of his bookcase were stuffed with

scripts and books. He sat behind his desk, rising, as did David
Levine, when Ty stepped in.

"Hey, Ty," Gary greeted, stepping from behind his oak
veneer desk, wearing jeans, loafers, a sports jacket and a tan.

"How's it going, man?" David offered.

Ty smiled. "I can't complain." He glanced at his watch.
"It's two o'clock. You mean you guys haven't left for the golf
course?" he joked.

"Hell, I wish," David said.

"When are you going out with us?" Gary asked.

"I can't hang with you two. I would look like a real handi-
cap trying to keep up."

They laughed. "Aw, come on. You're not that bad, are you?"
David asked.

"Let's just say I'm not that good," Ty said. "And I won't em-
barrass myself by telling you my golf handicap," Ty said.

"We'd love to go a few holes with you anyway." Gary took
a seat on the blue sofa. Ty sat at the other end, while David
sat in a matching mid-grade chair. "Hey, listen. Thanks for ac-
commodating us on such short notice," said David.

"No problem." Ty replied.

"Can I get you anything? Water? Coffee?" Gary offered.

Ty flashed his manicured nails as he waved his hand. "No,
I'm good." He was ready to get down to business, anxious to
talk about his creation. *Same Day Service* was like his baby.
He'd solely conceived the idea for the show, writing late into
the night for weeks until the story was just right. Then he'd
shopped the script for nine months, meeting with studio ex-
ecutives, discussing his newborn over lunch, and getting re-

jected over dinner. Finally, Rex Studios gave him the green light to develop his show, giving his characters life. His baby had grown into a hit show. But like any parent, Ty never wanted to hear anything negative concerning his brainchild.

Gary crossed his legs and leaned back, resting his arm across the back of the sofa. "So, David and I have been looking over the ratings and we're slightly concerned."

"Me too, Gary. Me too. But these things happen. We're up against tough competition in our present time slot. I think it's a temporary slump."

Gary shrugged. "Could be. But here's the thing. Do we want to wait and see what happens or do we want to be proactive?"

"I'm not sitting back and waiting on anything. The writers are working on edgier material and I'm booking the biggest names my budget will allow. That's why Cell Block is on the show this week."

"And that's a damn good idea. I told you that before. But honestly, I don't think it's enough. What if we can't keep booking a big name? Maybe they aren't available, or what have you," Gary said.

Ty's eyebrows rose slightly. "So far, so good. We won't know what impact it will have until the show airs."

David spoke up. "That's true, but we're just not sure that will be enough to save the show."

"At this point, the show doesn't need saving. My ratings are still higher than most of the shows on the air."

"We know and we want to ensure they stay high. You've got a hit show and we'd like to keep it that way. We were thinking about something more permanent than having a guest star here and there." Gary eased into the introduction of his idea.

"What could be more permanent? A change in time slot? If we switch nights, we'll lose half the audience, especially without strong promotions."

"No, no. no. Nothing like that, Ty," David said, reassuring Ty of their support.

Ty cut to the chase. "Then what exactly do you have in mind?"

"We were thinking a new cast member."

Ty rubbed his goatee. "Introduce a new character on the show? What difference would that make in the ratings?"

Gary continued. "We're thinking a white character is what the show needs. After looking over the demographics, it's clear we're losing the crossover audience."

Ty could feel his blood heating up. He only nodded as they elaborated on their bullshit idea. He hated the word "crossover." *We're not getting the white audience* is what they meant. They had a lot of nerve. They certainly weren't meeting with white producers urging them to put more people of color on their shows. Send in a white knight to save his damn show. They probably already had an actor in mind, and had checked on his availability.

"The new guy would be hired in the cleaners and become like a member of the family," Gary said.

Ty's eyebrows furrowed. "A white guy a member of a black family?"

"Well, a fixture in their lives at the cleaners."

Ty chuckled slightly and shook his head. "I don't think it's plausible. Here's a black couple with their own business in a black neighborhood and they hire a white boy when so many blacks are unemployed? I don't think so."

Ty had conceived the idea of the show because he'd wanted to write a show that reflected the reality of ordinary African-Americans. Not some silly show where blacks laughed at being poor, or a rich family whose lineage formed the talented tenth. He desired to show America what hardworking, dignified, middle-class black Americans were like. And a white character just didn't fit into his vision.

"It doesn't matter how he's written in. I just think a white character would help."

"Until he becomes the star of the show?" Ty asked.

"Naah. Nothing like that. We just think the introduction of a new character would help the ratings."

Ty wanted to speak his mind. Tell them both to kiss his ass and go straight to hell, but he couldn't without sounding even more racist than they did. They had just laid a race card on the table. He'd have to play something better.

His thoughts ran laps around his head. The suits had hit him with an unexpected move. Obviously, he'd been excluded from a previous meeting where this idea was conceived. He hadn't anticipated they'd take such drastic measures in resolving the ratings problem. He wanted to be politically correct by coming across as a team player. On numerous occasions he'd flat-out said no to things like script notes and story direction, skipping over the bullshit like he was playing a quick game of checkers. But this was chess. They were making well thought out, strategic moves and they were using him as a pawn.

Ty nodded again. "I see. Do you have anyone in mind?"

"A couple of names came up but no one in particular. So, what do you think?"

"I don't know. I'll have to give it some thought," he replied as he rose to his feet. They might have called the meeting, but he was ending it. "There are many things to consider in adding a new character." He paused. "Has this been discussed with the studio?"

Gary stood up. "No. It's only a suggestion, Ty. We want to see this show make it to a hundred episodes and go to syndication."

Ty gave a fake smile. "That's good to know."

"Let's talk later in the week."

"Sure," Ty said before stepping out of the office into the anteroom, anxious to get out of their presence and breathe some fresh air. Under no circumstances could he let them see him sweat.

Gary remained seated with his legs crossed after Ty left. He honestly wasn't as concerned about the ratings as Russ Tobin. Ratings tended to fluctuate at times. The show was fine. He liked it and thought it worked well. The real problem was Ty. He was always obstinate. Always determined to do things his way, never agreeable. To make matters worse, they had no one in place in the production office to report back to them what was going on. Ty had flat-out refused to hire any of the producers they had suggested, and at some points demanded, he hire. He'd put up a big fuss and later a fight, saying he could hire who he wanted. But Gary was getting tired of going unheard. Tired of battling with Ty. Frustrated that his ideas were not being used. There were creative differences every week.

Thus far Gary had just gone along, but now it was time for Ty to give or go away. All he needed was one good reason and Ty would be out of the door. He could easily be replaced. The studio had contracts with plenty of qualified showrunners.

"What do you think?" Gary asked.

"I don't think he's going to go for it."

Gary sighed. "Me neither." He paused, thinking. "What should we tell Russ Tobin?"

"I don't know. The truth?" David replied.

"Of course I'll tell him the truth," he almost snapped. David could irritate the hell out of him with his simple answers. "But we should offer a solution. Make it look like we're on top of this situation."

"There is no solution for Ty. That's his personality. Take it or leave it. The only thing we could do is get rid of him."

"Now you're thinking!"

"Is that what you're thinking?" David shook his head. "Oh, I don't know about all that. He may not kiss our butts, but he's a good producer. He never, ever goes over his budget. His show tapes are delivered to us on time and he's never bad-mouthed the network or asked for anything special."

"Well, that's how it looks from the outside. We don't know what the hell he's doing over there. He damn sure isn't listening to us. Apparently he's doing whatever he wants to do."

"But if it ain't broke, why fix it?"

"Because Russ Tobin wants it fixed." This was Gary's big chance to make a lasting impression on the head honcho. If he came up with a solution, perhaps he'd get a promotion and a raise. He was sick of these younger punks collecting million-dollar paychecks while he brought home pennies. "Ty has got to be screwing up somewhere, and we need to find out where."

David said nothing. Once Gary made up his mind to do something, there was no turning him around. People were hired and fired so frequently he could hardly remember who worked where, unless he checked the trades. Ty would be just another casualty of the entertainment wars.

10

ive minutes after Venus informed Ty that Naja was
refusing to go back into rehearsal he was in a golf
cart pressing the accelerator through the floor. Totally
frustrated by the slow moving electric vehicle, he maneu-
vered the cart past fake houses and storefronts on the back-
lot and rolled onto the narrow pathways between the stages
that were filled with crew people and extras. Naja shutting
herself off in her dressing room was unnecessary drama. Yet,
it was not unusual.

When renewing her contract at the beginning of the
season, Ty had outright rejected Naja's request for weekly
flower bouquets, organic fruit and a personal assistant. In
return she'd silently protested his decision on the first day of
rehearsals, allowing her hair to do all the talking. She strut-
ted in, greeting the other cast and crew members with a
brand-new 'do. Short tresses with bold, honey-blonde streaks

had replaced her long lioness locks. The cost of her six-inch weave had equaled the airfare to Paris, but it had been worth every dollar to see Ty sitting at the head of the table, seething, with steam pouring from his ears, ready to explode. She'd sat raking her painted nails through her hair, wrapping strands around her index finger to torment him further.

After the reading, he instantly grabbed her by her upper arm and yanked her aside. He spoke in a calm, hushed tone, struggling to keep his cool. "I don't know what's up with the new hair, but I expect it to be back to normal by the time we start shooting." She knew she couldn't make such drastic changes to her hair without permission from the producers, but she'd flexed her muscles and expressed herself. Ty might have turned down her wish list and stolen her thunder, but as an actress Mother Naja still had the power to create lightening.

Why couldn't she save the drama for the stage, where it belonged? Who did she think she was, shutting down rehearsal? He pulled up in front of the stage and slammed his foot on the brake pedal. He entered the building, breezing past the security guards posted at the door, offering them a quick wave of the hand.

As he headed toward the back of the stage, he walked into Leede, who was hovering over the craft service table, nibbling on chips and salsa.

"What's going on, Leede? What happened?"

Leede spoke with his mouth half full. "That's what I want to know. We're in the middle of rehearsal and Naja just walks off. I think her weave is too tight."

"What did she say?"

He swallowed. "She told the stage manager she was sick." There was skepticism in his voice. "Sick in the head. I'm glad I don't get PMS. You know it makes women a complete kook for a day."

Ty grinned slightly. He was surprised to find Leede being so selfless about this. "Where's Cell?" Ty asked.

"I guess he's in his dressing room with his boys. I was in there kicking it with them for a while. He's a cool cat."

"Yeah. How'd he do in rehearsal?"

"He was okay. More practice won't hurt."

Ty sighed, exasperated. "All right. Let me go see what's going on."

He tramped up the stairs and knocked on Naja's door. "Naja. It's Ty," he said.

When the door opened he was engulfed by a combination of fragrances: yellow roses, scented candles and Kors perfume. Aromatherapy used to intoxicate a brother and bring him to his knees. Naja had tried her magic on Ty, trying to seduce him on several occasions last season. He'd smiled and flirted and kept moving, quickly deciphering disaster wrapped in flimsy fabric and having the good sense to know nothing was free when it came to girls like Naja. This had better not be a setup or a diva prank, because he was in no mood for tricks. Naja quietly shut the door behind him.

Ty could feel sweat forming on the crown of his head. Though the room temperature was cool, he was steamy from anxiety and the golf cart ride. He took a seat on the low sofa and leaned forward. Resting his elbows on his knees, he clamped his hands and bypassed formalities. "What seems to be the problem?"

Naja flung her silky hair to one side of her neck. "I'm in the middle of a scene with Cell Block and when it's time to kiss, he puts his tongue in my mouth. Slobbering me down like I'm his woman. Not only was his behavior unprofessional, it was sexual harassment, plain and simple. I've worked too hard to have to deal with this type of indignation, Ty. And I'm not having it."

"I totally agree with you," he said, displaying support. He wanted her to vent and clear out her hostility. Only then could he rationalize with her.

"This is ridiculous. This is not a video shoot and I am not some video ho. I'm Naja Starr and I'll sue his platinum ass!"

Ty's expression turned from blank to thoroughly concerned in less than a second as he envisioned the headlines in the trade publications. *Rex Television Actress Naja Starr Sues Rapper Cell Block for Sexual Harassment.* The news reporters and paparazzi would start tailgating her. They'd bombard his office with calls for comments on the case. He and the other cast members would be subpoenaed to testify. The suits would piss in their pants because the network would be cited in the case, and Russ Tobin would drop the show like a hot grenade.

It was time to start reasoning with her. "I know you're angry, but consider your career."

She folded her arms. "I'm considering my dignity and my integrity and I will not tolerate some two-cent, lowlife hoodlum violating me," she argued.

"A lawsuit could hurt your career. Try to calm down and think this through rationally. Start from the beginning. What happened before the kiss?"

She primped her lips to one side. "His dumb ass was struggling to keep up. I said my lines and he kept looking down at the script, then back at me."

"Did you talk with him prior to rehearsal? Joke around with him or anything?"

"Well, yeah. Leede was late, of course. So I introduced myself because we never had the chance to chat at the table read. He made a mild, harmless pass, talking some nonsense about putting me in one of his videos. Ugh! Like I still do videos. Anyway, during lunch he gets more aggressive. He talked about joining me in my dressing room for acting pointers. Then he spoke of sex and ran his hand over my butt."

"And what did you say?"

"The first time I said thanks but no thanks as politely as I could. When he put his hands on my ass I told him next time I'd charge him."

"So, why would he make advances?"

"I don't know. You tell me why men are always horny." She paused. "Wait a minute." She pointed her finger at him, accusingly, her diamond studded nails reflecting light. "Are you trying to say this is my fault? That I provoked him? That I am somehow responsible for his behavior?"

Ty shook his head. "No. I'm just trying to get your perspective on this."

"Well, I gave him no indication that I would enjoy having sex with him or having his slimy tongue in my mouth!"

"All right. All right. But don't you think suing is a bit extreme? How about a formal apology and we all get back to work like professionals?"

"He should be fired."

"You're right, but how about a formal apology and you get back to work like your contract says?"

She curled her lips, pissed he'd have the gall to bring up her contract. It was just business as usual with Ty. They were all men standing up for one another and none of them gave a damn if she was Naja Starr. To them she was just another dispensable actress. A second-class citizen to be fondled. It would take winning an Emmy to get equal respect from them. Folding her arms over her chest and poking her lips out, she refused to be easily defeated. "I want the kiss taken out."

She stared at him, searching his eyes for disbelief. "I know what you're thinking. A kiss. A slip of the tongue. What's the big deal, right?"

Ty was silent. It sounded like a trick question.

"When I lived in Brooklyn I was seeing this guy name Billy Jett. He was a good-looking, clean cut brother. It wasn't too serious between us. We hung out a few times and made out few times. A couple of weeks after I met him, I wake up one day with a sore throat. It was July, not exactly cold season. So, I went to the clinic to get checked out. Guess what?"

Ty remained silent. It was another trick question.

"I had gonorrhea in my throat from tongue kissing Billy and exchanging saliva. I had to get a shot of penicillin in my neck. So while this may seem like a petty incident to you, I can assure you it's not."

"Wow," was all Ty could manage.

"Yeah, wow. So you need to talk to your little ghetto guest star. 'Cause I will bite his tongue off, if he puts it in my mouth again."

"I'm sorry you had to go through that. I really am. But in this business you are required to kiss unfamiliar people and the kiss is vital to the story." He paused, considering the options. "Listen. Here's what we can do. The kiss stays in the script, but you only kiss when we tape on Friday. That way, there will be two hundred witnesses if he pulls something. In addition, we'll have it on tape. Then you can take him to court and I'll go with you. Bet?"

If something similar had happened to Leede, she'd bet he wouldn't be negotiating and compromising his integrity. Leede was not only making more money than she, he garnered more respect based solely on gender. Leede wanted an assistant. He got it. Leede wanted a new dressing room. He got it. If Leede needs a private jet, he gets it. Ty *always* kissed Leede's ass.

Ty went on. "I'll go talk to him right now. One kiss on the night of the show, then he's outta here."

Her chest caved in as she acquiesced with tight lips. "Okay." There was no need to waste any more energy talking with Ty. He was as stubborn as a brick wall and he'd never given her anything she'd asked for. Ever. She hadn't forgotten how quickly he'd turned her down for the raise she'd asked for at the beginning of the season. She was hurt by Ty's attitude, but not at all surprised.

"I know this is not what you want and I don't blame you. Believe me, Naja. I'm on your side, but it's all I can do under the circumstances."

She politely shook her head, thinking, *I'll get you all back. Somehow. Some way.*

* * *

Ty stalled outside of Cell Block's dressing room, lingering in the hallway and massaging his temples as he contemplated his next move. As mediator, he was walking a thin line. In order for him to come out the winner and keep Cell and Naja working, he would have to play both sides. Under ordinary circumstances, Cell Block's manager would have been contacted so that he could confer with Cell and help iron out this situation. But there was no time for proper procedures. He'd have to deal with the situation himself.

From the hallway, he could hear rap music blaring from the other side. Ty knocked with authority, like he was the police, not knowing what to expect from the kid. One of Cell's homeboys opened the door. Cell Block was reclining on a chair like he was at the beach, his Nike Air Force 1's propped up on the coffee table next to half empty bottles of water and juice. Smoke from Newport cigarettes lingered in the air. The other two baby-faced cronies were sprawled out on the sofa across from him. One wore a red T-shirt underneath his platinum chain, the other a blue. Ty wasn't sure if he was in the company of Crypts or Bloods or *what*.

"Hey. What's up, Ty?"

Ty walked over and pounded his fist. "What's up, man?"

"These are my peeps. Little Felony and Black Mel."

Each of them lifted their chin as they were introduced. Ty responded in like and turned to Cell. "I need to rap to you alone."

His henchmen disappeared out the door and the room fell silent.

Ty took a seat on the sofa and rolled up the cuffs on his denim shirt. He was still overheated.

Though Cell Block hadn't so much as acted in a kindergarten Christmas play, Ty was depending on his casting to drum up extra Nielsen rating points. His latest CD had broken sales records, selling over five hundred thousand units in its first week of release. His success would benefit the show and hopefully blow the ratings through the roof. Once the promos aired and word traveled he was appearing on the show, Cell Block's face would be a credit card worth a hundred thousand added viewers.

Cell planted his Air Force 1's on the floor and sat up. His forehead wrinkled as his eyebrows curved inward and his jaws locked. His face transformed into an African mask designed to disguise the young, illiterate boy beneath it.

"How you doing up here? You feeling comfortable about performing on the show?" Ty asked.

"Yeah. I'm cool with it."

"Oh, yeah? That's not what I'm hearing."

"Rumors are spreading about me already, huh?" he chuckled.

Ty half smiled. "Rumor has it that you are having some difficulties on the set."

"I hope you don't believe everything you hear."

"That depends on the source. I happen to think Naja is a reliable source."

"Naja? Naja who?"

"Naja, the actress. You rehearsed with her today."

"Aw, man. You know you can't believe what women say. They're always trying to make something out of nothin'."

"I wouldn't exactly call forcing your tongue in her mouth and putting your hands on an ass that didn't belong to you nothing."

Cell smiled as if amused. "Is that what she said? That's bullshit."

"Is that right?"

Cell shrugged. "Hell yeah."

"Well, you're about to catch another case over some bullshit."

The word "case" caused Cell Block to freeze. He could sing and rap about jail all day long, but he didn't want to go.

Ty continued. "Naja is in her room threatening to sue you for sexual harassment. She could collect the royalties from your latest CD and the next. You know that, right?"

"Yeah, whatever. That bitch is trippin'. It's my word against hers."

"That's what Mike Tyson thought, and he served several years."

Cell instantly jumped to his feet. He tossed his hands around as he spoke. "I don't have to deal with this shit. Some girl lying on me and shit. I quit."

Ty gazed up at him. "You quit and Naja won't be the only person taking you to court. You are under contract." Ty was desperately afraid of losing Cell Block, but he couldn't bow down and beg. He had to communicate in a language Cell Block understood: street. He had to talk hard and tough to gain Cell's full attention and complete respect.

Cell cooled down, but he didn't sit down. He shook his head as he paced back and forth. "I don't know if this acting thing is me anyway, man. It ain't like I thought it would be."

"I know. For some reason everybody thinks it's a walk down Rodeo Drive, but it's not. It's work and it takes skill and talent." Ty paused as he watched Cell's mask crack, and he stole a glimpse of the scared young boy beneath. "I want you to do the show, man. That's why you're here. I honestly think you can pull this off and make your fans happy. And you can start building your acting credits."

Cell shrugged, not completely convinced.

Ty continued. "I'm going to send an acting coach over to work with you. He'll be here when you come in for rehearsal. You can work with him here in your dressing room if you want." Ty got up. "Now all I need from you is a formal apology to Naja. Admit you were wrong. Say it was unprofessional and you are sincerely sorry."

"Apologize to some chicken-head for something I didn't do? Fuck that."

Ty moved closer to Cell, but not close. "No, fuck you. This is my show and you will not disrespect any women, bitches or chicken-heads here. Rumored or real."

Cell tilted his head with his face contorted, still resistant. "I told you. I didn't do nothin' to that girl." He sucked his teeth. "Shiiiiit. She ain't all that."

"I'll tell you what. Since you're being paid to act this week, *act* like you disrespected her and apologize. Consider it a gentlemanly gesture. So, call your manager, your lawyer or whoever and have a letter drafted and signed. I'm on your side, Cell. That's why I'm offering you a plea bargain."

Cell Block turned away like he was deaf, but he understood every word.

Ty moved toward the door, resting his hand on the knob. "I'll see you tomorrow in rehearsal." He paused. "And one more thing. Naja likes roses. Either yellow or white. It doesn't matter."

He turned and walked out the door. He ran his hand over his goatee, knowing his tough talk and amateur negotiating could backfire in his face. Both actors seemed agreeable with the deal, but that was today. Tomorrow could be an entirely different story. They could wake up in the morning and flip the script on him. Actors had passive-aggressive ways of sabotaging a show. A Cell Block or a Naja could slow down production and drive up show costs by straggling in hours late, or worse, calling in sick.

In the worst-case scenario, Cell Block might just end it all by having his boys do a drive-by on him. Ty made a mental note to follow up with Cell's manager to insure a letter of apology was faxed over to Naja by morning. He'd order the flowers himself if Cell allowed him to live another day.

Sid was in his office wrapping up some paperwork when his phone rang.

He picked up. "Sid Porter speaking."

"Hi, Sid. It's Wendy downstairs in Publicity."

"Hey, Wendy. Long time, no see."

"I know. I can't seem to catch up with you these days. Where have you been?"

"Oh, I've been around. What's going on?"

"Listen, my buddy over at *The Tonight Show* just called me. It seems that Ashanti has canceled her date with Leno on Thursday night and they're looking for a replacement."

"Really?"

"Now, as a favor to me, she called me first. She thought it would be a good opportunity to have someone from one of our shows on. I know it's last minute, but it would be a simple ten-minute interview on the sofa. The actor doesn't have to have a movie coming out or anything. Just a clip from the show and friendly banter with Jay."

"So, who do you have in mind?"

"Leede Banks from *Same Day Service*. The show is doing well, and an appearance on *The Tonight Show* couldn't hurt. You think he could do it?"

"I don't know. He's tied up a lot with his stand-up."

"He's funny, that's why I thought he'd be best. Makes him easier to interview."

"I know what you mean. But listen, how about Naja Starr?"

"You mean the girl on the show?"

"Yeah. She'd be great. She's bubbly and she's got lots of personality. It might be a nice change. Leede is always promoting the show."

"Uhm, I don't know."

"How about as a favor to me?"

"What will I get out of it?"

"What do you want?"

"From a cutie like you? Let's see. A date."

"You got it."

"Okay, here's the deal. Leno tapes at five-o'clock sharp. She should be there by three for hair and makeup. I'll fax over the details. Have the clip sent over to me by Thursday morning and I'll make sure it gets there."

"Thanks, Wendy. I owe you."

"I know. I thought we already determined that. Dinner and definitely dessert," she said flirtatiously.

Wendy had consistently made obvious passes at Sid for

two years, since she'd been hired. She was a good-looking, smart girl, but not exactly his type. He didn't do blonde hair and blue eyes anymore, but he could suffer dinner and flirting if it meant getting Naja on *The Tonight Show*. The more attention she got, the closer he was to becoming a producer.

He picked up the phone and called Naja. She was sitting impatiently on the 405 freeway, banging on her horn at the slow moving traffic. Still fuming from the events of the day, her patience was as thin as a razor. Road rage was only an arm's length away.

"Hello?" She abruptly answered her cell phone.

"Guess what?" Sid's voice boomed from her surround sound speakers.

"I'm not in the mood for games, Sid. What is it?"

Sid sighed. "You are such a killjoy."

"That's because someone killed mine."

"What happened?"

"Nothing. What's up?" She didn't feel like reliving the horrible details of her day by talking about it. Besides, it would only make him mad. Just because her day was ruined, it was no reason to spoil his.

"You're going to be one of Leno's guests on *The Tonight Show*."

She smiled for the first time in hours. "What?"

"You heard me. Thursday evening, five o'clock."

"I swear to God, you had better not be fucking with me, Sid. Not after the day I've had."

He leaned back in his chair, proud of himself. "Seriously."

"Jay Leno?" she asked, still in disbelief.

"Yeah. Long-chinned guy. Comes on every night on NBC. You ever seen him?"

"Hell, yeah. Oh my God!" She screamed with laughter. "Baby, you have made my day."

"I'm planning on you making my night," he teased flirtatiously. "For this I figure you owe me one hundred kisses, seventy-five hugs and fifty blow jobs."

She laughed aloud. "Then you'd better go to Hollywood Boulevard and pick up a hooker 'cause I don't have time for all that." Suddenly, she had a million things to do. "I have to find something to wear. I'll have to get my hair done. I'll need some fly shoes. What will we talk about? I have to call everyone and have them watch. Oh my goodness. This is sooo incredible." She'd dreamed of the night she'd sit on Leno's sofa and watch his hefty chin go up and down. "Wait a minute. I'll have to leave rehearsal early. The producers will have a fit."

"Believe me, they'll figure it out. You're leaving to promote their show. It's not like you'll be promoting another project."

"That's true. I'm on my way to the gym. I'll see you later on."

"Hell, yeah. You gotta start working off this debt. The sooner, the better. So pucker up, Buttercup."

"Goodbye," she said with laughter in her voice. Naja disconnected the line. She lifted her chin, glimpsed at herself in the rearview mirror and smiled. She rehearsed, "Hi Jay." She gave a fake chuckle. "You know, I just love your band, Jay." The stress of the day vanished as she improvised. She now had something to look forward to rather than look back on. As a guest on Leno, she'd be a part of history.

Sid was doing more for her than her sorry agent, Lars Howerton, who still hadn't returned her call. Had she not feared being agent-less, she'd have called and fired him then and there.

11

Venus downshifted her Honda to second gear as she rolled up in front of the big brick house in McCarty Circle. The uphill street was lined with palm trees and homes built in the thirties. It was near sunset when she parked on the quiet street and approached the front door. When she rang the doorbell, she could hear it echoing through the house. A man with dark curly hair and even darker, mysterious eyes greeted her. He smiled, his top lip barely visible under his thick, bushy mustache. She imagined he still had a few crumbs from lunch lost in the hairs.

"Come in." He held out his olive hand. "My name is Paulo."

She gave a shy smile. "Hi. I'm Venus."

Her eyes panned the room as she stepped in. The furniture had been moved to accommodate the long, rectangular table spanning the center of the wood floor. It was covered with a white linen tablecloth, white candles and incense. Two rows of folding chairs lined its perimeters, and at the very center of the long table sat a framed photo of a man who could have easily passed as Paulo's daddy. A Brazilian guru maybe? She wondered if the person was dead or alive. Given the dark, candlelit room, the atmosphere was as fitting for a séance as a meditation.

She smiled as she carefully checked out the twelve or so people in the room, all dressed in white pants, tunics and button-down shirts. One guy looked like Rip Van Winkle. His beard was so long it looked like he'd slept for ten years, woken up and come to a meditation. There were three women with olive skin and dark hair and red-dot bindis centered above their dark brows. There were two Hispanics, representing LA's East Side. Four more men with long, dark hair and deep, dark eyes sat facing the table and two blonde women and two black guys with locks sat on the other side. There was an array of hair colors and features, all from various tribes around the world. Had they all been wearing suits, it would have looked like a United Nations summit.

Maxwell entered from a hallway at the rear of the living room. He was all smiles, his white teeth matching his white cotton pants and tunic. "Hey, Venus. I'm glad you came. How were my directions?"

"They were great. Didn't have any problems."

"Good. Have a seat. We're waiting for a few more people. Then we'll get started."

She placed herself in the second row of chairs surrounding the table.

"Here," he said, handing her a photocopied booklet. "It's a book of songs."

She flipped through the book with little interest. She wasn't going to sing. She was going to observe.

Fifteen minutes later, Paulo sat at the head of the table, looking like Jesus with his disciples in white sitting around him. From where Venus sat, she had a clear view of him and he of her. Everyone opened their photocopied pages and started to sing. She motioned her lips. The songs were more boring aloud than on the page. But she indulged, opening herself up to the new spiritual experience.

One by one, each person got up from his or her seat and stood before Paulo. In front of him sat a decanter and silver shot glasses. Paulo offered each person a glass. What was this, communion? They were probably serving real wine and not grape juice like in the Baptist church she grew up in back home. That's what she hoped, anyway. Then again she couldn't be sure. She rose when it was her turn, making her way to the head of the table. She decided whatever Paulo was serving, she'd say the Lord's Prayer before gulping it down.

Paulo nodded approvingly.

Taking the silver cup, she glanced down at the cherry-colored liquid. *Our father, who art in heaven . . .* She dropped her head back and drank slowly. It was flat and nasty to her tongue. It definitely wasn't wine. Her eyes shot over to Maxwell for some kind of a signal, but his eyes were shut. He was already ascending from earth.

She returned to her seat, closed her eyes and listened to the chanting around her. She tried to focus on her breath going in and out of her lungs. Slowly she relaxed. Her mind drifted and landed in Texas. Oh, how she missed her family. It seemed like months since she'd seen them. *What am I doing in California all alone, while they are all back in Texas? What if there is an earthquake? I'll be dead and all my family will live on. Why did I leave them?* Tears welled up in her eyes as she slouched in her seat. Feeling herself sinking, she looked up. Paulo's dark eyes were dead on her.

She sat up in her seat and lip-synched along with the chants, trying to keep her thoughts in the present. Soon, her eyes closed again and her thoughts jetted. She traveled to her ex-boyfriend's apartment in Texas. Eric Felder. *I poured out my heart to him and he treated me like a doormat. I loved him so much. I miss him so much. Why does love hurt, God? Why?* Tears rolled down her face as she focused on heartbreak two years passed. The pain was as real as it had been then. Her teary eyes opened and landed on Paulo. Now he was spooking her. She wiggled in her seat, trying to get comfortable. Her arms were tingling. Her heart pounded. She was nervous and paranoid under Paulo's watchful eye. She didn't feel like herself. Something was wrong. That's when it hit her. She was high! The realization caused her to panic. She couldn't breathe. She heaved in and out, sucking in smoke. The burning incense was cutting off her oxygen and Paulo was calmly sitting there, watching her suffocate.

She needed air, and quick. She glanced down the long hallway. With no other way to exit the room, aside from the front door, she got up and headed down the hall, her palms against the walls holding her steady. She found a bathroom, entered and shut the door. Several seven-day candles illuminated the green room. The small window was cracked open. Thank goodness. Using both hands she tried to shove it open more. She wrestled with the old, wooden window for a few seconds before bending over and placing her nose right at the two-inch crack, inhaling as much oxygen as she could get. She heaved in and out, hoping it would clear her head. It didn't.

Dropping her knees to the black-and-white-tile floor, she began to sob uncontrollably. *Oh my God! I'm high! I'm sooo high!* Fear and terror consumed her. Who were these people and what the hell did she drink? She curled up in a fetal position on the floor and closed her eyes. Colors appeared. Pink, green, purple psychedelic swirls and whirls panned back and forth. She opened her eyes and cried even harder. The motion potion was a hallucinogenic. She could be tripping all night. Tears poured down her cheeks as she cried so hard she could hardly breathe. She'd been high like this once back in college. Then, like now, she prayed. "If you bring me down from this, I'll never get this high again. Please bring me down." Her lunch started pushing up in her chest. She crawled over to the toilet and lifted the lid. Jamming her index finger down her throat, she tried to make herself vomit.

Suddenly there was a knock at the door. She panicked. Before she could stand up, the door creaked open. A woman peeped in, her straight black hair hanging down to her elbows, her third eye glistening between the two dark eyes God had given her. Now that Venus was high, the woman resembled a character in a scary movie and she, along with everyone in the house, was the enemy. They'd gotten her high. Now they'd chop her body up in small parts and use her as a sacrificial offering to their gods. That's it. The drug was supposed to numb her for the kill. This was some kind of trick. She knew her thoughts were insane and illogical, but she couldn't control them because she was high.

"Are you okay? You mustn't do that," the scary looking woman said.

"Yes," Venus lied as she pulled her soggy finger out of her mouth.

The woman eased closer and reached out to her. "You should come back in the room with the group. You will feel better."

Venus shook her head no and sat on her butt. "I don't want to."

"Please come. It is better to stay in the group energy."

"Leave me alone," Venus snapped. Witch or not, this woman was starting to get on her nerves.

Maxwell appeared in the door, craning his long neck in, his locks falling in his face. "It's okay. Let her stay in here," he told the woman.

"It's not good for her," the woman persisted.

"Just give me a minute. It's okay. She's my friend," he said as he eased her out of the bathroom.

He looked down at Venus. "You okay, Venus?" he asked.

"Noooooo," she cried, the tears falling again. "Do I look okay?" Her hair was all over her head, her eyes red and puffy and her lips as ashy as a crackhead's.

He shut the bathroom door and knelt on the tiled floor beside her. His brown eyes were glaring with concern. What had he done?

She gazed at him with soggy eyes, her lips turned downward. "You should have told me, Maxwell! Oh, God! You should have told me!" She leaned into his shoulder and rested her head as she sobbed out of pure fear.

"It's okay, Venus. Try to relax." He wrapped his arms around her trying to give comfort.

"Y'all are getting high in the name of God," she sobbed, sucking up snot.

"Sometimes drugs can be used to have a beautiful spiritual experience, Venus. It helps you work through your stuff quicker. That's all."

"But you should have told me. You should have told me." That's all she could say, feeling betrayed.

Guilt raced up and down his spine. He wasn't prepared for her to trip like this. Her cries revealed how distraught she was, broken down mentally and physically. Her drama was blowing his high. Within seconds, his head was as clear as an AA member celebrating his fifth year of sobriety. Maybe he should have told her. He simply had not thought about it. If he explained the process, no one would try it. Everyone would think it was insane and everyone reacted to the drink differently.

Still he defended himself. "It's all natural. The liquid is from the Brazilian rain forest. It's called the dime," Maxwell said.

The urge to vomit struck her like a bolt of lightening. In the same instant, she could feel her bowels pressing downward. "I want to throw up."

"That's good," he said. "It's called purging. You'll be cleaning out bad energy."

She gazed at him like he was an alien. He certainly sounded

like one. Everything that made her feel bad, he defined as good. Cleansing? Her body was clearly rejecting the toxic potion. What else but poison would make her want to vomit and defecate all at once?

"Just relax and go with it, Venus. Whatever thoughts come to mind, let them come and deal with the emotion attached to it. Remember, from darkness into the light."

"I can't see the light for all the colors. There's purple, orange, pink . . ."

"Try to focus."

It took too much energy to focus. This wasn't supposed to be work, she thought, feeling pure frustration. "I just want to go home. I'm sick of Hollywood. I wanna go home to my mama. That's where the light is for me." She broke down again. "All I wanted to do was be a writer and here I am high and working as an assistant. Being abused all day long. I have to get Ty's lunch. Move his car. Make appointments for Sasha to go to the spa. I have to tolerate Craig. And you know he's a pain, right? I'm just a simple girl with a simple dream. Out here there is no light! Only misery."

He slid his palm up and down her back. "It's okay, Venus. You're going to be okay. I promise." Maxwell's thoughts raced at ninety miles an hour. He hadn't expected the dime to affect her like this. He should have given it more thought, but it was far too late. He unfolded his legs and got up to leave, hoping a purging of anything would bring her down. Now he knew how a drug dealer must feel when a regular customer overdosed. It was an ugly scene, a scene that could cost him his job if she told. Ty had no tolerance for any airy-fairy notions.

He wouldn't like it at all and it would alert him to the fact that Maxwell was still sniffing snow. All seven of Maxwell's chakras were in shambles.

"I'm going to step out so you can use the bathroom."

"Don't leave me. I'm okay. I just need some air." She tugged at her sleeves. "I'm hot. I'm sooo hot." She ran her hand over her forehead.

"Come on," he said pulling her up by the arm.

He led her down the long hallway toward the back of the house. They entered a dimly lit bedroom that reeked of incense and continued to a doorway that led outside to a yard. Venus stretched out on the grass like she was home in her bed, the ground cooling and calming, the smell of plants filling her nostrils. This was the best she'd felt since drinking the nasty potion and getting dirty was not even a concern as she stared up into the sky and tried to count stars. Maxwell sat beside her and tried to count how he'd spend his last paycheck.

He broke the long silence. "I never knew you wanted to write."

"You know how it is. No one wants an ambitious assistant. They want an assistant who wants to be an assistant. Which is crazy. Who wants to do one job for life? It's where you start, not where you end." She rubbed her eyes. Her high was descending and embarrassment was setting in as she became more conscious of what she'd said and done. "What happened tonight is between me and you, right?"

Had she been able to see his face, she would have seen the relief he felt. "Absolutely. Mum's the word."

"Good. I can't wreck my career before it gets started."

"Have you written any spec scripts, Venus?"

"Heck, yeah. I've taken classes. Even sent them out to a few agents."

"Any responses?"

"You mean anybody blowing smoke up my butt? No. Not yet."

"Let me read them. I'll give you some notes and I'll see what I can do about helping you out."

She looked at him, searching his eyes for sincerity. "For real?" It took a whole heap of faith to believe people in Tinseltown. The streets were filled with flaky people who made careers out of making false promises. Like con men, they smiled and stole your dreams at once.

"I'm serious. I've got some projects in the making. I have higher ambitions too."

"Ambitions, huh? I've got news for you, Maxwell. Where I come from, you're already rich."

"It's not about the money. It's like the NBA. No matter the amount of your contract, you want the ring." He paused. "I want the ring."

She gazed at him and softly said, "Yeah, you know Sasha wants the ring too?"

The laughter that followed was a bonding moment. They were on the same page.

"Yeah," he nodded with a big smile on his face. "I've been hearing that. But seriously, I'll see what I can do for you, all right?"

"And you're not just saying that?"

"Nope. I'm saying it because I mean it." For the second time in one day, Maxwell had covered his ass.

Venus felt nauseous. She jumped to her feet. "I think I have to throw up now." She'd only traveled five steps before leaning over and purging the devil right there on the green lawn.

12

The studio lot was as silent as a cemetery when Ty rolled past the guard's gate at seven fifty in the morning. The sun was hiding behind a smoggy cloud that hovered over the Valley. He'd spent a long, restless night alone in his Hollywood Hills home that had left him groggy. Throughout the night he heard Gary Ackerman's voice echoing, *"It's clear we're losing the crossover audience."* Yesterday's meeting had unnerved him. Sound bites from the conversation had infected his dreams. Ty didn't take their so-called suggestion lightly. They could have phoned him to make a suggestion. But they'd called a meeting to see his face, gauge his reaction.

He suspected something else was brewing, and his sleepless night confirmed his gut feeling. Gary and David didn't have the authority to fire him, but based upon their recommendation and reports, the network wheels could be set in motion to cancel him out. The tragedy of it all was that there wasn't one minority person in a VP position or higher to lend him support or help keep his show on the airwaves. As the only black executive producer at Rex TV, Ty was a lone ranger fighting network evil.

Last evening he'd sat at his dining room table stretching his neck from side to side while on a conference call with his agent and attorney. After insisting they postpone for an hour whatever plans they had, he'd reiterated the details of the meeting and had them review the fine print of his contract. The agency was making a quarter of a million from him a year, his attorney at least a hundred thousand. So, when Ty wanted to talk, they cleared their schedules and listened. He needed to know if he had any rights in the matter and if he did, would his agency lend support and fight in his defense. According to the fine print, a fetus had more rights than he did. Contrary to his ego's belief, there was no HNIC clause in his contract. When he sold his creation, he relinquished all rights to the story and its characters, and the network could do whatever they pleased. Could he challenge them? Yes. It was his job to steer the story direction of the show. Would his agent back him up? He said he would. Did Ty believe him? He had no choice.

Brand-new producers like Ty rarely secured deals allowing them to control their shows. On occasion, the network or studio would only offer a show creator a co-executive producer position and give them a strong supporting cast, placing older, more seasoned producers at the helm. Had Ty's family lineage been that of Hollywood royalty, his agent could have brokered a better contract. But no one in his family cleaned a studio, much less owned one.

Ty was sipping a Caffè Americano from Starbucks when Maxwell tramped into his office, his Renaldi shoes leaving a trail of footprints on the beige carpet from the doorway to the sofa where he plopped down. When he'd arrived home from the meditation at one in the morning, there were two messages from Ty; one on his home phone, the other on his cell, both summoning him to an 8 A.M. meeting. It had been a draining night, with Venus scaring his high away. Even after she'd purged the first time, she was still flying high in the friendly skies. She'd laid out on the lawn under the moonlight, yapping his ears off, telling her own sorrowful, behind-the-scenes Hollywood story. Guilt still nestled in his spine as he listened. She'd appeared to be fine when she pulled off in her car waving good-bye, yet he'd fallen asleep wondering if she was okay. If she'd have nightmares. If she'd come into the office today mum or spouting off at the mouth with anti-Maxwell rhetoric. He was too close to making a deal to have it blow up in his face based on the testimony of an assistant.

His agent, Barry Reuben, had left a more important message on his home machine and Maxwell had called him back in the middle of the night and awakened him without an ounce of remorse. Barry drowsily repeated what he'd said on the answering machine. A meeting with the network had been set up for Friday morning to discuss his pilot and a possible development deal. After the brief but joyful conversation, he'd hung up the phone and dropped to his knees, praising the universe for the manifestation. He attributed his good fortune to the meditation.

While he sat in front of Ty seemingly insouciant on the outside, internally he felt like there were fifty miniature

Soul Train dancers lined up and down his spine, getting their groove on while his heart provided a steady upbeat tempo for them to dance to.

"What's up, man?" Maxwell greeted, noting Ty's beverage. "Drinking that poison is going to kill you."

"Yeah, yeah. We're all going to die from something."

"Eternal life, my brother. We don't have to die."

Ty raised an eyebrow. "I can't see you defying physics. If you get any skinnier, you're going to die of malnutrition."

"Don't worry about me. I've got good, sturdy bones, built to last."

But Ty was worried about Maxwell. Over the years, they'd spent hours, days and months together whether hanging around town, going to sports events or shut behind closed doors writing scripts. They'd surpassed being friends years ago and were tight as brothers, sharing what they had one minute and arguing over something the next. But over the past few months Maxwell had grown increasingly distant, hanging out with his new spiritual friends and forsaking his old one. He rarely visited Ty's home anymore, seldom found time to hang out with him, barely had time to share a meal outside of work. If he did, he'd insist on a tasteless vegetarian joint like Real Food Daily or A Votre Sante, places Ty didn't want to go. Shooting hoops at a high-school gym in the Valley had been a Sunday morning ritual for almost two years. Maxwell hadn't shown up at all in two months, always declaring himself to be tired or injured. Even Leede had attended more often. Sasha had questioned him about Maxwell's absence, but Ty had no answers and pretended to shrug it off. Something was driving a wedge between them and he couldn't identify the source. He suspected there was more to it than Maxwell's new spiritual life.

"So, what happened over at the stage yesterday?" Maxwell asked.

Ty shook his head. "A headache. Cell Block was creating scandals, trying to blow up the spot. He hit on Naja, then during rehearsal, he decides to put his tongue in her mouth. She hit the roof."

"That's Naja. You gotta give her credit. She never sways. Always true to the diva game."

"Yeah, for a minute I didn't think I was going to be able to calm her down. I think I resolved the issue. At least I hope I did. I'm expecting a formal apology to come across the fax this morning. I'm also having flowers delivered to her, signed Cell Block."

"He denied everything, huh?"

"To the hilt. Like every inmate in jail, he didn't do it."

"He's a big rap star who's used to having his way. Since he got out of jail, anyway."

"And I ain't mad at him for that, but his shit doesn't hold water over here. I had Venus get an acting coach to work with him. I think he's got a case of the jitters and he's afraid of being embarrassed."

"You're probably right. Did he get gangsta on you?"

Ty smirked. "Pu-leaze."

"Come on. You can tell me. Did he scare you, dawg?" Maxwell teased.

Ty laughed. "Hell, no. Not for a second, then him doing a drive-by came to mind."

They both laughed.

Ty switched gears. "Where are the writers? What's going on in the room?"

"We're straight. We've already gone over next week's script."

"Good. I want you on the stage today. Make sure this acting coach works out okay. One thing I learned yesterday is that Cell needs a little bit of supervision. I don't want him within pissing distance of Naja. Him or his friends, Grand Larceny and Assassin or whatever their names are. If Cell farts, I don't want her to smell it."

"No problem. I'm there."

Ty's expression turned serious. He tilted his head to the side, stretching his neck and shoulders that grew tighter with thoughts of the network. "Now for my meeting with Gary Ackerman and David Levine."

"What's going on with those stiffs?" Maxwell asked as he stretched his legs out.

"They're concerned with the dip in the ratings."

"Right. Right. But dips are normal. It happens to lots of shows."

"They want to add a white character to the cast," Ty stated.

"Come on, the drop isn't that serious. And if it were, that's a poor way to solve the problem."

"Would you like to call Russ Tobin and let him know that?" Ty got up from his desk and walked around it, unable to simply sit in a passive position while discussing the network. He propped his butt against the front of his desk and folded his arms across his chest. "If I cry racism, these crackers will nail me to a cross."

"I know, but it doesn't mean a brother can't get mad about it."

"I am mad. And when I've got three shows on the air like David E. Kelly or Aaron Spelling, then maybe, just maybe, a brother can talk trash. Right now I'm in no position to do so, but I am going to push the envelope as much as I can."

"So what do you have in mind?" Maxwell asked.

"I want you and the writers to come up with a white character for the show."

Maxwell pulled his head back, shocked. "What?"

"Slow down, Dick Gregory. It's just a precaution. I don't want you to spend a lot of time on it. Just a few scenarios. Nothing elaborate. I'm telling Ackerman hell no and kiss my ass to his suggestion but if they pin me against the ropes in the tenth round, I want to be prepared. I'd rather lose a round and retain the title belt. I'm going to have my say with them, but at the end of the day, I plan on keeping this show on the air by any means necessary." They sat in silence, turning this over in their heads.

Maxwell contemplated his own future as an executive producer. Like Ty, it would be his first time as a showrunner. He fondled his locks and tried to convince himself that things would be different for him. His spirit guides would protect him from such negative energies.

Ty interrupted the silence. "Say as little as possible to the writers. If they think the ship is sinking, some might jump overboard," Ty said.

"I feel you." *I might be one of them.* Maxwell could feel his words jammed in his throat. He wanted to spit out, *"Hey, man. I finally got a meeting with the network about my pilot."* He desperately wanted to share his enthusiasm with his best friend, but knew he couldn't mumble a word about the meeting until the deal was done. He had already visualized Ty pounding his fist with a smile. Congratulating him, then phoning his agent and having him fired by noon. That was Ty's style, his MO.

Maxwell knew Ty better than Ty knew himself at times. Every person in Ty's inner circle owed his or her job and good fortune to him, and he liked it that way, liked having people indebted and beholden to him. It reinforced his superior status and secured his place on the throne. Handing out blessings made him a god, and his one commandment was that there be no other gods before him. Those who dared to disobey and sought favor and blessings from others were deemed traitors and aptly extricated from his kingdom.

An old friend of Ty's named Steffon had come to Hollywood from DC, eager to become a writer. In their youth, the two had lived in the same apartment complex and attended junior high school together. Steffon was naturally funny. His sense of humor was quick and spontaneous, a gift from the comedy gods. Ty gave him recommendations for writing programs and helped him get hired as a writer trainee on another show. They were thick as thieves as long as Ty was the frontrunner and Steffon trailed several steps behind. Four years later, Steffon started making a name for himself in Tinseltown and production companies were courting him to write scripts for them. After Steffon made one successful deal too many, Ty completely cut him off, like he'd given him a deadly disease. He instructed his assistant not to accept any of Steffon's phone calls, to decline all lunch and dinner invitations, and under no circumstances was Steffon welcome to enter his office. And just like that, Steffon vanished from Ty's life as though he'd never existed, and his name rarely rolled off Ty's tongue again. If he ran into Steffon at a movie premiere or party, he was cordial and extremely distant.

Maxwell, like Steffon and others, was indebted to Ty. The studio and network execs had faxed over a list of available producers, all white, for Ty to select from as his co-executive producer. All of them were veteran producers under contract with Rex. Still, he had flatly turned them down, knowing these producers would not support him in tough times like these. Producers who would probably suggest he go along with adding a new white character. To avoid any disloyalty, Ty had gone out of his way and put himself on the line to hire Maxwell.

Maxwell readjusted himself on the sofa. Knowing he had a possible deal looming and neglecting to speak about it made him feel like a cheap counterfeit thief. But if he had to be a fake to win, then so be it. Life was about the bitter and the sweet. Besides, Ty had given him little choice. He'd mentioned his projects to Ty once before and Ty had glazed over the subject, giving it little credence. He made it abundantly clear he didn't want to hear about it, so Maxwell had no choice but to make a deal behind Ty's back.

Ty rubbed his puffy eyes. "Let's see. What else?" He twisted his torso and retrieved a white piece of paper from his desk that listed the names of all the actresses who would be coming in to audition for the next week's episode. Most of the names he recognized, a few he didn't. With so few acting roles for black actresses, or "blacktresses," as he liked to call them, he'd met a large percentage of them as they strutted into his office each week famished for work. A few he'd taken enough interest in to fuck. "We've got casting today at two. Rehearsal should be over by then. Hopefully."

"Yeah, I glanced over the list yesterday."

"You got anybody in mind for the two roles?"

"Sampson pulled me aside in the writers' room and said his girl was auditioning. I told him I'd see what I could do. I didn't make any promises. If she's decent, I'd just as soon give her one of the parts."

"Cool. I have no problem with that. I'd really like a big name for the second role."

"To help the ratings?"

"That's what I'm thinking. It's late, but maybe we can get someone. I'll talk to Nancy about it. I mentioned it to her before. Maybe I need to stress the point." Ty paused, thinking. "The last thing, which is the best thing: I got a call from publicity. Naja is doing Jay Leno tomorrow night."

"Really?" Maxwell said with surprise. "How'd she land that?"

"Don't know. Don't care. It's last-minute, so someone must have cancelled. Good, because we need the publicity. This could be a shot in the arm for this week's ratings."

"Leno tapes early. Around five in the afternoon."

"Yeah, we'll have to change tomorrow's schedule. Probably move the network run-through up a few hours."

"A change in schedule. The suits will love that," he said sarcastically.

"I hope so. What do I care about making Gary and David's day easier?"

"I heard that."

"We should chat with Naja today also. Let her know we need her to promote the show."

"She has nothing else to promote."

"Yeah, but I want her to be focused. I don't want her chatting Jay up about her damn dogs for ten minutes."

Maxwell smiled. "Can't you see her pulling out pictures of those mutts? Propping them up on Jay's desk so the cameraman can get a close-up."

Both men chuckled.

"Too bad we don't have this week's episode finished. It would be great to send a clip with Cell Block," Maxwell suggested.

"Aw, hell no. I don't want anyone mentioning the name Cell Block to her. Not after yesterday. There's no telling what she'd say."

Ty paused, his eyes roaming the room as he thought. "I think that's it for now. How's everything with you? You all right?" Ty was searching Maxwell's face for a sign, anything to clue him in on the changes in his friend.

Maxwell made eye contact just long enough to answer. "Yeah, man. I'm cool."

"You should come by the crib on Sunday. Mom and Pops are coming."

"That shouldn't be a problem," Maxwell answered as he got up from his seat and straightened out the wrinkles in his pants. Then he quickly excused himself before Ty could probe further.

Ty clenched his jaws, feeling helpless as he watched Maxwell exit. It was as if he'd just lost his woman and didn't know what to say in order to get her back. He longed for the close bond they'd shared in the early days of their careers.

He leaned back, remembering the days and nights they'd spent together, working for pennies as lowly production assistants.

Bam! Ty's size-twelve Nike shoe slammed into the side of a heavy-duty Xerox machine.

Maxwell arched his eyebrows as he entered the copier room. "What are you doing?"

"I'm unjamming this piece of junk," Ty said, his forehead wrinkled. "This is the third time this machine has jammed in half an hour."

Maxwell grabbed him by the shoulder and pulled him back. "These machines cost more than we make. You know, they'll fire us and keep the copiers."

Ty wiped his soggy face with his sleeve. "I hate these machines. When one works, the other doesn't. I swear they're on a mission. I think they dial up the Xerox gods at night and say, 'Ty had a meltdown today. We just need another week and we'll have his ass jumping out of windows.'" Ty half smiled and slammed his foot into the side of the machine again. "Motherfuckers!"

Maxwell smirked. "You should write that down. It could be a funny sketch."

"What do you think would happen if both machines broke and we couldn't get the scripts out?"

"I have no idea and I don't plan on finding out."

Ty opened the copier door, exposing its black metal gut,

and searched for sheets of paper jammed within the machine tunnels. "I'm just tired. I've been here since eleven this morning. What time is it now?"

" 'Round midnight," Maxwell said, as he watched Ty play doctor on the machine.

"Damn, and we've got fifty more copies to make."

Maxwell frowned. "Fifty? What have you been doing down here?" He'd been upstairs printing out the labels and chatting on the phone, flirting with some girl.

Ty pursed his lips. "What do you think? Fighting with this damn machine and losing."

"I made a run over to Paramount today and saw Nina Goode. She works in the publicity office. Have you ever met her?"

"Maybe once."

Maxwell rubbed his hands together. "Man, she is fine. I started rapping to her. We talked for a long time. She's into tennis."

"She actually gave you the time of day?" Ty examined the black dust from the machine now sticking to his palms.

"No woman can resist my charms, even in jeans and a sweatshirt. One day I'll open up a charm school and share my gift with all of mankind."

Ty struggled to pull two sheets of torn paper from the machine. "Why don't you use your charm on this stupid machine?"

"Move. Let the maestro handle this." Maxwell bent down on the gray tiled floor and wrestled with the machine for a few seconds. Then he got up and slammed the door shut. The machine started cranking and humming like a jet preparing for takeoff.

"How many copies have you made?"

"You asked me that already." Ty exhaled. "You must be as tired as I am. Just happier." Ty wiped the black dust off his hands on a white sheet of paper. "I don't see why I have to do this anyway. When Al West said he was hooking me up with a job, I thought I was going to be writing. I've got a bachelor's degree and I'm a damn PA." He shook his head.

"You have to pay your dues, son. One day all of this will be behind us. We'll be making C notes by the hour, and pretty girls like Nina Goode will be clamoring to be with us. We won't have time to sleep!"

"The life of a pimp, huh?" Ty said.

"Except you won't have to ask them nothin. They'll be begging you. Please, baby, baby, please, can I suck your dick?"

Ty waved his hand, dismissing Maxwell's wild notions. "I will have quit by then." Ty sat in the chair across from the copier, an Equal Opportunity Employer bulletin hanging on the wall behind him. "Seriously, man. I don't know how much longer I can do this. I know we talked about writing as a team and becoming producers, but these thirteen, fourteen-hour days are killing me. I don't see my friends. I don't have time to write. I don't have time to get my hair cut. Hell, I've barely got time to get laid."

"If we make it through one season on this pissy job, we'll be made men in this town. None can enter unto Hollywood heaven but by way of being a PA. It's in the holly book."

"You need to work on your jokes, partner."

Maxwell continued. "Think about all the free meals. Nigga, we eat good *every day*. Wolfgang Puck's, CPK, Cheesecake

Factory, Roscoe's. You're crazy. Ain't nobody quittin' nothin', especially not tonight. 'Cause I'm not delivering all of these scripts by my damn self."

Ty's forehead wrinkled. "Man, I'm putting stupid miles on my car too. They sent me to the post-production house three times today, from Burbank to West LA, three times. By the end of the season, my car won't be worth five hundred dollars."

"That's all it's worth now."

Ty smirked. "Go to hell."

Under the fluorescent lights, Maxwell clearly saw the exhaustion in Ty's drooping eyes. "Why don't you lie down on the sofa and get some Z's."

"Nah, I can't let you do that, man."

"You're not letting me do nothing. We're a team. Go sit your tired ass down somewhere." Maxwell was probably no less exhausted than Ty, but tonight it was Ty's turn to have a meltdown. The duties of being a PA got to them at least once a month. And like clockwork, once a month one of them threatened to quit.

Ty went into the next room as Maxwell placed the original script pages into the feeder and hit the START button. The battered machine cranked up and began spitting out pages like a loud, angry dragon.

Maxwell glanced over at Ty in the next room. During the day the room was used as a waiting room for acting auditions. After dark it was a bedroom for the PAs. Ty was laid across a sofa, his feet propped up on the armrest.

"Man, why don't you go upstairs? How are you going to rest with this loud-ass machine so close?"

Ty lifted his head. "I can let you know if the machine stops again."

"I'll be fine. I'm going outside and taking a hit."

Ty perked up. "You have weed?"

"I don't have weed. I have the chronic." Maxwell bragged as if he could scientifically prove the difference. "The question is: Do you want to flyyyyyy?"

They exited through the back door of the building and down the cement stairs before crossing the velvety, green lawn. Both men pulled at their fleece shirts for warmth against the cool night air. From the front seat of Maxwell's car they had a full view of the building. All four floors were vibrantly lit up with fluorescent lights like a car dealership, and the structure was as empty as a haunted house. Only Ty and Maxwell were left to finish up for the night.

Maxwell pulled out a big brown joint and a Bic lighter. The end of the joint glowed in orange as he lit it. He took one long drag and inhaled. Suddenly he coughed and a cloud of smoke burst from his lips. He began to choke, his lungs gasping for clean air.

Ty turned up the volume on the car radio. Too Short, a rapper, bellowed from the speakers. "You die in this car and you die alone."

Maxwell wheezed. "What do you care? You're quitting, right?"

"That was before I knew you had some chronic," Ty said as he loudly sniffed the secondhand smoke. "You know this shit is regional. Can't get it in DC."

Maxwell only nodded. "You think the *Hollywood Reporter*

would run a story about a PA found dead in the parking lot due to a drug overdose?"

"Hell, no. A website might have it, but not the trades. The studios are still protected. They'd look real bad."

Maxwell handed Ty the joint. "It seems like a PA somewhere in this town, at some point, would have committed suicide after being asked to do some dumb shit. Don't you think?"

Ty took a long drag. "Or better yet, commit murder. I came close when Nate asked me to make a third trip to West LA today."

Maxwell rested his palms on the steering wheel. "I wonder if they ever think about shit like that."

"Hell, no! Just like white people didn't think slaves would spit in or poison their food. These rich, arrogant bastards think they are beyond reproach." Ty passed the joint back.

Maxwell held the joint between his thumb and index finger. "Beyond reproach," he mocked. "What's that? The queen's English?"

"Nah. It's your mama's English."

Maxwell took a puff on the joint. "Check this, son. Remember Jason? He used to work over in building twenty-seven. He told me he did that once. This film producer he worked for over at the agency had him count out eight grapes and eight almonds each day for her, like she couldn't count. He finally started spitting in her food as payback for taking her shit."

"I am not surprised," Ty said.

"Yeah, man."

"When I'm a producer with a big-ass house in the hills and a slick Benz, I'm not going to have my PAs or my assistant running all over town and counting to eight," Ty said.

"Shiiiit. I am," Maxwell said. "I ain't going to get my own lunch."

"Me neither, man, but I'm not going to abuse them. That's what I mean."

Maxwell shook his head. "I know I'm new to this business, but there seems to be a thin line between what's normal and what's abuse."

"Here's an example. I'm not going to have my assistant pick up my dirty drawls."

"Or get watermelon at two in the morning," Maxwell added.

"Or pick up my kids from school. I'm staying true to my roots. I wasn't born living like that and I'm not going to front. And the only saliva I want on my food is mine."

"I heard that," Maxwell agreed.

"We'll never be nasty, condescending, can't-make-a-doctor's-appointment-without-an-assistant type of mothafuckers," Ty stated.

"I know that's right," Maxwell said. "We've only been on this job for how long? July, August . . ."

Ty cut him off. "Four months."

"It seems longer."

"That's 'cause we're making pennies. And like Michael Jackson said, 'They got me workin', workin' day and night. They got me workin', workin' day and night.'" Ty started dancing and singing in his seat. "That's when Michael was still a brother. You know, before he defected from us."

Maxwell chuckled. "Come on. I need to check on the scripts."

Ty slid his hand over the interior door panel, searching for a handle that was no longer there. "Nigger, where's your door handle? Oh, this is your charm, huh? Holding girls hostage in your broken-down car."

Maxwell walked around the car and opened the passenger door from the outside. "Ain't nothin' wrong with my ride." He affectionately patted the hood of his dated BMW. "She gets me everywhere I want to go."

"I hope she gets you to Pacific Palisades tonight," Ty said.

"Oh, no. That's your run, not mine. You should check your Thomas Guide. You might find a shorter route," Maxwell teased.

They headed back to the building to finish the scripts and deliver them. It was 4 A.M. when they finally climbed into their beds for the night.

13

By 10 A.M. the stage was bustling with movement as the crew hooked up lighting and completed construction on the set for Cell Block's concert performance. In the middle of the madness, Bernie, the stage manager, was running around with a clipboard in hand, taking attendance of the cast members. Bernie gave Leede a broad smile and resisted the unmanly urge to hug him simply because Leede had shown up promptly for his call time.

The residue from last night's booze and partying was smeared all over Leede's face. He'd closed down the Sunset Room and devoured a late-night meal at Kate Mantilini's on Wilshire Boulevard.

"What's up, Bernie?" Leede greeted. "Are we going to rehearse today or what?"

"I guess so, man. Everyone is here."

"We were all here yesterday, too."

"You got a point. But everybody's here and ready to work. I hear the rehearsal schedule will probably change, though. Either we'll go later today or earlier tomorrow morning."

"For what?"

"To make room for Naja. She's doing Leno tomorrow and they tape early, around four thirty. So we'll have to get her out of here by three o'clock."

Leede instantly grew incensed. Within seconds, his blood was hot enough to fry chicken. *How the hell did Naja get to do Leno?* He was the star of the show, not her. Yesterday she'd shut down rehearsal. Now she was changing the schedule for the next two days. She was getting out of control, flipping the script, and Ty was allowing it. He was probably sleeping with her, as he'd initially suspected. Leede stormed off in the opposite direction from his dressing room.

"Where are you going? You've got a wardrobe fitting in ten minutes," Bernie yelled amid the sound of clanking and chatter.

"I'll be back, Bernie," Leede said, not bothering to look back over his shoulder.

"God damn it," Bernie said under his breath, dropping his clipboard to his side. Leede was ruining his day at the same speed as he'd made it.

Venus sat at her desk, feeling amazingly clear and lightheaded. As much as she hated to admit it, the accelerated pace of working through "her stuff," as Maxwell had called it, and venting her subconscious thoughts and fears had left her feeling exonerated from internal burdens. Last night's nightmare seemed more like a dream today, kind of surreal and distant.

There were a few residual images of herself in the bathroom, Paulo's eyes and the scary woman, but she couldn't recall her exact words, couldn't put it all together to draw a clear sequence of events. She'd called her best friend in Houston first thing this morning, eager to share the shocking experience. At least what she could remember of it.

She remembered enough to bring her spec script in for Maxwell to read. She'd always liked him and his crunchy-posh gear, but she'd never see him as the same humble guy after last night. There was much more to this guy who walked around happy and smiling, speaking about intangible things. So what if he told someone about her behavior? To tell on her would be to tell on himself. In a calm and coherent state of mind, she realized he had a lot more to lose than she did.

She sifted through the stack of mail on her desk. It was the usual intake of resumes, headshots and benefit invitations. Her favorite envelopes were those from the fans. She studied the handwriting, colorful inks and return addresses. The penmanship on some was so bad, it was a wonder the mailman figured out where to deliver them. It fascinated her how many people took the time and energy to write to the show. Most were young women and, like her, they were in love with Leede. Naja got her share of letters from penitentiaries around the country, but Leede was the main attraction. Teenagers and even a few ladies sent letters of admiration, expressing their undying love and lust for him. Others simply wrote how much they liked the show and what they thought was the funniest episode. Many sent in pictures from their proms or in their best club outfit with fake cars in the background. Every now and again, a letter came with pasted letters cut from magazines, indicating there were definitely a bunch of kooks tuning in each week.

No one at the show expressed any interest in the fans and their letters other than Venus. She'd had publicity send over eight-by-eleven cast photos, like the big one hanging in the administration building, and mailed them out to the fans who had written in. Every now and then, she brought a letter or picture to the attention of Ty or Leede. They'd read it aloud, laugh and nonchalantly toss it back on her desk.

Leede barely spoke as he whisked by her desk and stepped into Ty's office, where Ty sat viewing footage of the show, playing, rewinding and making notes. He pressed the OFF button on the remote control when he gazed up and saw Leede. The huge screen propped inside the oak entertainment cabinet faded to black, and the room fell silent. His mouth started to form a smile until he felt the cool breeze that accompanied Leede. Ty's lips straightened, his forehead wrinkled in curiosity. "What's up, man?"

Leede closed the door behind him. "We need to talk," he said taking a seat on the cushiony mud-colored sofa.

Ty placed the remote control on his desk and leaned back in his chair. "I'm listening."

"Why the hell is Naja doing Leno and not me? You said on Monday, right here in your office, that it was my reputation on the line. That I'm the one carrying the show. Did you not?"

"I did," Ty agreed.

"Then what the hell is going on?"

Ty stretched his neck to the left. His office had become a freakin' complaint department. "First of all, I don't book talent for *The Tonight Show*. The publicity department hooked this up. As they should, since that's their job. So, all gripes should go directly to them."

Leede pursed his lips. "You expect me to believe you had nothing to do with this?"

Yeah, motherfucker. "That's exactly what you are to believe. You can call your publicist and confirm it. Secondly, the ratings are dipping and the suits aren't breaking their necks to run promos. So, I need all the free publicity I can get, and I don't care how I get it."

"Well, I do. I'm tired of being on Naja's schedule. Everything's about Naja. She held up rehearsal yesterday and then today Bernie says the schedule would be changed to accommodate her. She's making accusations against the guest on the show. She doesn't want to do this and that. She wants more screen time. Her dressing room looks like she's having a wake, with all them damn flowers. I said it before and I'm saying it again. Hurricane Naja is spinning out of control."

"Stop focusing on Naja and concentrate on yourself. What are you doing? Shouldn't you be in rehearsal?"

"I would, except I never know *when* rehearsal is."

Ty exhaled, surrendering to the moment. "Talk to me, man. What is it that you want? 'Cause I can't do anything about Naja doing Leno."

"I want some say-so in what goes on around here, because neither my interest nor my image is being protected. I'm in this just as deep as you are."

Ty nodded. "Okay."

"Just so you know, I'm having my agent set up a meeting with the suits and I'm going to ask to be an executive producer on the show like all the other actors are getting these days. And don't get it twisted, Ty. There are no hard feelings."

Ty gave an evil grin. "You'll be lucky if you get to keep your job."

"The studio and network knows how valuable I am to this show, even if you don't. No Leede Banks, no *Same Day Service*. Simple as that. I'm the face America tunes in to see every week. I'm the reason all of you have a job."

Ty stroked his finely trimmed goatee. "Let me tell you something. The studio doesn't think you're pale enough to keep folks tuning in each week. I had a meeting with Gary and David yesterday. And you know what? They want to put a white boy on the show."

Caught off guard by this latest bulletin, Leede was reduced to silence.

Ty pounded his point. "Yeah, a white boy to steal your show. Seems like they don't think America wants to see you after all. They think America would rather see a white boy. Who knows? Maybe they'll replace you with him. After all, this is not the Leede Banks Show."

"That's bullshit," Leede retorted, jerking his neck out.

"Like hell it is. I can get the suits on the phone right now. Don't underestimate the suits. You think they like you because they laugh at your jokes? It's all about the money."

"Then that's all the more reason for me to have some say-so in what goes on around here."

"Okay. But the white boy will replace both of us. Especially if they detect dissension among us."

"I'm not talking about dissension. I think we might do a better job together. That's all."

Ty shrugged. "Hey. Do what you gotta do, man. At the end of the day, you have to feel good about yourself. So that's on you."

"I'm just being up-front and open."

"And I appreciate that."

Leede left as swiftly as he'd come in, perfuming everything within a six-foot radius with his Aveda like a human air freshener.

Damn, Ty thought. That's all he needed now, Leede marching his narrow butt over to Building 130, giving the suits the impression he wasn't doing his job. Ty rubbed his temples and tried not to dwell on it. It was a waste of time. Leede would soon learn that Rex TV wasn't about to add a HNIC clause in his contract either.

Venus had missed every last incoming call in the last ten minutes because she'd been too busy eavesdropping on Ty and Leede. She'd tiptoed across the floor in her Pumas like a prowler and entered the adjoining office next to Ty's. With her right shoulder firmly pressed against the wall, she was able to comprehend enough of their muffled words to surmise what was going on. With her heart thumping in her chest like a basketball on a gym floor, the tension from the next room leaked through the plastered wall as the men exchanged threatening words.

Her eyes darted from side to side as her thoughts circled her head. *Mayday. Mayday. We're going down.* With internal bickering over who would be chief, all the little Indians like her were doomed. By tomorrow she could be answering phones for Leede. Hell, she could possibly be out of a job.

Then what? She missed home but she wasn't ready to go back just yet.

She had to get her script to Maxwell in a hurry. At least he wasn't asking for sex in exchange for a writing gig. She'd heard all the rumors about the only two female writers on the show, both LA hoochie mamas, with their stretchy pants and big boobs. One of them had allegedly slept with Ty and Leede. The other one had allegedly slept with Ty and Sasha. She wasn't coming up like that. She was country, not crazy. She'd seen how Sasha pranced up to the production office, kissing Leslie on the lips, for God's sake. She'd never told anyone, but once Ty had her drive to Sasha's house in Malibu to drop off a check and Sasha had answered the door wearing a lacy bra and matching underwear. Inviting her in for a drink like two o'clock was happy hour. Perhaps it was for Hollywood housewives and whores, but she was neither. So like the hired hand that she was, Venus didn't budge any further than the welcome mat, claiming she had to hurry back to work. She wondered how different her career would have been had she accepted the invitation.

As Ty and Leede's conversation had come to a close, Venus quietly rushed back to her desk piled high with fan mail, headshots and messages Ty would never read. When the door creaked open, she had the phone up to her ear, checking the voice mail, recording messages from the calls she'd happily missed.

Her forehead wrinkled as she listened. For the third time this week someone named Dominique had called for Ty. She deleted the message, searching her mind. Dominique? Venus thought she knew all of Ty's female callers, but she had no idea who she was or what she wanted. Dominique would never give anything more than her name and number. Had she told Ty someone named Dominique had called, he'd ask, "Dominique who? What does she want? How did she get my number?" He could be a pain in the ass like that. Hated an incomplete message and expected her to know the backstory of every fool, fan and friend who called him, like she was some kind of private eye.

"Get Gary's assistant on the line," Ty barked at Venus. "I want a meeting with him and David Levine today. I can go over there or they can come over here." He paused. "And call Al West and see if he has time to meet with me tonight."

Naja was spinning in orbit, breathing air of high altitudes as she strutted around the stage like a proud peacock, sipping Evian water, waiting for rehearsal to officially begin. She'd only glanced at Cell Block's letter of apology she'd found on her dressing room table before balling it up and ramming it into a trash can. The roses next to it had gotten even less of her attention as she glanced at them, then quickly turned away with her eyes rolling around her head in one swift move. Cell Block was a despicable, fat-headed creature. Surely he lacked the taste and etiquette to have thought of such a fine gesture on his own. That jailbird couldn't spell "rose," much less have the wherewithal to order a dozen of them. It didn't matter. Today, she would rise above any drama staged around her. Kiss Cell Block? Pu-leaze. He couldn't kiss nothin' but her ass.

Leede rode back to the stage on a golf cart feeling depleted of all his celebrity powers. He passed extras dressed in white nursing outfits and lab coats, standing near trailers, drinking coffee from Styrofoam cups and chatting. He looked from left to right, yet saw nothing, his anger blinding him. All he could feel was the gigantic hole in his chest where his ego once dwelled before being demolished in Ty's office.

He didn't have a blockbuster film or any other project lined up to shoot during his hiatus, and now he might have to compete with a white boy on his own show. How much worse could life get? Yeah, maybe Ty made the whole thing up. Maybe he was afraid of losing his power.

Nah. Ty wasn't a liar. And that's what was killing him. What would this mean to his career? How would this affect the show? Could he actually become a supporting cast member instead of the lead? Perhaps, especially if they hired someone with a bigger name than his, like Charlie Sheen. Maybe even his brother, Emilio. Maybe they'd hire a nut on drugs, like Robert Downey Jr. Hell, there were hundreds of white boys to pick from who were bigger celebrities than he. Actors whose parents were actors and whose parents' parents had been in the business. Maybe he'd change his name to Leede Eastwood, tell everyone Clint was his pa. In his distress, he came up with one implausible scenario after another in rapid succession.

He frantically punched his agent's number on his cell phone. The assistant patched him through to Steve Van Arden, who was having breakfast at the Beverly Wilshire Hotel in Beverly Hills.

Van Arden glanced at his watch when his assistant announced the call. It was a bit early for Leede to be calling.

Maybe it was that time of the month. Every thirty days or so Leede would read an article in one of the trades announcing Chris Rock, Martin Lawrence or some other black comedian was set to star in a film. He'd dial up Van Arden ranting and raving like a four-year-old, wanting to know why he hadn't auditioned for the role. Then he'd threaten to fire him.

Van Arden nearly choked on his latte when Leede just calmly stated, "I need you to set up a meeting with the network. I want to be an executive producer on my show."

"Sure, no problem," he answered.

It was the quickest and least painful conversation in the history of their agent-client relationship.

Naja was propped up in a director's chair on the stage floor reviewing her script when Leede stepped toward her, wearing the same Paper denim jeans he'd partied in the night before. She hadn't laid eyes on Cell Block as of yet. He was hemmed up in his dressing room with his cronies and acting coach.

"Hey, Naja," Leede said, his eyes gravitating toward her nipples that pressed through bra and shirt fabric like fingertips.

She smiled, glancing up from her script with the taste of baby food still on her breath. "What's going on? How are you?"

"I'm good. How is the leading lady?"

She rested her script on her lap. "Leading lady? What do you want?"

"Nothin'. I heard about what went down yesterday and I want you to know I've got your back."

She sheepishly smirked. "Thanks, Leede."

"Yeah. We can't let an outsider come in and break up our camp. We've got to stick together. This is our show."

"Thanks for the support, but it's done and over with. It's nothin' a Brooklyn sister can't handle. Cell sent me a formal apology and some roses."

"Okay. As long as you know, I'm here for you."

"Yeah, sure. I know that," she lied. She didn't know nothin'. Not even where this attempt at camaraderie was coming from.

"So, *The Tonight Show*, huh?"

Her face lit up. "I'm so excited. You know how it is, right?"

"Yeah, I've done the show twice. You'll be fine. It's no big deal."

"Not for you. You're a comedian. You and Jay can swap jokes all night."

"Yeah, well you know. I got the gift, so I got to use it. But you'll be fine."

"You think so? I'm not sure what they're going to ask me."

"They'll tell you, or you can tell them what you want to talk about. And get your flirt on with Jay before the show. He'll love it. And don't forget to holla at Brooklyn and your Uncle Roscoe."

She laughed. "You are so simple. Sounds like you want a shout-out. Don't worry. I'm sure I'll only be talking about the show."

"That should make Ty very happy, since he's sweating over the ratings."

"Well, you can't blame him. That's his job."

"But it affects all of us. Everything he does affects us in one way or another. I don't know about you, but I think he's holding us back as actors. I know you've got skills that you're not even getting to use here. It's our second season. Your character should be more developed than it is. There should be more story lines based on your character. You should have *been* on *The Tonight Show* last season."

She studied his face carefully. Leede was selling a dream and she couldn't decide whether to buy it. "You really think so?"

"You damn right." Leede moved in closer and lowered his voice, his shoulder against hers, his eyes scanning the stage. "Listen, I'm going to meet with the network and I'm going to ask for an EP credit. If I get it, I'll be looking out for you. We're in this together."

"What about Ty?"

He stood straight up. "What about him? He'll still be here. We'll be working together and an actor will have something to say about what goes on for a change. I'm tired of being treated like a hired hand."

EP, huh? He struck a chord. She went into a monologue as violins began to play in her head. "That would be a nice change. I feel like I have to fight for everything I get around here. You should have heard Ty negotiating with me yesterday. He didn't respect my feelings, my position. He did everything but accuse me of provoking Cell."

"That's what I'm saying. Things will be different around here if I become a producer. I got your back." He winked at her, sealing the deal.

Maxwell made certain Cell Block remained caged in his dressing room with his acting coach and cronies until rehearsal started. And Cell Block didn't put up the least bit of protest. He was content and happy to be in his own space, playing video games, where he had complete control and didn't have to stress about catching a case over a chick. His attorney and manager were expeditious in getting an apology over to Naja, but not before giving him a good talking-to. They made false assurances, blowing up the scenarios in hopes of keeping him in check and their fees rolling in. They told him his newly established career could not and would not survive such accusations. That P. Diddy and Snoop Dog had barely squeezed through their criminal ordeals, and they were hip-hop veterans. Sexual harassment charges would not only turn his gangster image into a gorilla, but also reverse his platinum coins into copper pennies. To seal their deal, they strongly implied that his record company would drop him faster than the speed of sound. Not to mention his endorsement deals. The only disadvantage they omitted was how much money *they'd* lose if he destroyed his career. Cell listened from his limo with tight jaws and a stiff upper lip. He might have been young and illiterate, but he wasn't stupid. He'd keep his distance from Naja.

The crew's movement had practically ceased when rehearsal got under way. Everyone onstage had been ordered by Bernie to be "quiet on the set." Maxwell jumped down from his high chair when his cell phone vibrated and quietly moved toward the hallway near the stage entrance. It was Barry, his agent, calling with an update.

"We're on for Friday morning," Barry said.

Maxwell grinned, feeling more euphoric than when he was numb from cocaine.

Barry continued, "Listen, the studio had some ideas of their own about casting," he lied. "They want to use someone already under contract."

"As long as I have final approval," Maxwell said.

"We'll negotiate your power when we got them hooked on the idea. For now we should play along."

Maxwell shifted his weight from his right leg to his left. "Drop a name. Who we talking 'bout?"

"Naja Starr."

"No," he answered flatly.

"Why not? You know her. Work with her."

"Exactly. She's low-budget talent with a high maintenance rider. Have you watched her closely?"

"No," Barry lied. He'd viewed videotapes of her that Sid had sent over to his office by courier. "But do you have any other choices? It doesn't matter who they have in mind. We make the deal and negotiate the terms when they're ready to write a check." Barry didn't give a gnat's ass if Maxwell donated both of his kidneys in exchange for a development deal. Writers always wanted autonomy over their creations, and in the big picture of things no one gave a hoot about the rights of writers. But it was hard to explain that to bigheaded, egotistical scribes.

"I don't know," Maxwell said as he watched the prop master roll a wooden cart past him. He weighed the notion. He'd have to give up something to get what he wanted. But Naja? She was an actress, an Aries and an only child. A troublesome combination. No one could give her the amount of attention she craved and she consistently produced drama on and off the stage. "Tell you what. You're right. We don't have to make a decision this minute. She'll be on Leno tomorrow night. Let's see how she does. Maybe I need to see her in a new light."

"Sounds good to me. This is what we've been working toward, buddy. Let's stay focused on the goal, not the details."

"Yeah, whatever," Maxwell said before ending the call. He liked Barry for the same reasons he sometimes disliked him. The exact same drive he used to protect his clients could ricochet and be used against them. Barry was an educated con artist, pandering writers whom he'd sell into slavery if it meant he'd collect a bigger check. Most of his clients believed he worked on their behalf. The swift ones like Maxwell knew chunky Barry Reuben worked only for his personal profit.

14

Sasha was stretched across the towel-laden table lying flat on her back. She drew her right knee to her chest and clamped her arms around her leg to hold it in place. She flinched as the almost too hot liquid was spread across the lips of her vaginal area. The heavy Brazilian woman giving her a bikini wax hummed an unrecognizable tune and went about her job as if methodically applying butter to toast. On command, Sasha switched legs as the woman applied more of the gooey liquid around her privates. It was a masochist's process but she was addicted to the result, a baby-faced pussy. "Yo' bouy-friend iz going too luuuuv diz," the woman said in her heavy accent.

Since arriving at the elegant Burke Williams Spa in Santa Monica this morning, she'd had a Reiki massage and an organic enzyme facial. After her bikini wax was done, she'd evaporate in the sauna for ten minutes or so. The midweek spa indulgence was a pricey effort to relax and help erase from her mind the dreadful vision of Ty and Dominique having intercourse in her dimly lit bedroom. The recurring vivid picture of the two left a lump in her throat.

If she ever loved any man, it was Ty. But the love housed in her heart had gradually been polluted by fear. As he had grown more and more evasive about marriage, her behavior toward him had become dominated and dictated by trepidation. Fear he may *never* marry her. Fear he'd string her along until she was gray. Fear he'd one day leave her and another woman would replace her. Fear of being on her own. Ninety percent of her day was spent living in fear of fear.

The youngest of three siblings, Sasha had grown up in Long Beach, California. She had no desire to attend college, but her father, a professor at UCLA, insisted she go because it was free. Clueless about her true aspirations, she followed her parents' urging and found herself hanging out at the student union, flirting with ball players. Her college experience became nothing more than groupie training. Eventually, she withdrew and got a job at a retail store in Westwood, hustling clothes for rent on a small apartment in LA. It wasn't until a semester later that her parents realized she'd moved off campus. By that time, she'd gotten caught up and captured by the glitz and glamour of the LA party scene and hanging out with tall men with long money. Her mother always stressed being an independent woman, but Sasha didn't yearn for that type of control. With a type B personality, she was content to let others make decisions. And though she had the looks and height to become an actress or model, she wasn't ambitious enough to pursue either, didn't need all the attention that came with the job. The night she and Ty met at a party, he had presumed she, like every other pretty girl in LA, wanted to be in movies. But she desired nothing more than to love hard, marry rich and birth babies. A simple life filled to the brim with luxuries. An old-fashioned girl on the inside, a fashion plate on the outside.

She should have never agreed to swinging with him, should never have been afraid to say no. She was no Swazi woman, and they damn sure weren't living in Swaziland, where polygamy was lawfully allowed. She'd gone along, figuring he'd keep his affairs with other women to a minimum. She knew there were others, but there was no tangible evidence. No photos or definite sightings, but she didn't need any. Her gut told her and her gut whispered only truths. Ty was too young and too tall, his money too new and too long for him to be monogamous. In the past she'd turned a blind eye to the clues, but fucking in front of her face was outright insolent. So what if she had sexed women in front of him? It wasn't the same and it certainly wasn't cheating. He could name every woman she'd bedded, in alphabetical order.

The *ménage a trois* with Dominique had been a big no, a colossal faux pas. She'd played along, sucking Dominique's honey nipples and sliding her tongue up and down her neck, disguising her discomfort. In those dizzy moments in the darkness she had been confused, but with the morning dawn came clarity. She was pissed, hurt, angry and of course afraid. In retrospect, she wished she'd responded differently. Wished she had the guts to get ghetto on them, yelling, kicking and cursing until someone called the police. But in a mind where fear ran rampant, she only did what she thought would please him, rather than herself.

Ty wasn't fooling her for a single second. He wanted Dominique. She tried to recall the painful specifics. Who touched whom? Who provoked whom? If memory served her correctly, it was Dominique who had perpetrated the situation. The bitch! A bitch she knew absolutely nothing about. Ty had constantly warned her, "Be selective. People know who I am. And definitely no actresses. They'll screw us both trying to get work." Yet, still she hadn't asked Dominique anything about herself. Why should she? That was the point of a one-night stand: discreet, carefree and noncommittal. Half the pleasure was the anonymity, but now it was half the problem. She wanted—needed—to know who Dominique was. What was her story? What did she want? And more importantly, *whom* did she want? Her? Or Ty?

Sasha had placed the piece of paper Dominique had written her number on in her Fendi wallet. She'd phone her before going into the sauna. See if Dominique was free for lunch.

Sasha bit her bottom lip and waited for a subtle gesture from the humming Brazilian that the wax was about to rip. She cringed, her muscles contracting in anticipation of the pain. Finally the woman applied pressure to her inner thigh ever so slightly and in one quick, devastating stroke, ripped away what felt like wax, hair and flesh. Her mouth flew wide open. "Fuuuuuuck!" she screamed, her back arching, the lips of her pussy burning, virtually in flames..

* * *

Sasha maneuvered her Benz down the palm-tree-lined pathway to Ivy on the Shore in Malibu. Like its sister space in Beverly Hills, the place was a posh restaurant with beach décor and island prints where well-to-do patrons dined on seafood and salads in a tranquil garden patio. Dominique was standing in the lobby entrance when Sasha arrived, her naked crotch tingling from fresh air and cotton and her hair still dark and damp from the shower. Both women smiled, exchanging their customary Hollywood grins. It was a fraudulent display of happiness designed to match the sunny weather and manicured lawns. Sasha leaned forward and smacked a kiss across Dominique's cherry lips like they had been intimate friends for years.

Dominique was having a wonderful day and it was only one o'clock. This morning she'd had a good sweat at the gym. She had on a pair of her favorite thongs and she'd gotten a call-back for an audition, something that hadn't happened in weeks. Then, only moments later, Sasha had called and she'd been smiling ever since. The closer she got to Sasha, the closer it put her to Ty, the true prize.

Sasha clutched the tan leather bag hanging from her shoulder. "It's good to see you. I'm so glad you could meet me on such short notice. I had no idea what your schedule was like."

"Your timing was perfect. I had just finished my workout. I'm free until two thirty."

"Oh, good," Sasha said as the maitre d' led them toward their table.

The women sat down in the cushiony seats, giving each other a once-over, noting in daylight what they might have missed under the darkness of night. Dominique's hair was glued to her peanut skull like Elvis. Her sultry, emerald eyes were more pronounced with her hair off her face. Dominique radiated femininity in her large hoop earrings and gray hip-hugger slacks. Yet her nails were cut as close and butch as her hair. Sasha was perplexed over whether the girl was a lipstick lesbian or not. Either way, she was as sexy as Sasha had remembered, making her crotch tingle for another reason.

"What gym do you belong to?"

"West LA," Dominique said as she placed her crisp white napkin across her thin thighs. "How about you? With that body, I know you work out," Dominique said, looking out of the corner of her eye.

Sasha smiled sheepishly. "We have a gym in the house. It's just a small one and the trainer comes three times a week. But I cancelled today and went to the spa instead. Sometimes you need a break from the routine, you know?"

No, but I'd like to. Dominique nodded as if she understood. Damn, she wanted Sasha's life. Not to mention her man who afforded her that life.

"So, do you do weights, Pilates or yoga?" Sasha asked.

"I use the machines at the gym. And I do hatha yoga twice a week for a really good sweat. It loosens me up and keeps me limber. At least that's how I feel when I'm done."

"You don't have a trainer? Wow. You must be disciplined. I admire that."

In Dominique's eyes, Sasha led the life of a movie star. Her best friends were probably actresses. She more than likely had a plethora of designer dresses for attending movie premieres and benefits. Paparazzi pointed their cameras in her face whenever she was with Ty. She undoubtedly had every celebrity privilege without having the job. And she needed a break from the routine.

"Did you ever try acting?" Dominique asked, curious of how Sasha had landed Ty.

"Noooo. I'm way too shy for that."

"Well, many actors are shy people. It's not uncommon."

"I know. Let's just say I prefer being myself."

Dominique gave a fake blush, choosing her words with care. She could feel Sasha's eyes roaming all over her skin like a laser beam, reading her lips like a hawk, and committing her words to a memory bank. "It's really good to see you again. I had a blast hanging out with you and Ty. You guys make a great couple. You're lucky to have him."

"I guess I am." *When he's not being an asshole.*

"How long have you two been together?"

"Three years."

"Three years? That's a lifetime in this town. Any plans for marriage?" she asked, glancing at Sasha's left hand where there were no rings.

"We're working on it," Sasha said with all the courage she could gather within a second's time. "So, how about you? Are you spoken for?"

"Naah. LA is a tough place to date. But I'm sure you've heard the horror stories."

"I hear my single friends complain about it all the time. As my grandmother would say, the pickings are slim. Especially if you're looking for a brother."

"Well, I haven't narrowed my search down to just brothers, if you know what I mean," Dominique said with a sly smile.

Damn. What did she mean? Sasha wasn't sure. What was she supposed to ask? Are you always bisexual? Was the other night out of the ordinary? Do you prefer women to men? She couldn't think of a diplomatic way to ask if Dominique preferred males or females in bed. So to avoid embarrassment, she changed the subject to something lighter, less puzzling. "So, where are you from?" she asked. It was the first of a battery of questions she would ask Dominique throughout lunch, interrogating her as if she were on trial for committing a crime. Unbeknownst to Dominique, she was. Her crime was having intercourse with Ty. Others were guilty of the same, but they had not been caught.

By the time their waiter, Brock, had placed their appetizers before them, Sasha had discovered Dominique was from Chicago, the South Side. She had a sister named Leigh. She'd survived a Catholic school education and she'd flown to LA like many, chasing birds and dreams. She'd done a play here and there, and a few bit parts. But she was confident her big break was just around the corner. In her spare time, she worked out and dabbled in abstract painting, watercolors and acrylics.

Sasha listened intently, smiling here and there, uh-huh-ing in response. "Acting. Oh, really?" Ty was adamant about his "no actress" rule. What the hell? If things went her way, he wouldn't see Dominique again until they were reincarnated as camels in Egypt. Ty didn't believe in heaven and hell.

Dominique's eyes narrowed as she watched Sasha. She personified confidence on the outside, yet she smelled Sasha's fear. "So, we'll all have to hang out together again. Maybe catch a show at the House of Blues or something."

Sasha rested her fork on her plate, her hair nearly dry from the ocean breeze. "Or maybe you and I could hang out. I'm really attracted to you, Dominique, and I was struck by your beauty the moment I saw you in the bathroom at the Playboy Mansion."

"Thank you. I find you attractive as well."

"Good, then let's keep this between the two of us. Ty and I have an understanding. Sometimes we swing together. Other times we swing separately. It's all good."

Dominique's eyebrows rose. "Ah, you have a generous partner. I'm too jealous to share."

"We know where we stand with each other. Our relationship is a rock." *So, if you have any ideas, forget about it.* "So, if you want to hang out and get down with me, cool. I'm always ready for a party."

"I knew I liked you for some reason. You're a woman after my own heart." Dominique winked and raised her glass of Perrier to toast.

15

Ty eased into Gary's office, his chest protruding as if armored, the rest of his body following. He took a deep breath and surveyed the room, preparing himself for the unexpected. This could be unfriendly territory. Leede might have been bluffing with his cries for an executive producer credit. After all, he was an actor seeking attention, an artist not savvy in business affairs. But Ty couldn't be too sure of anything right now with hothead Leede on the loose, breathing flames like a dragon. This was no time to be uncompromising and challenging. That's what the suits would expect. His game plan was to proceed with caution and see how hard they'd push for the white character.

Gary stood in the middle of the floor in his cargo khakis with a golf club gripped between both hands. A putting cup was strategically placed several feet in front of him. The golf set had been a Christmas gift from his kids. Now he played putt-putt daily on company time.

David sat on the sofa with his corny loafers planted firmly on the floor, looking on as he sipped from a bottle of water.

"If I had your hands, I'd turn mine in," Ty teased, with a smirk on his face.

Gary turned toward him and smiled. "Come on in. I'm just working on my stroke."

David rose from his seat to shake Ty's hand, as did Gary. Greeting one another like amiable colleagues.

David sat back down on the sofa and edged his glasses closer to his face. He looked like the kid in high school who never got a date. Gary was probably the smart-mouthed bully.

"So, Ty. What's going on with your home team? The Redskins," David said.

"Had I known we were going to discuss the Redskins, I'd have worn my burgundy and gold," Ty said.

David smiled. He *liked* Ty.

Ty sat down. "But as a card-carrying fan I am required by loyalty to represent regardless of my gear. The Redskins have got a great team. They just need a little practice playing as one," Ty said.

"Yeah, man. They've got loads of talent on that team but they're not winning. Something is missing," David said.

"A good coach is what they're missing. That and a backup quarterback. Just give my team a little time. I guarantee you, they'll make it into the playoffs," Ty said.

"They somehow always seem to finagle their way into that," David said.

"And I'm sorry your Dallas Cowboys don't fair as well," Ty said.

"I've given up on that damn team," David sighed.

They all laughed. Gary had dropped his club and taken a seat across from Ty and David, who were seated on the sofa. A coffee table divided them.

Gary folded his arms across his chest and got straight down to business. "So what's on your mind? How are you feeling about our idea?"

Ty twisted his lips, faking uncertainty. "I don't know. I guess I'm just not convinced adding another character would be worth all the effort. There's a lot of work involved in adding a character." Ty started counting off the fingers on his left hand with the right and extended his vowels to make it sound laborious. "Developing the characteeer, casting for the roooole and wardrobe desiiiigns. All of which will come out of my budget."

"I want you to understand. We're working with you, not against you. Maybe we can work with you on the money issue," Gary said.

"I'm clear on that, Gary. But the fact remains that adding a new character does not guarantee higher ratings. I see it as a high-risk investment, and I'm not all that concerned about gaining the crossover audience. That's never been the demographic of the show. I think it would be to our advantage to build on the audience we already have."

Gary chewed on his bottom lip. David nodded.

"I'd like to see the network run more promos for the show. It's only been a one-share dip, and I see that as no reason to panic. At this juncture, I think running promos would suffice."

"We're airing a few now," Gary said. The network was running the same amount they did for all the shows.

"Let's run some more in heavy rotation. I'm talking about a commercial campaign as if *Spiderman VII* was coming to network television," Ty said.

"Sweeps Week is coming and we're prepared to air numerous promos for your show. It's in the budget. You've seen the marketing reports."

"Great. But how about running commercials now like it's Sweeps Week? This would be a more cost-effective way to promote the show. Either people want to see the show or they don't. I'm confident they do. My writers have been working hard to make the show edgier. Let's promote those changes. Refresh the memory of our audience. Remind them when to find us. Give them the best highlights, the funniest moments."

"We're not trying to force your hand with the character," Gary said.

"And I'm merely asking the network to put more marketing dollars behind the show."

"I don't know if we have the budget. We'd have to put some new promos together," David said.

"Okay, let's say we get approval for a commercial campaign. What if it doesn't work?" Gary said.

What an asinine question. Ty paused, taking a deep breath to control his increasing anger. He cleared his throat and forced a smile. "Advertising always works."

Gary shrugged. "It's not my decision to make. I'll have to run this by the big boys."

"You mean Russ Tobin?"

"Inevitably, yes."

"Okay. Well, I have another suggestion as well."

Gary and David made eye contact. Ty smiled. He might have come in unprepared in the first round, but he was ready to go the distance this time.

"What's that?" David asked.

"Encore episodes. Air two shows in one week so we can build more of an audience. It's been done many times before." Ty rested his back against the sofa, covering his humiliation as he pleaded his case. He wasn't telling them anything they didn't already know. How many shows had they written blank checks for? *Ft. Greene Park* had been an episodic show about a hip, artsy community in Brooklyn with an all white cast. The show had suffered poor ratings since its premiere, but the network kept airing episodes, running them back to back, then airing a third "encore episode" for so many weeks that people eventually had to watch because it was the only damn thing on. Then Rex TV proclaimed it a hit.

Had Ty been a white man this discussion would not be taking place. He'd be in his own office playing a casual game of putt-putt and shooting the breeze. Instead he was arm wrestling for his show and they were playing him for a chump. Taking him for stupid and treating him with prejudice.

Ty could feel the weight and agony of an entire racist system that stretched far above and beyond the two suits sitting in front of him. It was a system controlled by rich, white advertisers who refused to fork over the same exorbitant amounts of cash to advertise during black shows as they did on white shows because they (to put it nicely) did not consider the black audience a hard-to-reach, target audience. Black people watched TV more than anybody on the entire planet. Like the Democratic party assumed the black vote, television advertisers assumed the black dollar.

The only ammunition Ty had was the fact that *Same Day Service* was still generating substantial advertising revenue. The ratings might have dropped slightly but advertising profits during his show had remained stable, the advertising sponsor still signing checks. But they didn't know Ty knew that. Didn't think he had the good sense to investigate that aspect. Had no clue he had connections through Al West to get this type of confidential information.

Gary pinched his nose. "Encore episodes, huh?"

"I think it's a great idea," David said.

Of course it's a great idea. The network can sell ad time every time *Same Day Service* ran, creating three times more revenue. "Look, I'm not saying a white character won't work. I'd just rather explore other options first," said Ty.

"That's fair, Ty. David and I will see what we can do from our end. We'll do all we can. We want this show to make it for the long haul."

Ty nodded.

"We like the changes in the script."

"Good."

"So, are things going okay? Cell Block working out?" Gary asked, digging for dirt.

Ty stroked his goatee, wondering if they'd gotten a whiff that Leede wanted an EP credit. Perhaps he should speak up, tell his side of the story first. "Leede's a little hot under the collar because publicity booked Naja on Leno instead of him.

Other than that, everything is good. You'll see tomorrow at the run-through."

"Wait a minute. How hot are we talking?"

"Hot enough to throw a small temper tantrum. I think it was the initial shock. He was talking about not having enough say about what goes on. I've heard all this before. He was just letting off steam."

"Well, let us know if we need to do some damage control. We always want to keep our stars happy."

"I think he's okay."

Gary stood up. "Good. I'll get back to you by the end of the week and let you know what's going on."

Ty rose. "David, I'm going to invite you over my house when the Redskins play Dallas."

"Hell, that's as good as Super Bowl Sunday! I'll be there."

They all shook hands and Ty left, temporarily satisfied. They'd listened to reason, but he intuitively knew the battle had yet to be won. They weren't likely to budge on their marketing budget, and he was less likely to budge on adding a white character.

Gary shoved his hands in his pockets and stared out the window.

"I told you he wouldn't go for it," David said.

Gary turned and faced him, "Do I look surprised?"

"He's right, you know. With a commercial campaign, the ratings would probably go back up."

"At what cost, though? Russ Tobin wants to add a new character. He didn't say anything about increasing the marketing budget."

"Maybe we can get him on the phone."

"I'm going to hold off for a day or two. We're scheduled to meet with Maxwell on Friday morning to discuss his pilot. Let's see how badly he wants his own show."

Gary was under constant pressure to keep the ratings up on existing shows while developing new shows for the next season. He was expected to successfully gauge what Americans wanted to watch when they came home from a hard day's work. Hell, even a psychic couldn't predict a hit show, but no one cared. In a business where ratings equaled profit, the studio wouldn't waste a New York minute firing him if he guessed wrong.

Just two days ago, he'd read about the demise of one of his colleagues at Paramount. Another VP thrown out on his ass, like he'd sat behind his desk Instant Messaging hookers all day. Executives like Gary were shuffled around from one studio to the next as they were hired and fired like fast food workers. The turnover at Rex TV was daily and swift. Many had come up the ranks with him at Rex, but the majority were gone, working for another studio or a production company. Gary was one of the last men standing in his department. After only five years of service at Rex, he was already considered a vet.

Reared in a small town in Vermont, Gary had done little more than roam the planet after graduating from Boston University with a degree in communications. Allowing his hair to grow past his shoulders, he traveled the world on a budget and worked menial jobs here and there. One day he awakened in a hut on a beach in Thailand with a new lease on life. He bought a one-way ticket to LA, chopped off his hair, bought a suit and reentered society. Now he had two kids, a wife who thought shopping was a national sport and a mortgage on a home his family had outgrown. He'd done eight years in the business, and he still had a ways to go if he was planning on taking over the helm, replacing Russ Tobin one day. But he was at a crossroads. He could feel it in his veins. The call from Russ was a sure sign, if he'd ever seen one. He'd have to use this rare opportunity to make his mark and prove his worth. If Russ wanted changes, then that's what he'd get. He'd be damned if he'd lose his job over *Same Day Service*. At the age of thirty-six, his priorities had reversed. Once he could have cared less about a job. Now his entire life depended on one.

16

The caterers were folding up serving tables and throwing away utensils from lunch when the black-tresses, as Ty called them, started filling up the outer office, where Venus sat on guard as gatekeeper with a sign-in sheet placed in front of her. One by one they sashayed in, grinning at Venus like she was the casting director and could persuade the powers that be to hire them. They obviously didn't have a clue about the rank and file in a production office. She didn't have the power to convince Ty to use a black pen instead of a blue one.

Venus studied these artistic women weekly and upon sight could readily distinguish between what she called the thespians and the Halle Berry wannabes. The thespians were formally trained individuals who'd invested time and money in honing their dramatic skills. They usually showed up either dressed for the part or very casual. Their makeup was done but

not overdone. They reviewed their lines while patiently wait-
ing their turn to audition. Their smiles were bright and brief.
No questions asked. They knew the drill. It was all business.

The Halle Berry wannabes showed up nearly naked, in
halter dresses, pumps, miniskirts and tight yeast-infection
jeans, advertising everything the good Lord gave them. They'd
most likely been voted the cutest girl in high school, home-
coming queen or won a local beauty pageant and decided
they had what it took to be a big star since they'd been one in
their hometown. These desperate-looking girls hung around
Venus's desk, eyeing the audition list and tossing their butt-
length weaves from one bare shoulder to the other. They asked
directions to the restroom to touch up their hair and makeup.
They did yoga poses in the hallway and continuously asked
how long it was going to be before their name was called, as if
they had better things to do.

Maxwell was in the hallway explaining to a half-naked
wannabe that Senator Clinton was Hillary, not Bill, when Ty
trekked down the hall headed for his office.

"Let's get started. Is Nancy here?" Ty said.

"She's just down the hall," Maxwell said.

Ty strolled into his office anteroom, which was wall-to-
wall with women. He maintained a straight face as he paced
through, avoiding direct eye contact. He didn't like being too
friendly before an audition. He didn't want to give someone
a false impression that they would be hired. He momentarily
stopped, barking a command at Venus, "Find Nancy so we
can get started," and walked into his office.

He took a seat on the sofa. Maxwell trailed behind him, his
locks pulled back into a ponytail.

"How'd it go with the suits?" Maxwell asked.

Ty shrugged. "Damned if I know. They listened and gave very little rebuttal. That could mean anything."

"Word."

"I gave them the commercial pitch. Recommended encore episodes to get the ratings up. I told them everything they already knew. Or should know anyway," he paused. "How was rehearsal?"

"It was smooth."

"That's good. Leede was in here this morning having a meltdown because Naja is doing Leno instead of him. I don't know. He's been edgy, quick to anger. And I'm a little concerned. He's been in my office twice this week with issues and hella attitude."

"What is it that he wants?"

"Everything. Now he wants to be an executive producer. Says he's tired of being treated like a hired hand, that Naja is out of control, correction, 'Hurricane Naja.'"

"A hired hand? He must be trippin'."

"That's what I'm saying. The more we kiss his ass, the more he demands we kiss his ass."

"Could be the alcohol altering his personality. He's out a lot, drinking."

Ty shook his head as he pondered. "I don't know. Maybe the pressure is mounting and he's having trouble carrying the weight. It's his name that's out there big and strong, you know. The dip in ratings. And on top of that I ended up telling him about the network wanting to add a white character to the show."

"Why'd you do that? It's not definite."

"'Cause he pissed me off. Talkin' about he's the reason we have a job. I needed to take him down a few notches."

"Well, I'm sure that made him feel better," Maxwell said sarcastically.

"I know. I know. But it's not like I made it up. And either way, Leede might get worse before he gets better."

"Leede tends to wear his emotions on his sleeve. And he was fine in rehearsal. But you really think he's in trouble, huh?"

"Yeah, I do. I think we should stay alert. There could be more drama." Ty paused. "How is my other problem child?"

"We've got Cell in check today. Stayed in his room with his boys and worked with Aaron on the script. He does better when he's locked down. That's probably what he's accustomed to."

Ty smiled. "That was cruel."

Maxwell laughed. "I'm just saying."

"How'd he do in rehearsal? Has he improved?"

"Yeah. I think it's as good as it's going to get."

The moment Ty glanced at his watch, Nancy, the casting director, entered and they called the first actress in. With Nancy feeding them the lines, each actress attempted to read through the scene with animation, as if onstage before a huge audience. Once done Maxwell and Ty commented, "Nice read." Or, "Thanks for coming in." Then they jotted down notes as the talent left.

Ty's head was hung low, making notes, when Dominique Brooks sashayed into his office to audition with a slippery smirk spread across her face. Maxwell gawked like she was an unknown species. Where had this beauty come from? Was she new in town? He'd never seen her before. Where had she been hiding? He nudged Ty with the point of his narrow elbow.

Ty gazed up from his notes and paused for a few seconds as he ID'd Dominique's face with DSL quickness. A picture of the Playboy Mansion flashed in front of him. An image of Sasha's bed appeared in Technicolor. His lips parted and he stammered, "Hey. How are you? Good to see you again."

Maxwell's neck jerked in Ty's direction, giving him a how-do-you-know-her look.

"Hi. Good to see you too," she replied.

For some stupid reason Ty never expected to see the people he crept with during the day. As if he sexed vampires. His penis awoke from an all-day slumber, taking charge of the situation and shutting down central controls in his brain. Damn, he'd love to taste that ass again without Sasha tagging along for the ride. If he was reading the gleam in her green eyes correctly, and he was rarely wrong about these things, she was going to toss some sex his way all over again because he was the HNIC.

Bolts of electrifying energy jolted his system. She was having the same effect on him as she had the night they'd met, but for some peculiar reason he felt slightly vulnerable. This woman had been in his home, in his bed, and was now in his office, and he knew next to nothing about her, not even her last name. His eyes scanned the sheet in front of him. Dominique Brooks. He exhaled in relief. At least now he had enough information to Google her on the Internet.

Dominique cleared her throat and jumped into the part. The audition took less than four minutes. "That was good," Ty said. She smiled and was out the door. Ty would have followed her out the room if possible. He scribbled a comment by her name. "Not bad." Yet he wasn't blown away, and that's what he needed in these days of low ratings: performances that knocked him off his feet. He made another note. Call Sasha. He couldn't wait to tell her who'd come by his office today. Couldn't wait to reprimand her about picking up actresses.

The entire process had taken about forty-five minutes. Nancy, the casting director, had weaned out the bad talent during the first casting session in her office. Ty and Maxwell got to pick from those who'd been called back. They compared notes and discussed who would be best.

Maxwell pursed his lips as he glanced over his list, but was casting with his dick and not his mind. "Man, we should hire Dominique. She is fiiiiine. I wouldn't mind getting with that."

"We can't hire her because she's fine," Ty quickly replied with a frown on his face.

"She gave a good, solid performance. Dude, she's got all the goods," Maxwell argued.

Ty shrugged. "She was decent."

"Hold up. Since when do we *not* grade on a curve for those with curves?"

"Since the network started breathing down my drawls."

"I thought you knew her?" Maxwell asked.

"So? I met her at Al's birthday party at the Playboy Mansion. You'd have met her too, had you shown up like you were supposed to."

"Did you hit on her? I mean, how did this happen?" Maxwell asked.

Ty smirked and glanced over at Nancy. "We can talk about that later. Pick somebody else. Dominique is not the one."

The two quickly agreed to hire Sampson's girlfriend as a favor, but the second role was up for grabs.

"As for the bigger part, I think we need a big name. Honestly, we need a big name in here next week and every week after that." Ty paused. "Nancy, can we get Queen Latifah?"

Nancy shrugged. "I'll call her agent and see. It's last minute, but you never know. Who's your second choice?"

"I'll take anyone with a name who's not a thugged-out rapper."

"Then you don't want Latifah," Maxwell teased. They all chuckled.

"Venus or Serena would be good," Ty said.

"What? We're going to get a resident acting coach or something? Those sisters can play hella tennis but they can't act."

"I'll see what I can do," Nancy replied.

When Ty's door opened, they were all laughing and joking around. Ty went straight to Venus's desk. "Did my agent call?"

"Ah, no. But there's someone here to see you."

Ty frowned as he turned, following Venus's eyes into the conference room. He detested unannounced visitors. He eased over toward the door. There she was again. Miss Dominique Brooks. He gave an easy smile, disguising his surprise. "Hey. What's going on? I didn't know you were still here."

She stood up and gave him her best whispery Marilyn Monroe voice. "I just thought I'd say hi. That is, if you're not too busy?"

"Oh, no. I got a minute. Come on in," Ty replied as he

moved toward his office. He ignored Venus, so she assumed he was okay with the unexpected guest.

She just stared at him. *I got a minute.* Two minutes ago he was pissed. Now he's got a minute. She vowed not to be a two-faced hypocrite when she became a producer. It seemed as though everyone in Tinseltown was exactly that, though. Could she really swim upstream?

Ty entered his office. "You did well in there. I didn't know you were an actress."

She shrugged, flashing her gorgeous smile. "It's nothing. And I don't go around bragging about it."

She entered Ty's office and he closed the door.

"Why not? It's an honest profession."

"I'll put it this way. I'd prefer you know that I was an actress from seeing my work."

"Yeah, but I just saw your work. Auditions are a great way to work out and hone your skills."

She smiled. "That's true."

Her eyes scanned the room, quickly noting everything in sight. "Nice office you have. An interior decorator, right?"

"Right. Some things are best left for the professionals."

As she sank into one of the down seats, she could feel his eyes on her like heat. "They did a good job." She nodded approvingly at the room. "When I get callbacks, they never say who I'll be auditioning for. I had no idea you were a big-time producer."

"I'm just earning a living. And it beats stealing," he joked.

Dominique left her purse on the sofa and moved toward Ty's desk where he sat. "I didn't take you for a modest guy. I find that to be an attractive trait in a man." She paused. "I had a blast with you guys the other night. And trios aren't usually my thing."

"Me too," Ty said, his nose wide open, her Jil Sander perfume intoxicating him, her gray hip-huggers taking his breath away.

She leaned against his desk next to where he sat. "I'd like to do it again soon."

Ty couldn't help but smirk. "That shouldn't be a problem. You did well today in the audition." He didn't know what else to say in the moment of heat.

"You told me that already. Does it mean I got the part?"

"Not this week, but I'm sure there will be another role in the future that's right for you." It was his customary answer when turning actors down. But he'd have lied if he had to.

"You're the boss," she said, her voice soft and sultry. "I like men who are large and in charge. Between the other night and today, I know you're both. Remember, I got to try you on for size." She looked down at Ty's crotch, watching it lift and come to life.

Ty licked his lips in anticipation. He couldn't believe the gift standing before him. And it wasn't even Christmas.

"I thought it was a good fit," Ty said.

"I think it was, but I might need a second fitting to be sure."

"I'm sure I could work something out."

Dominique ran her long, slender fingers across the crotch of his double-pleated pants. She began to unbuckle his brown leather belt to unleash what lay beneath. Ty relaxed, and swiveled his chair to face her. She pulled his penis out of his pants and held it in her hand. "Mmmm. I remember you," she said as she knelt down beside Ty's desk and took him in her mouth. His lips flew open. "Oh shit," he whispered, unable to control the instant escalation of his excitement. Ty sat reclined in his chair, completely lost in a sexual trance, when there was a knock at the door. Initially, it was a tap and then a more aggressive knock, a fist pounding hard like there was a SWAT team about to bust the door down. "Ty. Open the door," he heard Sasha yell. His heart paused. In one split second, the central controls in his brain were up and running again as blood climbed upward and his penis collapsed. His eyes locked with Dominique's, both of them stunned. Here he was trying to do something spontaneous and rewarding, and here comes Sasha, banging his door down like a fire marshal smelling smoke. *Wasn't she supposed to be at the spa or something? Where the hell is Venus? Why isn't she guarding my door?* He sprung out of his seat, zipping his pants and running his palm over his head like he'd messed up his hair. He'd have to think on his feet. "Come on in," he said, wondering how he would explain Dominique's presence. His ego told him he didn't have to, but he knew better. If his relationship with Sasha lasted beyond today, he'd be explaining this situation for the next forty years.

Dominique took three gigantic leaps across the carpet with the grace of a gazelle and grabbed her knockoff Prada bag from the sofa, her heart beating so hard it felt too small for her chest. Sasha was sabotaging her plan.

The doorknob snapped, *click, click,* back and forth as Sasha sought to enter by force. "It's locked. Open the door," Sasha huffed, her fears causing her left eye to twitch. She turned to Venus for answers. "Who's in there with him?"

Venus sat, paralyzed. Only her mind and lips moved. "I don't know. They were having auditions and I went to the restroom. And . . . and . . . I don't know, Sasha." Her instincts told her Ty was about to get a serious beatdown. Had she been able to move, she'd have run up and down the hall yelling, "Fight! Fight!" so everyone could form a circle and watch, like in high school.

"Well, don't you have a key to his office?" Sasha insisted.

"No, not anymore," Venus lied. Ty would turn back time and fire her *yesterday* if she opened that door for Sasha.

Sasha turned, balled up her left fist and banged on the office white door again, her body trembling. A second later, Ty flung the door open, his jaws squared. He was pissed to the high heavens.

Sasha pushed past him, her eyes sweeping the room, her face red with anger. Her heart sank down to her Manolo Blahnik heels when she saw Dominique, the evidence of all of her fears. She demanded answers. "What are you doing here? What's going on? And why is the door locked?"

"Chill out, Sasha," Ty said with irritation ringing in his voice. "Ain't nothing going on. We just finished a casting session. Maxwell just left out of here. I don't know why the door was locked. Maybe Venus didn't turn the lock this morning when she opened my office door."

"What do you think? I'm stupid?" Her hands were planted firmly on her hips.

Her head swiveled toward Dominique who stood to her left. "What are you doing here?"

Ty spoke up again. "I told you. There was a casting session. She auditioned for the show. Go ask Maxwell."

Sasha narrowed her eyes and shot him an evil look. "I wasn't talking to you. I was talking to Dominique." She turned her attention back to Dominique, her chest heaving in and out.

"Hey, girl. I auditioned for the show," Dominique said, giving an uneasy smile. "You didn't tell me Ty was a producer. Girl, I was shocked when I walked in here and saw him. I mean, to meet you both the other night and then see you both today? You two are like spiritually connected."

Sasha's eyebrows rose slightly. "And you were what? In here, fucking for your part?"

Ty stepped to Sasha. "Look, this is my job. Don't come up in here, trying to blow up the spot."

Sasha glared at him, dying to pick up the phone receiver and give him the worst beatdown of his life for being such an idiot. Sometimes he was a genius. Other times he was just plain old dumb. "You'll be lucky if that's the only thing I blow up, because I feel like blowing up your ass. You don't know who this girl is, *fool*. Did she tell you she had lunch with me a few hours ago?"

Ty's eyes quickly panned between the two women before landing on Sasha. "You've been talking to her and didn't tell me? I guess you've been sleeping with her too?" Ty said, his imagination running wild.

"Oh, don't you *dare* turn this around. This is not about me. This is about you. You didn't walk in and find me with anyone."

"Oh, but I could, though, couldn't I? How many lovers have you had Sasha? How many times have you been behind my back?"

"I haven't been with anyone behind your back, negro. That's why we swing."

Dominique slowly inched toward the door, making her escape as they argued.

Sasha caught a glimpse of her shadow through her peripheral vision. "Don't you ever let me catch you near me or my family again," she threatened, waving her index finger like a weapon.

"It's not what you think. He's telling you the truth," Dominique said, backing out of the door.

"Get the hell out of here before I call security and have you thrown off the studio lot."

Dominique clutched her phony purse as she left. "I'm sorry, Sasha. It's really not what you think."

Sasha tightened her lips in disgust. "Don't apologize. Thank me for being a lady and not kicking your ass."

The second Dominique was out of sight, the tears Sasha had been suppressing broke like a dam. Her feelings were so hurt, she physically ached. Now that she had privacy, she could rip into Ty's ass as he deserved.

Ty stood near the door as he shut it. Sasha charged toward him and started swinging, flaying her arms through the air like a windmill, continuously striking Ty. "How could you do this to me? How could you? You gave her a part on the show? I hate you, Ty. I fuckin' hate you." She kept repeating herself, working through the pain that hit her every time her heart tried to beat.

He held his arms up in defense. "I didn't give her a part." He began wrestling with her, trying to pin down her arms, but there was bionic strength in her aggression. Every time he grabbed one arm, he'd lose hold of it trying to get the other. "Calm down! It's not what you think!"

"I'm not dealing with your shit anymore. Do you hear me? I'm not dealing with this shit anymore. I'm sick of you. You can't treat me like this." She'd sacrificed too much of herself to be with Ty and she hated him for it now.

"Why were you having lunch with her, Sasha? What is going on between you two?"

"That's what I want to know, Ty. What's going on with you?"

Perspiration lined Ty's temples. He couldn't get a grip on her. Couldn't calm her down and it alarmed him. He'd never seen her so enraged, so violent and he didn't know what to do. He hollered for help. "Venus!"

Venus sat at her desk like Helen Keller, playing blind, deaf and dumb. She was going to stretch out on the dirty floor and play dead if she had to. She felt sorry for a brother, but Ty was on his own. She didn't *do* domestic disputes.

Sasha's propeller limbs slowed. She was tiring, wearing down from all the swinging and heartache. Her strength diminished as exhaustion set in.

Ty grabbed hold of her upper arms and hugged her tight. "Calm down. It's not what you think. I swear it's not. I swear."

Sasha surrendered to his embrace, her head resting on his chest. "You don't know what I think. Do you even care what I think, Ty? Do you?"

"Come on, baby. Don't let some girl come in our world and destroy what we have."

"What do we have, Ty? What is this? Why are we living like this?"

"We have each other and we have Taylor. And if Dominique had someone she wouldn't be doing what she's doing."

Sasha pulled away from his embrace and sat on the edge of the sofa. She gazed up at him with soggy eyes. "I need more. I need more. I don't think I can do this anymore. I need stability."

"I'm here. I've always been here."

"When it's convenient for you. I want a home with my man. With my husband."

He cringed and ran his palm over his face. It was back to the M word. "I've told you. I'm not ready. I'm just not ready."

Sasha bent over, cupping her face in her hands. "And I can't walk into your office anymore not knowing what to expect. I can't give my all and have you giving me fifty percent in return."

"I'm giving you all I can at this time." He paused. "I've got a lot on me right now. The network is riding me bareback over the ratings and I cannot deal with this right now."

"You're always running. And it's always work."

Ty lowered his voice. "You're not being fair. My job comes first and you know that. And I've always been up-front about it. That's who I am."

Sasha got up, clearing her smeared mascara with a tissue. "Yeah, I know who you are. And you have no idea what fair is."

Ty was unable to articulate his feelings in regards to Sasha sleeping with women. He didn't think *that* was fair. He knew it was silly, but he honestly felt she was cheating on him, betraying him in the worst way. And to discover she'd had lunch with Dominique only heightened his insecurity. He couldn't possibly express his true sentiments without sounding like a vulnerable and pathetic wimp. In order to protect his masculinity and his deepest fears, he mentally mixed some cement and built a brick wall so Sasha couldn't see his weakness and he couldn't feel her pain. "Go in the bathroom and get yourself together, Sasha. We'll finish this conversation at home."

She got up and wobbled into the bathroom. It would be useless to argue further. Not now, anyway. If she pushed and prodded him, he would only get madder and eventually hurt her feelings. Her heart had suffered enough damage for one day. One more blow to the heart and she'd need a new one.

17

Ty's brother Craig was sprawled across the green iron bench in front of the production building as if he owned a controlling interest in Rex Studios or at the very least, the bench. His jaws caved in as he took a long drag from a Newport cigarette. Lounging in this spot under the California sun was as comfortable as being back on the block in his old hood. Were it not for nepotism that's where he'd be. But hanging out at the studio lot afforded many more luxuries than the streets, like free meals, a gym and basketball courts with nets not made of metal chains. In addition, he could get his tapes dubbed, watch *Judge Judy* and have daily interaction with celebrities and high rollers. He wiped sweat from his brow. He wouldn't trade his Hollywood life for all the oil in Iraq.

He cocked his head to one side and dropped his palm to his knee when he caught sight of Dominique rushing out of the building's double glass doors. Craig sucked his gold teeth. "Hey, pretty lady. How you doin'?"

Dominique's radar detected a nuisance. She cut her eyes at him, afraid to look him head on. "I'm good."

His eyes ran up and down her body as he mentally measured her butt and bust. "Ump, ump, ump. You sure look good too."

Dominique kept stepping.

"Slow down. Why you walking so fast? You ain't got a minute for a brother?"

Not even a second. She eased her sunglasses onto her face, hiding from the sun and Sasha. There was something familiar about this hoodlum who was now standing before her. She took a good look at him through the tinted lenses. Ty. He looked like an older, shorter, broken-down version of Ty in a jersey that was five years retro and Converse that looked like Ty's hand-me-downs. He had the same eyes as Ty, except these looked liked they'd witnessed more pain; same head but with hair; same silhouette, yet thicker. She spoke up now that he had her full attention. "Do I have time? That depends on what a brother has got to say for himself."

"Plenty. How much time you got? 'Cause I could talk all day long about how beautiful you are," he said, flashing his gold teeth, hoping to impress her. "You know my brother is the executive producer and creator of *Same Day Service*. I'm his right-hand man. I can get you tickets to the show any-time you want. Now that's the best deal I've offered anyone all day."

She paused, contemplating the offer. Why not? This could be a detour leading back to Ty. She wasn't about to give up on him. She'd been too close, had his nose too open. Had they spent five more minutes alone, he'd have been clay in her hands.

Craig stamped out his cigarette butt. "My name is Craig. What's your name, beautiful?"

"I'm Dominique. You work on the show, Craig?"

"I'm an actor," he replied with bass in his voice. He was no actor. He was an extra, earning minimum wage. "You've probably seen me on the show."

"Can't say that I have, but I'll look for you next time I watch."

Craig squinted his eyes against the sun. "You should come on up to the taping on Friday. I'll put your name on the guest list. No problem. Maybe we could hang out after the show. Get a bite to eat or what have you. Why don't you slip me them digits and I'll give you a call?"

"How about you give me your number and I'll call you?"

He sucked his gold teeth. "Oh, it's like that? Why you tryin' to play a brother?"

She checked her watch. "Look. I've got an appointment. I'd love to come to the show on Friday."

"Well, I need a number to call you in case of emergency. You never know. The show might get cancelled and you'll have come all the way to Burbank for nothing."

"I live here in Burbank, so it's not a big deal."

"Burbank, huh? You in the phone book?"

Dominique cut her eyes at him. "Are you going to get me into the show or not? I don't have all day."

"Well, I guess I could hook you up anyway. What's your last name, Dominique?"

"Brooks. Dominique Brooks," she said.

"To show you I'm on the up and up, I'm going to put your name on the list for the show and I'll take you for a ride in my Range Rover afterwards." He pointed to the gray truck parked in the space reserved for Ty's vehicle.

She twisted her lips. "Thanks. What time is the taping?" she asked.

"Six o'clock. And don't be late. You're in for a treat. I'm going to give you a backstage Hollywood tour. You're going to meet all the stars."

Dominique forced a smile. "I'll see you on Friday."

He grabbed the crotch of his sagging jeans. "And I can't wait. Damn, you pretty. I'mma marry you, girl."

Dominique rolled her eyes as she walked away. She'd be there on Friday night with bells on. Wouldn't miss it for the world. She'd been close and intimate with Ty, had his penis wrapped around her tongue and he loved it. There was a connection between them and, if given the time, she could steal him away from Sasha. All she needed was another opportunity and now she had it, thanks to his ghetto brother. She wondered what the rest of the family was like.

Inside the Mondrian Hotel on Sunset Boulevard, glamorous-looking employees draped in white linen served rich and famous people cloaked in haute couture garments. From its magnificent glass walls and sleek, all-white décor to its obscurely shaped chairs and eclectic art objects, the hotel was nothing if it wasn't a Soho art gallery in the middle of West Hollywood. Everything in it was so ultra expensive the place smelled of crisp, new money.

Al West was seated inside the hotel's famous Sky Bar, taking in the hillside view of the city and looking over the pool. His diamond pinky ring sparkled as he twirled his wineglass, soaking up his drink and the happy-hour ambiance. Technically, he was off the wagon for the fiftieth time, except for a bit of Merlot here and there.

Al was gawking at the drum-tight ass of a brunette patron when Ty came in, wearing weary like a sign on his forehead.

Al gazed over. "Damn, Youngblood. You look like hell," he teased.

Ty slid onto the sleek bar stool next to Al and forced a smile. "Then I look just the way I feel." He rested his elbows on the bar, noting the blonde, blue-eyed bartender, who was fashion-model perfect. "Give me a double shot of Hennessy and a Corona." He turned to Al. "My drinking isn't going to bother you, is it?"

"Naw, I only wish there was such a thing as secondhand alcohol. You know, so I could get a buzz and still go to my AA meeting professing to have been a good boy."

"What are you on these days? Wine?"

"Yep. I'm a certified wino. It's the least I can do and still keep my kidneys intact." He paused. "So, what's going on? Only two things can have a man looking like you look. That's either money or pussy."

Ty smiled. Ah, the street wisdom of Al West. Lessons learned on the streets of Chicago's South Side would never leave him. Ty tilted his head back and gulped his cognac. The empty glass made a clicking sound when it landed on the bar. "I'm not agreeing with your theory, but if I had to narrow it down to one word, it would be *pussy*. I met this chick at your birthday party the other night."

"Who?"

"Dominique Brooks. You know her?"

Al thought for a moment. "Nah."

"Sasha and I met her and we did a little swinging, you know. Anyway, she shows up at my office today for an audition."

"Was she any good?"

"She was decent. But then she stays behind after everyone has left and she's kicking it to me."

Al nodded his salt-and-pepper head.

"No, I mean she was really kicking it to me. Hard. An old-fashioned casting couch session."

Al grinned. "But you were cool with that, right?"

"Well, I was until Sasha came banging on the door."

Al's eyes widened. "Get outta here."

"That's exactly what I wanted to tell Sasha. She never pops in like that. Thank God the door was locked."

"Well, you'd better get busy or you'll never be able to live this down. Women don't forget a damn thing."

"She's still talking about getting married. In fact, that's all she's been talking about." He paused, his chest burning from the cognac. "I'd never seen her like she was today. Never. She was straight-up trippin'."

"Was it a girl fight?" Al eagerly asked.

"No. She tried to beat *my* ass." Ty massaged the wrinkles on his forehead. "I can't marry Sasha. Not now. But I don't want to lose her either."

"Then you've got to buy yourself some time. What has she been asking you to do that you didn't want to do?"

"Marry her."

"Besides that. If she's been bugging you about going to

Brazil, then it's time to buy first-class tickets to Rio. You need a big-ticket item to show you care. You feel me? You're going to have to give up something to smooth this over. Make it worth her while and make it seem like you're trying."

Ty swallowed the remainder of his shot. He sat still, thinking, the alcohol setting him free from stress and fatigue.

"You have to get her to appreciate your honesty. And take it from me, a man who's been married twice, if you ain't ready, don't do it. Marriage is like fire. It is not to be played with."

Ty only nodded in response. He ran his finger over the frost on his beer glass. Sasha wanted to be Cinderella and live a fairy tale, get hitched, ride off into the sunset on a white horse and live happily ever after. But Ty didn't believe in fairy tales, had never ridden a horse in his life. The realities of his world didn't afford him such lighthearted views. In all the fables he'd read, Prince Charming had never been born in the hood and never wore Timberlands. He'd never sold drugs or seen his sibling shot and killed. And never once had Prince Charming pulled out his sword to fight racism. The Prince profile didn't fit Ty. Where he came from, there were no perfect beginnings or endings. He was a guy from the street, where happily ever after meant not dying in the street.

Ty loved Sasha. She was the first woman to stand by his side and take him on and all his flaws. He wasn't an easy person, but she knew him better than anyone. So well, at moments she was able to tell him what he was about to say. As a result she knew when to push and when not to. She knew how to get what she wanted and when to give him space. He loved how her nose crinkled when she was mad. Loved the big smile on her face when she danced. Loved her positive disposition, always able to see light when he saw darkness. She was easy and treated him like a king, and more important, she treated his kid as if she were baby Jesus. There was kindness and love in every word she spoke to Taylor and in every hand that touched her. If anything happened to him tomorrow, Sasha would take good care of Taylor. For that he worshipped her, in his own way.

Al gulped his wine, wishing it were hard liquor. "A prenuptial. It's a must these days. I didn't have sense enough to do it because I was whipped."

"Twice?"

"Okay. All right. I was whipped the first time and a fool the second. But I didn't have as much to lose each time."

"It's not all about the money."

"If you divorce her, it will be. Trust me," Al quickly replied.

Ty's reluctance to marry ran deeper than his pockets. He treasured his freedom and he had enough cash to truly know what freedom was. He wasn't ready to marry and give a daily report of his time, didn't want to bother getting his trip slip signed every time he jetted out of town. Commitment was one thing. A lifetime contract gluing him to another like a Siamese twin was another. It was more responsibility than he wanted at the present time. One day he'd be ready to jump the broom. He wanted a traditional family like the one he'd grown up in. He wanted to grow old with someone, have someone to fuss at and fuss over, but at the age of thirty-four, growing old seemed as far away as Pluto. He had more urgent matters pressing, like stabilizing his career as a producer.

"I'm more concerned about work right now. Leede says he is going to ask for an executive producer credit."

"He's out of his damn mind," Al said.

"Maybe so, but he could make things more difficult than they already are. As it stands, these crackers are trying to lynch my ass. Leede could plead his case by saying I'm not doing my job. That would be tightening the noose around my neck."

"First, he'll have to prove he's doing *his*. Only a bona fide fool would ask for a raise while a show is on shaky ground. 'Cause a raise is really what he's asking for.

"He says he wants more say-so, more control," Ty said.

Al turned his glass up. "Bullshit." He took a swig. "The suits will count the cost first and foremost. An executive producer credit would mean an extra twenty grand an episode in his purse. It doesn't matter who's running the show, because the suits will still want to control."

"That's true."

"What you are going through is not out of the ordinary, Youngblood."

"So I've heard."

Al went on to give Ty examples of other black producers who'd fought battles with their networks and lost. Just last season, Jason Manning struggled with NBC over his hit show. Jason, like Ty, was the creator and executive producer. His show had earned an Emmy in its first season. The show's ratings were solid and even had a strong crossover audience. Yet the network battled with him over the characters and the stories because they wanted every line to be funny. Jason saw the black characters one way and the executives, who'd never lived in black skin for a day, saw them another. At the end of the second season, he was fired. The network only cited creative differences. "'Creative differences' means he didn't do what they wanted him to do," Al said.

Then there was Tamara Collins. She too had written a sitcom the network was excited about. They wined and dined her, filling her head with their vision for the show. But when it came time to hire the staff, they opted to make her the co-executive producer and placed two white guys at the helm as the executive producers. While Tamara maintained some power, they harassed her over every detail of the show, down to the props. "They didn't trust her to make one decision on her own. The situation grew so stressful, she eventually quit," Al said.

"I'm not quitting. They can forget that," Ty said as he nursed his beer. He was as emotionally attached to his project as a mother to her newborn. "I met with the suits again today. I told them I didn't think adding a white character would make a difference. They didn't say much in response."

Ty was all ears, waiting for Al's wise words. He'd given Ty his start and with years of producing on his resume, Al was a voice of experience and his confidante.

"And what about the encore episodes?" Al asked.

"They said they'd see. Said the decision wasn't theirs to make."

"Ump. Black shows stifle the executives. Movies too, for that matter. They don't know how to market them to the white audience 'cause they don't fit into one of their pre-fixed categories." Al poked out his lips, the truth of his words unsettling him. "Don't be fooled by these so-called liberals. They are far from being colorblind. And don't get me wrong. I don't think it's intentional. It's damn near unconscious. We were all raised in the same racist society and it's hard to break the cycle."

If Al were still a betting man, he'd bet his firstborn the network was searching for a way to make Ty disappear. But he didn't want to alarm Ty, didn't want to agitate him further. Over a span of twenty-five years, Al had fallen victim to many unfair practices of the business. White characters had been placed on his shows against his wishes and he'd been forced to hire white writers he didn't want. Back in 1991, one of his shows had been cancelled in less time than it took him to blink. The network suits had called his office and said, "The show has been cancelled. A new show will be moving into your offices in two days. You can be out by then, right?" And just like that, he and the other two hundred or so people working on the show were instantly eligible for unemployment.

Ty shook his head. "Here's the worst part of it. Last night I had this worked out in my head. I was going to go into this meeting and tell the suits, hell no. There's not going to be any new white characters on my show, that I didn't need the crossover audience. That black people alone had made my show a hit. I had made up my mind. Al, I was going to tell them motherfuckers to suck my dick, that I wasn't taking their shit no more!" His shoulders dropped a notch. "Instead, I went in there today grinning like a cheshire cat in front of them crackers. Talking as if unsure of myself. Playing down my intelligence. I did everything but said Yessah, Boss." Earlier he might have felt the weight of a racist system, but tonight he felt its humiliation and it pained him.

"You cooled down after a good night's sleep, huh?" Al

chuckled. "Man, niggers been doing that since we got here. Don't beat up on yourself. You gotta give to get."

"Yeah, I know. But I'm giving up more than I thought I would."

"You have a choice. You can be self-righteous and poor or compromising and rich." His eyebrows rose. "Look, Youngblood. The suits are going to do what they want to do, regardless. I know it's unfair and you have every reason to be pissed. But sit back and watch and wait," Al said. He cleared his throat and continued. "Fluctuations in ratings are normal. The problem is you had an early success. Your show ratings rocketed on the Nielsen meter during the first season, so that leaves nowhere to go but down. It's hard to sustain those kinds of numbers."

"Especially when I'm up against *American Icon*. The world loves that damn show."

"Come on. All shows experience dips, even *American Icon*. You know that. You've got to ride this out. I've been around long enough to know these things usually fix themselves. And when it does, the suits will ease up."

Ty's eyes narrowed. "So I'm paying for my success, huh?"

"One way or another, we always do, Youngblood. We always do. You just keep booking big talent. And if they force your hand with the white character, make them put their money where their mouth is. Insist they hire a white boy with a name. Not some white kid on the rise. A no-name punk is unlikely to boost ratings. But . . ." Al paused and pointed his index finger, "he can't be bigger than Leede." Al motioned to the model-perfect bartender and ordered another glass of wine.

18

"Hey, wassup?" Leede whispered. The phone had awakened him from a comatose sleep. He looked around the semi-familiar hotel room and then at the less familiar brunette sleeping next to him. He glanced at the clock on the nightstand for the time, then at the stationery to see where he'd been snoring and whoring all night. The Argyle.

"Hey, man. How was the movie?" Van Arden asked. He'd placed Leede's name, plus one, on the guest list for the movie premiere of *Jaded*, starring Kevin Costner. It was his comeback.

"It sucked. But it's Kevin, so it will make some money. The party was nice though. Sometimes the studios are better at throwing parties than making movies."

"Did you get some snapshots on the red carpet?"

"For sure," Leede said.

"Good." Van Arden was obsessed with keeping his clients

in the public eye. "Listen, I spoke with Gary Ackerman about meeting with you."

Leede flung his ashy legs from under the covers and sat up on the side of the bed. He yawned long and wide. The mystery woman next to him stirred in her sleep. "This morning?" he asked.

"No, we spoke yesterday. I wanted to catch you before you got to the studio."

Leede's cell phone was off, so Van Arden had called several hotels on Sunset asking for Elmer Fudd, Leede's ridiculous check-in name. He firmly believed Leede would someday be a huge star because he thought like one, using secret code names as if paparazzi all over the globe were hunting him down. Many late nights had ended on hotel mattresses when Leede was too pissy drunk or dreadfully tired to drive to his home in Encino.

"Gary said he'd like to meet with us to address your concerns about your character and the direction of the show, etcetera, and he's eager to hear your ideas," Van Arden said.

Leede rubbed his eyes, perking up at the news. "When is this going to happen?"

"Three o'clock. After the network run-through."

"Damn. You could have called me later?"

"Later when? While you're rehearsing?" Van Arden paused. "I spoke to him briefly about you becoming an executive producer."

"What did he say?"

"Not much. Something about the ratings being low and the budget being at its maximum."

"And what did you say? Did you fight for me? Tell them

that I make that show the success it is? That budgets can be changed? Did you? Huh?"

"I made a few arguments for your case, but I'm not even sure I know why you suddenly want an executive producer credit. We have to look at this logically. The show is still in its youth and you didn't create it. It would be wise to wait for the ratings to go back up before asking for more money."

Leede rubbed his forehead. Van Arden was serving him the same bullshit Ty had shoved at him yesterday. "If you had more time to spend on me and my career you'd know that my interest was not being protected on the show. Egos are flying all over the place. Naja is out of control. Ty is out of control. Now *you're* tripping."

As a rule, Van Arden didn't yell or call his clients names, though it was not always easy. He took deep breaths and counted to ten, remembering the clients paid his bills. "If you hold on until next season, I'll get you a better deal. I'll guarantee you an executive producer credit."

Leede had been waiting all his life. "Are you listening to me? The show has not yet been picked up for next season. I'm hearing rumors that a white character will be added to the show. I've got to make something happen now. If a character is going to be added, then I want to take part in casting." Leede looked at the woman sleeping next to him, trying to remember her name.

"Don't worry. I'm on the case. You'll have a movie to shoot by hiatus."

Leede clenched his jaw. Van Arden made a lot of verbal promises, but Leede needed to see some tangible results. He was too insecure to have faith in anyone, too afraid to trust.

His life had been a string of one letdown after another, starting with being deserted by his mother. His father? Leede wasn't sure he even had one. When the show became an instant hit, he'd expected a vagabond to crawl from under a rock, claiming to be a sperm donor. Leede had gone so far as to prepare a statement to give to the press in the event that it happened. But no stubble-faced drunks came forth. Leede was half relieved, half disappointed. Not even after national success and a hefty paycheck would a man claim him as an offspring.

"I haven't been on an audition in three weeks," Leede angrily complained.

"I called you about a movie role you were offered two days ago. And you didn't want it."

"That's right. I want a role that's going to blow me up. A part that will get me an award nomination, that will take me to the next level."

Van Arden silently sighed. Actors were all alike. One job and they wanted to own the town, wanted Rome all in one day. Every client he had expected him to part the Red Sea so they could cross from anonymity to stardom. "Have you bothered to read the scripts I sent you?"

Leede frowned. "I have to memorize a script a week! I don't have time to read scripts! And if you bothered to come to a taping you'd have some idea what is going on. But I guess you're too busy with your high profile clients to be concerned about me."

Van Arden conceded. He'd only made one appearance on the set since the new season started. "Okay, maybe I haven't been around as much as I should, but I'll be there for you today."

"That's okay. Don't worry about coming to the meeting. I don't need you!"

"You can't talk to the execs by yourself. I mean, you can, but I wouldn't advise it. Nobody meets with them without a rep."

"You're not my manager anymore and I don't want your damn advice."

"You're firing me?"

"Hell, yes!"

"But we have a contract."

"Not anymore," Leede said before hanging up the phone, infuriated with Van Arden, Ty, his unknown father and himself for thinking any of them cared about him or his career. The brunette rolled over and stretched like a kitten. "Good morning," she purred. "You were so good last night."

"Make sure to tell your friends," he quipped. Leede got up and went into the bathroom. It was time to start his day. His call time was earlier than usual because "Cyclone Naja" was doing *The Tonight Show*.

As soon as Naja's feet hit the floor, she removed cucumber slices from the refrigerator and placed them on her eyes to eliminate any and all puffiness. Last night she'd rolled back the silky sheets on her sleigh bed and silenced the ringer on her phone at 9 P.M., intent on getting her beauty sleep. She'd slept flat on her back, her arms folded across her abdomen like a corpse in a coffin, allowing her honey skin to fall taut over her high cheekbones. She'd read in a magazine once that sleeping on one's back kept the skin firm and youthful and prevented early wrinkles. Before going to bed, she'd spent the evening at the spa, getting the works; a manicure, pedicure, massage and sauna. When she walked onstage at NBC Studios for *The Tonight Show*, she would look and feel like the Queen of Egypt.

Naja was the first to arrive at the studio and the first cast member to have her final fitting for Friday's show. This last fitting was to be brief. Two outfits had been altered to fit her ever-expanding breasts. The costume designer swore her bust had increased a cup size over hiatus. When the fitting was completed, she insisted on rummaging through the racks of clothing for another outfit to don on Leno. To no avail, the costume designer had wasted two hours with her on the previous day, determining what dress met all of Naja's criteria. It had to fit like a second skin, match her complexion, look tailor made, could look nothing like a Halle, J.Lo or Jada replica, blend with Leno's sofa and make her look like a divine diva. Yet somewhere between yesterday and today her insecurities had flared up and haunted her and she was distraught over her choice. It took thirty minutes of her primping and posing in front of a full-length mirror and the designer repeating, "That dress makes you look sexy. You look fabulous, girl," before her insecurities were once again temporarily laid to rest.

Back in her dressing room, Naja cocked her head back and gulped down Pepto Bismol as if it were a thirst-quenching beer. During the fitting, her stomach had started rumbling and cramping mildly, and she could feel a common case of diarrhea coming on. If she didn't know any better, she'd say it was a bad case of nervousness over the Leno excitement. The intestinal earthquake was the damaging price she paid for dining on jarred baby foods. She was tossing the pink stuff into her tote bag when she heard a tap on her dressing room door. She grabbed a bottle of water and took a sip, then opened the door. Her eyes met Ty's. She stepped aside as he entered.

"I just wanted to make sure you're all set for this evening."

Naja smiled. "I think I'm covered."

"A clip was sent over this morning. It's from episode four of this season, when you spray air freshener on the homeless guy."

"Oh, yeah. I liked that one."

"I think it was one of your best shows."

"Thanks."

"I just wanted you to know, in case you want to set it up for the audience. Did they tell you what you would be discussing?"

"I had a phone interview with one of the producers yesterday. She asked about my background, my hobbies and personal interests. You know. The regular."

"I'm sure they'll bring out something interesting and witty based on what you told them. It should be fun." Ty checked his watch. "I'd better go. Run-through starts soon." He turned toward the door, then looked back over his shoulder, feeling uneasy. "Oh, and Naja, thanks for being so cool about the incident with Cell Block."

She batted her false eyelashes and nodded.

"If he tries any bullshit tomorrow, remember, I'm going to court with you." He flashed a smile to reassure her. "Break a leg."

"Thanks," she replied. What was he doing kissing up? Damn

near apologizing for his behavior. Uhm, apparently he'd gotten word Leede was about to be the next executive producer.

The network run-through started on time. After Bernie yelled, "Quiet on the set," and peace was restored onstage, the cast read through the script exactly as they'd rehearsed over the past two days. This was a private showing solely for the benefit of the network suits to give final approval and their last opportunity to make comments and suggestions. Walking through the scenes on completed stage sets, the network and studio got a good idea what the show would look like when taped. Following each sentence with their scripts in hand, the writers dutifully burst into phony laughter after each and every joke, just as they'd done at the table read. Much to the satisfaction of the writers and producers, the reading ran smoothly. There would be no late night rewriting session. When the reading ended, Bernie released the actors and gave them call times for the following day.

Gary and David were already seated at one of the patio tables at the studio commissary when Leede walked up with his baggy sweatsuit waving in the wind. Leede adjusted his sunglasses though the stripy umbrella above protected him from the sun. He flashed the same sparkling smile that had landed him the leading role on *Same Day Service.*

"Hey, Leede. How's it going?" Gary lifted halfway up from his seat, as did David.

"I'm good," Leede answered, as he shook hands.

"Great script this week," Gary said.

"Hey, how's the new house coming along?" David asked.

"Mmm, you know? It's a slow process. I don't have much furniture. Only the essentials."

"It's hard to fill a big house," Gary added.

"I figure, what's the hurry. I've got thirty years to pay for the damn thing. So I've got thirty years to furnish it."

Gary and David smiled.

"But I've got plenty of patio furniture. The pool is the main attraction. You guys will have to bring the kids over one day. Maybe they can teach me how to swim."

"Don't you swim?" Gary asked.

"Let's put it this way. I can do the breaststroke, but not under water," Leede joked.

The men chuckled.

"Hey, I don't mean to rush, but we've got another run-through. Do you think Van Arden is running late?"

"Uh, no. Something came up. I don't think he's going to make it," Leede said. It was none of their business he had no manager representing him at the present time. He still had an agent, but they rarely spoke, since Van Arden was the middleman.

Gary glanced at David. "We can reschedule for another day. It's no problem."

"I'm here. Let's do this."

David raised a brow. "You sure?"

"Yeah," Leede answered confidently.

Gary shrugged. "Alright. So what's going on? Van Arden says you're not happy, and if you're unhappy, we're unhappy. And Ty told us about your being slightly perturbed earlier this week."

"I don't know what Ty told you, but I want more say in

what goes with the show. I'm committed to this show, my character and the network and I have my own creative ideas I'd like implemented."

Gary and David nodded.

"Are you saying you're unhappy with the way Ty is running the show? You can be honest. This conversation is between the three of us," Gary said.

"Look, I have no problems with anyone." He chose his words wisely, steering clear of the politics.

"You wouldn't be the only person. We hear things. And from what I'm hearing there are some problems in the production office."

Leede innocently shrugged. "I don't know anything about that."

Gary wouldn't be deterred. "Well, if you want to be a producer then you certainly can't be satisfied with the producers we have in place. As you probably already know, we are less than pleased with the ratings."

"Hey, I just want the show to be the best it can be. And that means having some input. I want approval on the story lines of the episodes."

"We think you can make the show better. This show has the potential to make the long haul into syndication. So, let's explore this because maybe there should be some changes if you want to become an executive producer," Gary said.

"Changes? What kind of changes?" Leede asked.

"I think you are a gifted actor and funny as hell, Leede. Isn't that right, David?"

David nodded.

Gary continued. "I could be wrong on this. It just feels like something's been missing lately. I don't know. Like you're not as funny as you used to be. You know, like you might not be putting your all into it."

His heart missed a beat as a surge of heat ran through Leede's body. "I'm not sure I know what you mean."

Gary sat back in his chair. "We're all friends here. Let's think about this. 'Cause there is always room for improvement, in front of the camera as well as behind it."

David jumped in. "Okay. We're just talking this out. You know, maybe you could be more conscientious, Leede. I don't know. Perhaps setting a good example could be a goal."

"I have set a good example."

Gary shrugged. "By being late. I don't know."

"I don't know what you're talking about. I'm not always late."

"Really?"

"Really."

"Hmmm. That's not what we heard."

"Maybe you heard wrong."

"It's possible but unlikely." Gary paused. "How about being prepared and knowing your lines?"

"What? I'm always prepared," Leede argued.

Gary shook his head. "I'm not sure you're making the extra effort here. You've got a lot of responsibility as the lead character on this show. Everyone is looking up to you and you're carrying a whole lot of people on your back."

"I know that! I've been carrying this show from day one. Me and me alone. So I'm late every now and then. So what? When it comes to rehearsal I'm there and I'm doing my job."

Gary gave a coy smile. "Listen. This is a team effort and

we're all in this together. As a team, I think we should see some improvements before we start handing out promotions. That's all."

Leede stood up in a rage. "A handout! You know what? I think y'all can kiss my ass. Who in the hell do you think you are?"

"There's no need to get mad." Gary stood up.

"Too late. I passed mad thirty seconds ago. Who the hell do you think you're talking to? Huh? I'm Leede Banks. I've got million-dollar movie offers. I don't need y'all or this show. Y'all need me. 'Cause I'm the one carrying this damn show. This show would be nothing without me and my skills. I'm the glue holding this shit together."

Gary tried to get a word in. "It was not my intention . . ."

"Y'all don't know me. I suggest both of you step up your game and show me some respect. 'Cause I'm the star of this show. I'm the reason people watch every week. I'm the reason either one of you has a job. And if I wanna be late there ain't a damn thing you can do but wait on my black ass." He paused. "If either one of you come to me with any of this bullshit again, I'll be in Russ Tobin's office quicker than you can say, 'That nigger's crazy.' And I'll have your low-rent asses fired. This is my damn show, you got that? I'm fucking King Kong up in this piece and don't y'all ever forget it."

Leede stormed off in a rage. The only thing he could think of was ramming his right sneaker up both their asses. He could see the headlines now: "Actor Leede Banks, best known for his role on *Same Day Service*, was found guilty for assaulting two studio executives. It is the first time anyone has been convicted for using Adidas sneakers as a weapon."

19

Sid was already standing in front of the guest entrance at NBC Studios in Burbank, located just a few blocks from Rex Studios, when Naja's limo pulled up. She could have easily walked the distance in less than ten minutes. But now that she resided in Tinseltown and lived the glamorous life, walking was no longer an option.

Sid stepped toward the car to greet her. "What a waste of good money sending a car to pick you up."

She rolled her eyes. "Ugh! They better had," she said as she slid out the black sedan and sashayed toward the entrance.

The receptionist greeted them and then directed them to the green room. As usual, there wasn't a trace of green in the room. The term was merely entertainment lexicon for guest quarters. It was about a five-hundred-square-foot space with two burnt-red sofas, a coffee table supporting a vase of white tulips and a long table filled with water and juices. A TV monitor hung from the corner and one long mirror surrounded by round lightbulbs ran horizontally along the back wall.

Sid opened a bottle of Evian water and handed it to Naja. "Are you nervous?"

She smiled. "Nervous with excitement. It's a good nervousness." She rested her right palm over her tummy, feeling a volcano moving inside. The Pepto Bismol wasn't potent enough to cure diarrhea and excitement. Nevertheless, she pulled the pink stuff from her purse and gulped some down.

Sid looked on in awe. "Wow. You're drinking that stuff like its water. You *are* excited."

A studious-looking woman in glasses, a ponytail and jeans entered and introduced herself as Judy, one of the producers on the show. Judy extended a warm welcome and profusely thanked Naja for agreeing to do the show on such short notice. Judy then instructed Naja on the shooting schedule and what time she'd go on. Naja would be first. The latest reject on a reality show would appear second. And a comedian would be last. Judy left quickly, leaving Naja to attend to her erupting stomach for the next hour. With any luck the Pepto Bismol would be working overtime by then.

"So, I've got good news," Sid said.

Naja looked away from the mirror, where she touched up her makeup. "I'm ready."

"I think I might have landed you a leading role. I've been in talks with Barry Reuben, the agent, and he's got a show he's selling and he thinks you'd be perfect."

She turned to him, ecstatic. "Barry Reuben is one of the hottest agents in town. What kind of role?"

"A female detective who busts cheating husbands. A heroine, if you will."

She heard violins playing in her ears. This was her dream. She didn't like to get her hopes up about things like this, projects could be shelved quicker than Superman transformed back into Clark Kent, but she couldn't stop the visions of money and fame that flashed before her in Technicolor.

Sid baited the hook. "It's a package deal. You're the star and I'm the producer. We'll be a team, babe, if everything goes right."

Overwhelmed with emotion, she said something she never said to men. "I love you, Sid." She didn't love *him*, of course. She loved what he was doing for her career.

"You'd better," Sid teased as he hugged her.

She stiffened. "Careful, careful. Don't wrinkle the dress."

Sid didn't move.

She pressed her palms against his shoulders. "Come on. Stop playing. Someone might see us."

"So what?"

"So, I'm not ready for people to know about us yet."

"Who cares? I'm not going to lose my job over it."

"I'm not ready, okay?" It had nothing to do with his career. It was about hers. Naja was deeply concerned about losing her fan base, which was predominately African-American. They'd possibly shun her if they knew she had crossed the color line in her personal life.

He backed away, fiddling with his tie. "You get all pretty

and then you don't want to be touched. Women." He shrugged it off. "Anyway, the deal is looking good, but it's not sealed yet."

"What about *Same Day Service*? I'm under contract," Naja asked.

"Only for this season. You've got to position yourself for the future. Let's face it. The ratings on the show are dropping and there might not be a next season."

She looked at him thoughtfully. "I guess you have a point."

Ty was lying on the king-size bed wearing boxers and a T-shirt, his back supported by a mahogany headboard and three fluffy pillows. Sasha was on the other side of the bed, a whole three feet away from him, wearing long-sleeve cotton pajamas that left only her hands and feet exposed. She didn't want Ty to so much as dream of having make-up sex. Still bitter from finding Dominique in Ty's office, her lips were sealed in a silent protest. The only voices in the room were those blaring from the television. She folded her arms across her chest, physically present but mum. After one entire day of letting his phone calls go unanswered, she'd hoped her silence would send a strong message that she was still angry and hurt and unhappy with his response to the situation. It was the first time in their relationship they had gone twenty-four hours without communicating. On the night they'd met, they'd talked the night away in a booth at Kate Mantilini's restaurant on Wilshire. Now, three years and a baby later, she'd been forced to zip her lips.

But a day of silence hadn't evoked the smallest confession

of wrongdoing. Not even a lousy rendition of an apology had slipped past his lips. He'd hugged her tightly, kissed her passionately and professed love, then carried on as if nothing happened, as if nothing had changed. Classic Ty behavior, she called it. He was reluctant to discuss intimate issues, always expecting her to pinch her nose and keep on moving, pretending not to smell the stench of all his shit. This time she was too stubborn to budge and too angry to give him anything resembling a peace treaty. So after inviting him over, she handled him like an unwelcome guest in his own home. Classic Sasha.

Today had been the easiest, most trouble-free day Ty had had all week. No one had stormed into his office with a complaint. No women had shown up unannounced. No one from the network had phoned with any suggestions. And there had been no fires for him to stamp out. He'd been hemmed up in the editing booth for the majority of the day, watching footage rewind and fast-forward over and over again. Several phone calls had been made as he went back and forth with the Mercedes dealership on Wilshire, negotiating the price and delivery on a new car for Sasha. The vehicle would be equipped with everything except Direct TV. A brand-new Mercedes CL500 would say everything he couldn't. As Ty accumulated wealth over the years, he'd learned to replace words with gifts. The expensive vehicle he ordered today would say, "I'm sorry," and he had little doubt Sasha would accept his expensive apology.

Ty decided to speak, chipping away at the invisible ice between him and Sasha. "I've been thinking. We should give up the threesomes for a while."

She cut her eyes at him. "A while? How long is a while?"

"Until we get ourselves together," he said, pressing a button on the remote control.

"Swinging isn't the only problem we have. There was one woman in your office, not two."

"I told you, nothing happened."

"And why should I believe that, for God's sake? You fucked her in front of me."

"That's why I don't have to do it behind your back."

Sasha stared at the flat-screen television on the wall, pissed.

"So no more swinging. End of story," he stated.

Sasha pouted. Sometimes Ty treated her like a child, giving orders, making demands regardless of her thoughts and opinion. She didn't want to give up her female lovers. It had become such a part of her life and she so enjoyed them. Who would keep her company while he worked twelve hours a day? Who'd cuddle her and talk to her in the middle of the night? She bit her bottom lip, wondering if she could curb her lesbian desires. But in her heart of hearts she knew she had to. No matter how deeply she tried to deny it, she realized her actions were almost as deplorable as his. She'd gone behind his back just as he'd gone behind hers. And seeing Dominique in Ty's office was karma, plain and simple. She'd reaped no less than what she'd sown.

Ty watched the last fifteen minutes of the eleven-o'clock news as usual, intentionally missing the crime stories. News regarding homicides and shootings gave him flashbacks of his brother's shooting and other friends who'd died on the streets of DC. After the puff-piece news stories about celebrities' comings and goings, NBC would air *The Tonight Show*, taped earlier in the afternoon.

The television was on, but Leede wasn't watching it. Not yet anyway. He'd snap out of a drunken trance the moment Naja's face flashed across the screen. He'd consumed so much alcohol since his meeting with the suits that if a match had been lit anywhere near him, his body would have instantly gone up in smoke and flames. He sat on his oversized, cushiony sofa, staring at the walls of his empty bachelor pad, feeling lonely and betrayed.

He'd been a fool to put absolute trust in Ty. Based on Gary's comments, Ty had met with the suits, spoken out against Leede and made him out to be difficult, lazy and lacking professionalism. Ty had stabbed him in his back, made him look like an idiot and betrayed him as a friend and a colleague. Why else would they mention Ty's name? Ty probably told the suits Leede is losing his edge. Leede is always late. Leede isn't a team player. Leede wanted to be on Leno. There was no telling what else he said, but apparently he'd said enough for the suits to doubt his abilities and damaging enough for them to think they needed a white guy on the show. He should have never mentioned becoming an executive producer to Ty. Apparently, he'd run like a rat to the suits. Ty was probably afraid of him becoming an executive producer. Ty feared losing his power to Leede so he sabotaged Leede's chances.

After such a horrific day it seemed appropriate for it to end with Naja sitting on Leno's couch. Perhaps Ty had had a chat with her as well. What would she have to say about him? "You know Jay, Leede is one late motherfucker. It's damn near noon when he shows up for work. We have to wait on his ass every day. And you know the ratings have dropped. All because of Leede." He turned up a half-empty bottle of champagne to his lips and took a swig, drowning himself in alcohol and self-pity.

20

Naja's heartbeat resonated throughout her entire body as she stood on the edge of the stage watching a TV monitor, hearing Leno's voice boom from every direction in the room.

"From Rex Network's hit TV show, *Same Day Service*, please welcome Naja Starr!"

The applause from the audience and band instruments drowned the pounding of Naja's heartbeat as she stepped onstage, her glossy pink lips spread from one shimmering chandelier earring to the other. The pink peasant Versace halter dress she'd borrowed flowed like ocean waves across her thighs as she carefully stepped onstage wearing strappy, four-inch pumps. Her hair was teased high enough to punch another hole in the ozone layer. She was half sex kitten, half supermodel. When she reached the guest chair and the applause ceased, she sat down with the grace of a queen and crossed her toned, sexy legs for the world to see.

Jay smiled. "How are you?"

She smiled more, her jaws locked. "I'm good."

"Naja Starr. Now is Starr your real surname, or is it a stage name?"

"Starr is actually my middle name."

"So where are you from? Where did you grow up?"

"I'm from Brooklyn, the biggest borough in New York," she said looking directly into the camera. There were yells, whistles and some applause from the audience.

"How did this whole acting thing come about for you? Did you do any acting in high school? Did you always know you'd be in Hollywood?"

"In a way. I was a performer. I studied dance for many years and I was a cheerleader in high school."

More whistles and applause. Naja moved her arms as if doing a cheer, egging the audience on. When the applause died down, she said, "Woodrow Wilson High! Go big green!" There was one whistle from the audience.

The camera panned to the man who'd whistled. He looked sixty years of age, slim with mostly gray hair and a beard. Jay said, "One of your classmates is here." The audience laughed.

Naja patiently waited for silence before speaking again. "I have a question, Jay."

"Wait. You've got it turned around. I'm supposed to be asking the questions, but go ahead. I'll give you one."

She stared into the camera as if asking the audience. "Why do guys love when a girl says she was a cheerleader?"

"It probably has something to do with those short skirts. And the cheerleaders were always the hottest girls in school."

More whistles and applause.

"So, you live in LA now. How much of a shock was it, moving from New York?"

"Two major changes. One, I had to give up walking, because there's a city ordinance or something that people can't walk the street in LA. Two, I had to learn how to drive. I was resistant at first, but have you ever tried to hail a cab here? It's impossible. So, I decided I'd better get with the program."

"This is definitely car country," Jay agreed. "So, you're single, married, attached?"

Naja tilted her head to one side and rested her elbows on the arm of the chair. "Very single. It's just me and my two puppies. But I'd like to find a daddy for them."

"A lot of people are getting hooked up online. Have you considered that? Ever done it?"

"I tried it when I first moved here because I had a hard time meeting people. So I got a friend to take pictures of me to post on Match Dot Com. It wasn't a complete disaster, but I never connected with anyone."

"You should have used your cheerleader picture and said you were looking for a daddy. You'd have gotten a million hits."

"Or a million kooks." They both laughed.

Jay stared into the camera, responding to the stage manager's cue for a commercial break. "We're gonna take a break and we'll be right back with Naja Starr."

The band started playing the moment Jay said break and in

exactly three minutes, enough time for two commercials, the on-air lights flashed and they were back.

"My guest is Naja Starr of the hit show *Same Day Service*." Jay turned toward Naja. "We have a clip from the show. Do you want to set it up?"

"On the show, my ex-husband and I own and operate a dry cleaning business. I think the clip speaks for itself."

The cameras panned to a small screen and the clip begins. Naja is standing behind the counter when a homeless man walks into the dry cleaners. His stench causes the customers to frown. Leede tries to put him out, but the man insists that he'd come to see Naja, not Leede. Naja starts sweet-talking him, drawing the man closer to her. "How's my buddy doing today? Come on over. I've got something for you." When he nears, she whips out a can of air freshener from behind her back and blasts him until a cloud forms. The audience laughs and applauds.

Naja grinned and smiled, displaying her North Pole white, veneered teeth. She was high from all the attention and floating on applause. If there really was a heaven, this had to be it.

"So, how did you get the part on the show?"

"My agent called me in New York and asked, how quickly can you get to LA for an audition? I said, 'I'm there. Why are you still on the phone?'"

"So, you like working on a sitcom?"

"It's a lot of fun. We're like a family and I get to work with some great people. Leede Banks is the funniest man I've ever met."

"Yeah, he did stand-up on our show. He's very funny. Now *Same Day Service* was an instant hit. You got an Emmy nomination the first season. Did you guys realize this might be something special when you started? Could you feel it?"

"Every opportunity to work feels good to me, Jay. Was I surprised? Not really. We've got a talented cast. The writers are excellent, and Tyrone Hart, the creator and executive producer, is a gem."

"You guys have been having some big name guests appearing on the show. I hear Cell Block is doing the show. He was here last week and my audience went wild. What's it like working with him?"

Naja sat in a stupor as she fell from heaven. This hadn't been part of the phone interview and she certainly didn't have anything positive to say about Block-head. There was an unspoken rule in the entertainment industry; an actor didn't badmouth another actor, at least not on camera, and definitely not on national television. It was a major faux pas. But oh, how she would have loved to use this opportunity to get back at Cell and Ty. She smiled. "What are you trying to do, Jay? Get me in the middle of an East Coast, West Coast feud? When you say *anything* about a rapper, they rap and rhyme about you on their next CD."

Jay laughed out loud, giving Naja the last words of the interview. He reached for Naja's hand. "Thanks for coming by, and continued success with the show."

Naja smiled. "Thanks."

Applause, applause, applause. She waved to the audience as Kevin Eubanks and the band played Jay into the next commercial break, ending Naja's dream.

21

Maxwell's breakfast meeting with the suits got off to a late start. While he'd shown up promptly, eager and anxious, Gary and David had apparently taken their time, arriving at Art's Deli in Studio City a full twenty minutes late. Maxwell stood up and greeted them as they approached the table.

"Good morning. Sorry we're late," David offered as he walked in savoring the smell of Art's fresh-baked bagels.

Maxwell forced a smile. "No problem." The waiting had been unnerving and had left his palms damp.

The men seated themselves across from Maxwell, making small talk as they looked over the menu. Art's was an outdated landmark, decorated in vinyl and Formica with massive photos of sandwiches along the walls. The only notable change in the place over the years was the beefy prices.

"Hey, did you catch Naja on Leno last night? She looked great," David said.

"Yeah, she gave a solid interview," Maxwell said.

"I'm hoping we can get some ratings mileage out of this," Gary said.

"Did you see the look on her face when he mentioned Cell Block?" David asked.

"No, I didn't notice," Maxwell said, knowing he too had stopped in his tracks, stunned by the question. He'd phoned Ty immediately after the interview.

"If I didn't know any better, I'd think something had happened between those two," Gary said.

"Maybe a bit of romance gone wrong," David pondered aloud.

"Really? I didn't notice," Maxwell said. "But it went over well with the audience."

A waitress came over to take their orders. Maxwell lightly tapped his foot under the table, impatiently waiting for the discussion of his deal to begin. Gary and David ordered bagels and lox. Maxwell only ordered a cup of herbal tea. He'd sniffed two lines of cocaine before he'd left home, leaving him with no appetite to speak of.

"So what's going on? How are things over at the show?" Gary asked.

"It's going well. The writers are ahead of schedule and we're working on some new story outlines to hand in for approval," Maxwell said.

"It's quite an asset that you have experience running a writers' room. Ty is very lucky to have you there," Gary said, as he fattened Maxwell for the kill.

Maxwell smiled. "I like the creative process of it all."

"Do you want to be that hands-on when you get your own show? You'll have a lot of other things to supervise as well," David said.

"Definitely. Everything starts with the writers. We put the words in the mouths of the actors. No words, no actors, no show."

Gary nodded.

"How has it been working with Ty? He's set an example for you, I imagine," Gary said.

Maxwell's eyes darted from side to side as he wondered where the conversation was going. "Absolutely. Ty and I have been working together for years. We wrote as a team for three years. He's a good, solid producer."

"Interesting. Not everyone would agree with you. Certainly not I. We've had a few concerns. And our concerns are growing."

Maxwell sat up. "You mean the ratings?"

"That too," Gary said.

"I'm not sure what you mean," Maxwell said.

"If things are so great and you and Ty have such a good working rapport, why abandon ship?" Gary bit into his bagel.

"I can assure you that it has nothing to do with my relationship with Ty. You know better than I how these things go. There's no guarantee the show will be picked up next season. And I don't like sitting at home. I want to be working," Maxwell said.

Gary paused. He wanted to push further but he couldn't gauge Maxwell, couldn't discern his reaction. Maxwell was more easygoing, laid-back and compliant than his partner,

Ty. Maxwell was a crossover baby from the Bay Area who wanted there to be no color lines and for everyone to get along peacefully. Gary categorized him as easier to work with and more controllable. If Ty was Malcolm X, then Maxwell was surely Martin Luther King. And like Presidents Kennedy and Johnson, Gary preferred to get in bed with Martin, a nonviolent, Bible-preaching peacekeeper.

David got down to the business at hand. "We really like your script. The characters have a fresh voice. We feel it has lots of potential and we'd like to work with you on it. Give you some notes for the rewrite. And once it's tight we'll give it to the department heads to be voted on. If all goes well, we can shoot the pilot in April."

Maxwell grinned and nodded. He could feel the *Soul Train* dancers warming up his spine, ready to bust a move.

David swallowed before speaking. "Now here's the thing. I'm sure you have some actors in mind, but we're under a lot of pressure from the network to pull talent from our pool, the people already under contract. You know, try to keep people in the Rex family long term. So here's the pitch. What do you think about casting Naja Starr? You work with her. You know her. How would you feel about that?"

Maxwell was so close to making a deal, he could already feel crisp, clean money sliding through his bony fingers. At close point range of his dream he didn't care who was cast, as long as he got his show. "I don't have any problems casting Naja for the pilot, but if the show gets picked up, I'd like to make the final decision on casting for the series."

Gary gazed at David. "That's fair," he answered, knowing

the network would have the last say in casting if they were going to kick out all the dough to make it. "If the pilot is approved, we'll offer you a development deal."

Maxwell's body tingled with excitement. Gary had spoken the magic words: development deal. Finally, he'd be the HNIC.

It was crystal clear the suits were framing him and setting him up by interrogating him about Ty and taking control of the casting of his show. He knew it was a low-down, crack-house-crooked deal, yet he'd gladly sign his first and last name in blood. He was so desperate and hungry to get ahead in Hollywood, he was willing to sell his organic soul to the devil, C.O.D. He wanted to walk the red carpet and be recognized as a force to be reckoned with. He wanted to arrive to work whenever he woke up and have a PA get him breakfast from a place twenty miles away. He wanted to have a mansion photographed for *Ebony* magazine. He wanted everything he'd ever seen in Tinseltown.

Maxwell extended his long arm across the table and shook hands, making a pact with the devil.

Gary had placed a call to Russ Tobin the moment he walked into the office from his breakfast meeting with Maxwell. And in true Hollywood style, it had taken Russ two hours to return his call. When Gary's assistant, Cheryl, announced Russ Tobin was on the phone, he dropped his putter on the floor and leaped to his desk as if the president of the United States was calling from the oval office. Gary cleared his throat.

"Gary. Russ Tobin here."

"Hi, Russ. How are you?" Everyone called the president by his first name.

"Busy as hell. What's the status of *Same Day Service?*"

"I met with Tyrone Hart, the executive producer this week."

"I know who he is. What happened?" Russ didn't have the time or the patience for foreplay conversation.

"Just as I presumed, he doesn't like the idea of adding a white character on the show."

"How opposed is he?"

"Extremely opposed."

"How do you think he'd react if we forced the issue?"

"Honestly, I think he'd go to the trades, screaming unfair treatment. He's got a real chip on his shoulder."

Russ sighed. "*American Icon* is kicking our ass. I can't just sit around and wait for this show to tank. I'd rather pull the plug and cut my losses." He said this knowing he hadn't lost a dime thus far, but TV was all about the ratings. A competitive ratings game, and Russ always played to win. His job depended on it. "I guess we could switch the night. We could air it on Saturday night. There'd be less competition."

Gary said nothing. Saturday nights were a death sentence for any show. It was the least-watched day of the week. Most people were out and about with their families; single people were at bars and clubs; teenagers were running the street and hanging out at malls with their friends. Practically no one was at home watching television but the young kids and their babysitters.

"We discussed switching the night briefly. He's opposed to that as well." Gary took every opportunity to make Ty out to be a difficult employee, rather than a producer deeply concerned about his show.

"I don't want to cut this show from the prime time line up just yet. You got any ideas?"

"I've been losing sleep trying to come up with a solution to save this show," he lied, trying to make himself sound overly dedicated to his job and the network. "If we're going to give the show a chance, why not run a few encore episodes and run a few extra promos in the markets where we did well last season? It worked for other shows. Why not this one?"

There was a long silence on the phone as Russ turned this idea over in his head. "You think this show can make it to syndication?"

"It was a smash hit last season and earned us an Emmy nomination."

"Yeah, yeah, yeah." Gary could almost hear Russ frowning at the thought of investing more money, mostly because he was a tight old bastard who guarded the network purse strings as if it were his personal life savings. He was both cheap and cautious. And when he got right down to the point of the debate, he couldn't see investing too much more in a black show because of the limited advertising revenue it generated. "I'd need you to be on top of production over there and be very hands-on." Russ was seeking to protect his interest, his money.

That was exactly what Gary wanted, more control. "I'd be willing to do that."

"Is everything else okay over there?"

"Ty is coming in on budget as always, but there was a

little shake-up with Leede Banks. Nothing for you to worry about."

"Good. I'll get back with you." Russ disconnected before Gary could say good-bye.

Russ decided it was time to drop by the show to get a feel for what was going on. He was long overdue for a visit to the set anyway.

22

Bernie anxiously paced the backstage area wearing headphones and with clipboard in hand, ready to count heads and take attendance. He brushed sweat from his brow. The doctor had told him to slow down and take it easy in order to keep his blood pressure under control, but he couldn't help it. His nerves wouldn't rest until everyone was exactly where they were supposed to be. If he should suffer a hypertensive cardiac arrest, it would be no one's fault but Leede's. Perhaps he'd take Leede on his next doctor's visit and let him get the lecture.

It was tape day and as usual it would prove to be hectic. More than fifty AFTRA extras had been called in for the Cell Block concert performance scene and another ten for background. There was a tight schedule to keep, with little room for delays. With union scale workers crawling all over the place, time was literally money. Bernie had to get the actors to hair and makeup and wardrobe before nine thirty, when camera blocking began.

Leede arrived at the studio on time. He'd fallen asleep on the sofa right after Naja's interview and slept some of the alcohol away. He entered tired and sluggish, but Bernie didn't care. He shoved him into a makeup chair without a second thought.

Leede sat in the black leather chair suspended two feet above the floor. He gazed at his reflection in the oversized mirror as Lily, the makeup artist, piled concealer under his eyes where exhaustion had pitched a tent and settled in. Within the hour, Lily would have him looking six years younger.

Naja entered the makeup and hair room feeling overly perky for seven in the morning. Last night she'd accomplished a childhood dream and she was still basking in the limelight. Her phone had rung all evening yesterday as friends and family from the East Coast called, ecstatic she'd given a shout-out to Brooklyn. They were generous with compliments on her dress, her hair and her interview. She'd received enough accolades to make the most insecure actress confident for at least a day.

"Hey, cheerleader of PS 20. You know Jay was scoping out your breasts," Leede teased.

She propped her hands on her hips. "I never hold that against you. So why should I fret over Jay?"

"Somebody is feeling special today." He paused. "Thanks for the compliment. I know I'm going to owe you for that act of kindness."

"It's on the house this time," Naja teased.

"And you're not going to ever let me forget that, are you?"

"Never," she said as she stepped onto one of the high chairs. "And how'd you beat me into the makeup chair?"

"I'm uglier than you. I need more time and more makeup."

She smiled, examining herself in the mirror, running her fingers through her weave. "You know that little conversation we had the other day?" She was referring to him becoming an executive producer. "What's going on with that?"

Leede shrugged, knowing exactly what she was asking about. "Nothing yet. These things take time."

She gave a sympathetic look and nodded. Now that she had a stab at getting her own show, she couldn't have cared less about Leede becoming an executive producer. She could hardly wait until the deal was done.

When Ty entered the anteroom of his office, Venus's desk was empty. He'd sent her to pick up Sasha's new Mercedes from the dealership in Beverly Hills, but figured she should have been back by now. Heaven forbid he'd have to answer his own phone. He picked up the trades from her desk and went into his office.

Maxwell had called Ty around 9:15 on his cell, wanting to know what time he'd be in. He needed to talk with him.

Maxwell's conscience had gotten the better of him. He wasn't as comfortable as he presumed he would be, meeting with the suits behind Ty's back. Ty didn't deserve such deceit from him or the suits. Like everyone else, Ty certainly had his faults, but he always played the cards in his hand. He never pulled cards from his sleeve.

Maxwell stepped into Ty's office, guilt oozing from his pores. He was anxious to confess his sins.

Ty greeted him with a faint smile, disguising his curiosity. On the phone Maxwell had made it clear there were no problems at the office, pending or otherwise. So what was this little chat all about? Subconsciously, Ty hoped Maxwell was coming around to his old self again, that he was ready to confide in him so their friendship would be as tightly knit as it had been before all the success and before Maxwell fell in love with Buddha.

Maxwell took a seat on the sofa. "I've got some good news and I've got some bad news."

"That saying has always confused me. I don't know if it's supposed to make me feel better or worse."

Maxwell leaned forward and rested his elbows on his narrow knees. "Look, I need to level with you about something. I had a meeting with the suits this morning."

"What suits? You mean Gary and David?"

"Yeah. I have a pilot they are interested in perhaps shooting in April."

Ty's face was expressionless. "Good for you."

"I'd have told you earlier . . . well, I tried to say something before . . . but all that doesn't matter now. Here's the thing that bothered me. The suits asked me how I felt about working with you. Wanted to know what kind of job you were doing. Basically, it was like they were looking for dirt on you."

Ty locked eyes with him. "Did you give them any?"

Maxwell wiped his nose, paranoid that residual cocaine lingered on his nostrils. "Of course not. There is none to give. They had the wrong dude if that's what they were expecting.

I know things haven't been the same between us like in the past, but I'd never sell you out like that, man. We are still a team." His emphatic denials made him sound guilty.

Ty reared back in his chair. "So why you here, man? What do you want from me? A thank you?"

"Nah, man. Why you being all sarcastic and shit? I want you to watch your back. I know you've been meeting with them about different things, mainly the ratings issue, but I got a funny vibe from those cats."

"What kind of vibe were you detecting?"

"You want the truth. All right. Here it is. I got the distinct feeling they might be trying to get rid of you."

"Thanks for enlightening me, but that scenario has occurred to me."

"You haven't said anything about it."

Ty couldn't cover his fury. "And you haven't said much yourself, nigger. You've been a ghost since last hiatus. Which leads me to believe something is wrong. You've barely said anything about what's going on in your life. You're not exactly confiding in me. So why should I bare my soul to you?"

"Because business ain't always connected to pleasure. This is work we're talking about. Our paychecks. I know you're not into the type of shit I'm into, but I'm still the same person I've always been. Underneath these locks, I'm still your writing partner. Spirituality has changed my life and lifestyle, but not who I am. I'm still me."

"The Maxwell I knew would not have gone behind my back." Ty sucked his tongue. The betrayal left a bitter taste in his mouth.

Maxwell jumped to his feet and spread his arms. "Come on, man. I tried talking to you about it before and you didn't want to hear. More than once I tried."

Ty sat in denial with imperial posture. "I don't remember that."

"Of course you don't. 'Cause you don't wanna. Man, I want my own show as bad as a junkie wants a hit. When the suits started talking about a deal, I was foaming at the mouth." Maxwell stared into Ty's blank eyes. "Don't you remember what it was like to be hungry for a deal, Ty? Wanting to get ahead and get paid? I've learned a lot working with you, but it's time for me to grow up and move out of the house. I need my own space now. And I'm willing to sell *my* soul to the devil for it, but I wouldn't sell *yours*. You've fought too hard for me." He beat his hand on his chest. "You made me a multimillionaire. And I'll never forget that. Can't forget it."

Ty was touched by Maxwell's goodwill confession, but not enough to forgive him. Maxwell could no longer be trusted because he was half loyal, half sneak. The fact of the matter was, Maxwell would not have uttered a word about his deal if Ty's name had not come up in the meeting. He'd have signed a deal behind his back and Ty would have read about it in the *Hollywood Reporter*, along with the rest of the world.

"Are you done? 'Cause I am."

Maxwell frowned. "Aw, man. Come on. That's exactly why this has happened. You just shut down whenever you feel like it."

Ty didn't want to hear Maxwell and he damn sure didn't want to hear the truth. "I've got a show to tape today and I don't have time for the bullshit."

"We'll talk after the show, all right, man?" Maxwell pleaded.

"I'll think about it."

Maxwell backed out of the office. "It didn't have to be this way. This was your call, not mine."

"You live with your decisions and I'll live with mine."

Sid balled his fist and pounded on Naja's dressing room door. She dropped her script on the sofa and answered. The music blasting onstage seeped into her sanctuary as he entered.

Her eyes panned up and down the hallway. "Did anyone see you?"

"I don't know. I wasn't looking. Why? You afraid to let the world know you've got yourself a white boy?"

She shut the door abruptly and sighed. "Don't be funny."

He moved in closer to her. "What's wrong with you? You nervous?"

"Be careful. I don't want to mess up my hair and makeup." She sniffed for air. "Where have you been? Happy hour?"

He backed away. "I had one martini. Dirty," he said with a sly grin.

"Yeah, well, I'm sober and my workday is just starting."

"I've got a tape of last night's show. I thought you did great, at least up until the part about being single."

She sat on the sofa, smiling. "I was pleased with the interview. Look out world, *The Oprah Winfrey Show* will be next."

Sid sat down, pulling his suit jacket to the sides of his body. "So, I spoke with Barry Reuben today."

Naja stopped and stared at him.

"It looks like they are going to move full-steam ahead with Maxwell's pilot."

"Maxwell?"

"Yeah, he's the writer of the show I was telling you about. Now he and the network have agreed to cast you for the pilot." He shook his head. "But it's not the deal I asked for, and we might have to pass on it. I'm sorry. I know you had your hopes up. I waited until the last minute to tell you, hoping to prevent this."

Her eyebrows furrowed. "But why?"

"Because they are not interested in our package. He wants to split our team and I'm not going for it. Don't worry. There will be another show. I promise. I came close this time. Next time I'll nail the deal for sure."

"Wait a minute. What do you mean? Our package? What part of the package?"

"They're willing to give you a shot at the leading role, but they're not going to give me a producer credit. I told Barry Reuben we're a package deal and he doesn't get one without the other."

She stood up and began to pace. "You're not my manager. You have no right to do that. You didn't even discuss it with me. This isn't fair."

"I'm not your manager in writing, but I brokered this deal, acting as your manager. I found the project and I went after it."

Naja made a sad face. "Maybe it was your doing, but why would you stand in the way of my success? You don't want to see me make it, do you?"

"Don't be absurd. Of course I want you to make it. I want us both to make it."

"Then why am I to pay for your shortcomings? It's not my

fault they don't want to make you a producer. I don't have anything to do with that."

"I thought you loved me. I thought we were working toward building a future together."

No longer able to disguise her anger, Naja flipped the script. "Oh, come on, Sid. Be for real. Love doesn't have a damn thing to do with this. You don't love me any more than I love you. You think I don't realize what you're doing? You go throwing my name around town, pimping me."

He bolted up to his feet. "A pimp? Is that what you think?" He paused, his face getting redder by the second. "So many men have treated you like a whore, you now think like one. You know that, Naja? It's all about you. That's the only person you love. You think I don't realize *that*? You've profited from all of my so-called pimping and I didn't hear you complaining about it yesterday when you were on Leno. All this time you seemed to enjoy being pimped." Sid's ego was bruised. He desperately wanted to become a big-time producer just as desperately as Naja wanted to be a larger-than-life star.

She was no different than the other half-talented chicks in LA. Once you made something out of their nonexistent careers, they kicked you to the curb. They walked out after you had struggled and sweated to make a somebody out of a nobody. "Now you can try and land this deal without me if you want, but I can guarantee you, it won't work. I practically begged for you to be considered for the role. Now that I won't be around to press them, they'll drop you like a hot grenade."

"Oh, stop making it sound like you've done me such great favors. You were busy doing favors for *yourself*." She pointed her index finger at him. "You didn't make me, Sid. And you damn sure can't break me. I'm Naja Starr. I was already on a show when I first fucked you. You remember that!" She picked up her script, reared her right arm back and threw it at the door with all her might when Sid stomped out of the room. She yelled behind him, "Don't you ever come back, god damn it." Pages floated to the floor like leaves falling from a tree. She folded her arms and paced the floor. Damn him for riling her before a show. She hated Sid. Truly, truly hated him.

She'd call her agent and see if he could salvage the deal. First thing tomorrow she'd have someone pick up her things from his house. As for the few things he had at her place, she'd torch them. Next time, she'd choose a man who had already conquered Mount Everest, instead of someone still trying to climb his way up.

23

Every audience member entering Stage Six for the taping was required to go through a metal detector and have their bags searched by the studio guards. With a little more than two hundred civilians attending the show, security was as airtight as check-in points at LAX. There was always the threat of a demented fan showing up with the intent of harming one of the stars or someone in the audience.

The DJ blasted the top forty hip-hop songs of all time as the audience spilled into the bleachers. Between songs, a plump comedian ran up and down the metal bleacher stairs telling jokes, handing out CDs and candy, entertaining the crowd. The energy was high as kids and adults sat in anticipation of seeing the show and their favorite television celebrities in person. At six in the evening, the show taping was a cross between a happy hour party and a Broadway show.

Ty entered the chilly stage, bypassing the metal detectors, and was instantly hit by the airborne adrenaline and excitement that swooned about. He loved being at the stage, in the big, open space with all the lights and a live audience. This is when and where it all came together, where all the details he'd worked on all week merged. Here, he forgot about the meetings with Gary and David, and the ratings. Here, on Stage Six, he reigned supreme.

He tugged at his tan suede sports jacket and straightened out the collar on his white button-down shirt as he headed for the control booth. Throughout the taping he'd go from the booth, watching all the monitors, back to the stage again.

The heated discussion with Maxwell had left his head spinning and his blood racing at high speeds through his veins. On the exterior he was insouciant. On the inside he felt the despair of losing a dear friend. He lifted his chin, greeting Sid and David as he passed them.

Craig ran up to Ty and threw his arm over his shoulders. "Man, I've got the finest honey you've ever seen up here tonight."

Ty nodded, maintaining his stride. His eyes roamed the stage, checking the lighting and reviewing the sets. It may have appeared to be a party, but it was work for Ty and he didn't want to overlook one detail. "Maybe I'll get to see her later. I don't have time right now."

"All right," Craig said eagerly. "I'm going to bring her backstage to meet you."

Ty waved and kept walking, leaving Craig behind.

People mingled behind the stage. Everyone working on the show had invited a friend or family member to the taping.

Ty panned the premises and glanced at his watch, wondering if the director would start on time. His thoughts switched to something more troubling: Leede. He hadn't conversed with him since Wednesday when he'd stormed out of his office talking about becoming an executive producer. At yesterday's run-through, Leede had been cordial yet aloof. Where was he now? It was close to showtime and Ty didn't see him onstage. Leede never passed up an opportunity to have an audience. He usually came out early, before the rest of the cast, and clowned around with the audience, told a few jokes and exchanged a few "your mama" insults with the warm-up comedian. Given the kind words Naja had bestowed upon him on Leno, he should be in a hearty mood, but his absence was a sign that all might not have been well.

Ty made his way past the craft services table and up the isolated staircase that led to the dressing rooms. Leede's was the first door on the right. Ty stretched his neck to one side and knocked on the door. A nondescript white girl with sandy blonde hair answered. Another girl, Ty assumed her buddy, was seated on the sofa. Cigarette smoke stood still, suspended in midair, and beer bottles lined the coffee table.

"What's up?" Ty greeted them.

Leede was dressed for the first scene of the show. "I don't know. You tell me."

Ty shrugged off the tension he suddenly felt. "You set for the show?"

"I'm always ready, aren't I? Even if I am late sometimes."

"What's going on, man? Why are you so salty?"

Leede looked at the girls and gave a direct order. "I need to talk to Ty. Go comb your weaves or something."

Both girls scrambled for the door as Leede turned his back to Ty and rummaged through a duffle bag that rested on his vanity. He slipped a small .38 into his sweatshirt pocket. It was the same one he kept in the glove compartment of his car for protection against stalkers.

Ty stood still, watching and wondering.

Leede faced Ty, motioning with his hands as he spoke. "Cut the bullshit, Ty. Don't act like you don't know what I'm talking about."

Ty shrugged. "I seriously don't know what the problem is. So why don't you tell me?"

Leede inched toward Ty, his fury building by the second. "You couldn't wait to snitch on me to the suits, could you? Couldn't wait to tell them? 'Leede is late. Leede needs to step up his game.' You'd tell them anything to keep me from becoming an executive producer, wouldn't you?"

Ty quickly added two and two. "The suits are lying, man. I never spoke to them about you. Never. They are trying to fuck with the show. They did the same thing to Maxwell."

"I thought we were friends. You sure had my ass fooled. What did you say, Ty? There should be no dissension. Ain't that right?"

"You've known me long enough to know that I am not a liar. I would never go behind your back. You were honest with me and I'd never disrespect you like that."

Without another word Leede charged toward Ty like a bull. Using the entirety of his weight, he body-slammed Ty against the door. The door sounded off from the impact. Leede grabbed Ty by the lapel, crumbling the suede fabric under his grip. His breath was heavy and hard.

Ty leaned against the wall with a frown on his face, struggling for whatever oxygen he could get to his lungs. The body slam had knocked the wind out of him.

Leede leaned against him, pressing his weight, his fury and his pain. "Why the fuck did you betray me, man. Huh? Why the fuck would you sell me out like that?"

The two men stood locked like boxers in a ring. Ty, a full three inches taller than Leede, couldn't see Leede's face but he could smell alcohol escaping from Leede's pores.

Sweat lined Ty's forehead, each bubble threatening to trickle down his face. He finally caught enough breath to speak, his words deliberate and slow. "Calm down, man. You're not thinking. Ain't nobody betrayed you." Ty could feel his stainless-steel watch stabbing his wrist as he pressed his weight in opposition, but Leede didn't budge an inch.

"You're a motherfuckin' liar. You told the suits I'm always late. I wasn't doing my job. I wasn't funny. All that shit was a lie. You wanna hold me back." Leede was terrified, certain he'd be nothing without his acting gig. He'd become one of a thousand unemployed actors and his fans would quickly forget him.

In an instant, Ty felt something hard and heavy pressing through Leede's sweatshirt, poking him in his rib cage. It felt like steel, like a gun. His anger instantly peaked at the threat of a gun. "I don't know what your problem is, but you'd better raise up off of me." With a sudden rush of emotion, he locked his arms in a tight grip around Leede's neck as they both struggled for air. "I will kill you, motherfucker, if you don't kill me first. So, if that's a gun you've got at my side under your shirt, you better use that shit right now or your ass is mine." Ty completely lost all sense of time and space. "I will fuckin' kill you. I will fuckin' kill you. Right here. Right now."

Leede pulled the gun from his sweatshirt. "I'm not afraid of you. Niggas die on the street for snitching on a mother-fucker. I've carried this show on my back and this is how you thank me."

"And you won't be shit if you don't take your god damn hands off of me. How the hell are you going to believe the suits over me? You have lost your god damn mind."

Both men reeked of pure fear as they exchanged deadly threats. Neither had the heart to kill and neither had the courage to die.

"Take your hands off of me," Leede demanded, clutching Ty as tight as he could.

Ty squeezed more, choking him as hard as he could. "You must think I'm a punk. I will kill you just for thinking that. You think you gonna chump me with a gun?"

"You thought I wasn't going to find out. I thought we were boys and now you want to get rid of me."

Suddenly Ty remembered he was not on the street. He was on Stage Six at Rex Studios and two hundred people in the audience were waiting to see a show. Studio execs were swarming the place. Stage Six, he remembered, and he had a lot at risk, a helluva lot to lose. Otherwise, he'd have beaten Leede into oblivion, then stomped him through the floor. "I have bent over backwards for your black ass to keep you happy. And every time I do, you come up with some new shit. This week you wanted my job. Now my life." Ty pushed Leede as hard as he could, shoving Leede away with the force of a tornado wind. Ty pounded his chest. "You want my life motherfucker? I'm sorry, you can't have it."

Leede stumbled backward, a good three feet away from Ty. He frowned as his lungs grasped for air. "You could have talked to me, man. I came to you. You could have talked to me," he pleaded.

"Don't you see what they are doing? Divide and conquer, Leede. Don't play into their hands. Don't fuck up this opportunity. We're out of the hood, man. We made it out."

Being at the top felt a whole lot different than Leede had imagined. The struggle shifted from How do I get there? to How do I stay there?

Leede dropped his arms, the .38 pointed toward the ground. He confessed with self-pity. It was as close to an apology as he could reach at the time. "It's so much pressure. People come at me from so many directions and I just started trippin'. The suits told me I wasn't funny anymore. If I'm not funny, then I'm nothing. You know how it is, man."

Ty bent over, trying to catch his breath and wake up from the bad dream. "I never told the suits anything. I swear. It's not you they want, it's me." He paused. "They want me gone and they are campaigning for votes."

Leede plopped down on the sofa, looking like a lost, confused little boy who was in a lot of pain. Ty should have hated him for what he'd just done, but he didn't. Instead, he felt sorry for Leede. Leede, like his brother, was weak, and Ty was always drawn to the cripple. He always wanted to help and hold people up. Ty needed to be needed and Leede needed him.

Ty eased the gun away from Leede and began his pep talk.

"There's an audience out there waiting for you to make them laugh. Prove the suits wrong. Go out there and do what you do best." Ty made a mental note: from this day forward every single person would be required to pass through the metal detectors, including the cast. If Leede had a .38, then Cell Block probably had an Uzi.

Ty looked at himself in the mirror over the vanity. He pulled out his cell phone and dialed Venus while Leede sat in a chair looking dumb.

"I've been looking for you and calling you. Your cell phone has been off. Russ Tobin's assistant called for a drive-on. He's coming to the show tonight," Venus said.

Ty wiped sweat from his forehead. Negative thoughts bombarded his brain. Why tonight? What hadn't Gary and David told him? Russ had not shown up to a taping all season. This was no coincidence. And he damn sure wasn't coming to get his photo taken with Cell Block. The son of a bitch was probably coming to fire him in person. Ty grew numb. He couldn't feel the phone in his hand. "I'm in Leede's dressing room." He made another conscious effort to breathe before giving orders. "Now pay attention. Go and let the director know Leede needs fifteen more minutes. You got that. Not twelve, not seventeen. Tell him I want this show started in exactly fifteen minutes. Then go to wardrobe and see if they have a white shirt that will fit me. They have all of my measurements." He looked down at the smudges of makeup Leede had smeared on his shirt. "Then come up here. No. Meet me at the backstage door."

"You might want to know something else." Venus paused. "That actress is here, walking around with Craig."

"What actress?" he snapped.

"Dominique Brooks. You know. Your friend that was here the other day," Venus said.

Ty dropped his head and exhaled. Leede should have just shot him. Then he could have escaped all of this misery. He was about to lose his job and his woman. An hour earlier, Sasha had accepted the brand-new Mercedes as a peace offering. If she spotted Dominique on stage, she'd use the car to crush every limb in his body. He thought swiftly, pushing his mind into fifth gear. For the first time in a long while, he put his pride aside. His lifted his chin. "Listen, Venus. I need your help. If you work with me on this, I'll hook you up with a nice bonus when Christmas rolls around."

Venus spoke up, taking advantage of the weakness in Ty's voice she'd never heard before. "I don't want a Christmas bonus."

Ty paused. "You don't?"

"No. I want a freelance script."

Ty bit his bottom lip and acquiesced. "I can do that."

"What do you need me to do?" she asked.

"Get Dominique out of here. Pull Craig aside and explain. Get Rojas from security to escort her out of here immediately."

"Okay, but there's one more thing."

"What now?" Ty snapped.

"Bernie is hyperventilating. He says Cell Block is in his dressing room smoking weed."

"Fuck it." Ty was tired of needy stars. What they all needed was some professional counseling. And first thing Monday morning that's exactly what Leede would get. "I can't do everything. Tell Maxwell. Let him handle it," he yelled. He slammed his flip phone shut. Life was closing in on him, had hemmed him up in a corner. He tried to weigh what would be worse, losing his show or losing Sasha. He crossed the room, thinking, plotting and planning as best he could under duress. "Leede, get yourself together, man. You've got a show to do. You get paid a lot of fucking money to do this shit. So, do it. I'll see you onstage in fifteen." Ty left and paced outside of Leede's dressing room door, his underarms wet with per-spiration, his emotions completely disheveled, but his brain still ticking like a bomb.

Venus stepped with purpose, her adrenaline pumping up her ego by the second. This was what she'd been waiting for, a chance to write and a chance to give some orders instead of taking them from everybody. Her first command was for the director. Yes, it would be *her* telling him when the show would start. Damn, she felt important.

The control booth was dark when she entered, only the ten monitors lending any light. She smiled at the assistant direc-tor, who was conversing with Maxwell. "Excuse me," she said, interrupting.

Maxwell stepped closer to Venus. "What's up, V?"

"Listen, there's a situation in Cell's dressing room. He's smoking the place *out*, sending smoke signals to his homies on Crenshaw. And Russ Tobin is on his way up here. Need I say more?"

"Does Ty know?"

"Yes, but you need to go and take care of Cell. He doesn't

have time and neither do I. I have to go talk to the director about the starting time."

"No problem. I'll handle it."

Thirty seconds later she was standing in front of the director, staring at his black eyeglass frames and brown Hugh Grant hair. His name was George and he'd successfully made the transition from child star to drug addict to sitcom director. Her chest sat out an inch as she proudly announced, "We'll be ready to start in fifteen minutes. Ty says the show should start in exactly fifteen minutes. Not twelve, not seventeen." It was a reminder for herself as well. She had only twelve minutes to kick Dominique to the nearest curb.

Venus could feel her blood bubbling with excitement and nervousness as her eyes frantically searched the stage for Rojas. He was far too big to miss, even in a crowd. She motioned for him when she found him near the stage doors, munching on something. As he came closer, she saw he had a handful of nuts.

He smiled. "What's up, Venus? You're lookin' nice today."

She threw him a stiff smile. Everyone dressed better than normal on tape days. "Thanks. Look, Rojas, Ty needs a huge favor."

"That's my man. Anything."

"There's a situation here tonight and her name is Dominique. She's a real pretty girl. Close-cropped haircut, green eyes, maybe about five feet, nine inches with fair skin."

Rojas nodded, committing the description to memory. "Uh, huh."

"Ty wants her out of here ASAP."

"Off the stage?"

"No, off the lot. If his girlfriend sees Dominique, she may never allow him to see his child again," she lied. She thought the story needed more weight to be convincing.

"Ty is a playa. Daaayum. This is good!"

"Okay, you're not following me. This is bad, Rojas."

"Maybe where you come from, but in El Segundo this shit is good."

"We're wasting time and we don't have much."

"So where is this home wrecker? What reason do I give her for tossing her off the stage?"

Venus hadn't had time to consider this. She shrugged. "I don't know."

"Well, we usually throw people out for having a weapon, or drugs or disorderly conduct."

Venus said what she thought Ty would have said in this situation. "Look, tell her whatever you want to tell her. I don't really care. Just get her out of here."

Rojas nodded. "Show me the honey."

The honey was standing several feet from Craig, who stood in the middle of the green room like it was his home. Holding a bottle of Snapple in one hand, he laughed and talked with Sid like he was a big shot. Dominique had obviously put some distance between her and her host. She wore a pair of fitted jeans and a tie-died wife beater. A light sweater was tied around her small waist.

Rojas stood near the door while Venus approached Craig and grabbed him by the arm. "Can I talk to you for a minute?" she said, steering him away from Sid.

Craig flashed his jeweled teeth. "What's up, Big City?"

"The girl. Is she your guest?"

"Yeah. Ain't she gorgeous?"

Venus shrugged.

"Aw, don't be jealous. She's just a friend. It has nothing to do with what me and you got."

Venus gave him the evil eye. "Ty wants her gone."

"What are you talking about? Ty don't even know this dame. She's with me." He patted his chest.

"Look, your friend is a friend of Ty's and he wants her gone. So, you're gonna have to get her out of here."

Craig sucked his teeth. "Why does he always get the girl? Why does he always have to get everything? That shit ain't fair."

"I've got nothing to do with your sibling rivalry. The girl has to go before Sasha turns this stage out. Am I making myself clear?"

"Sasha? She knows her too?"

"Perhaps you should have a chat with your brother about this."

He fondled his crotch and twisted his lips, feeling like a pure fool for pretending to be a shot caller. If he didn't follow Ty's instructions, he'd take his new truck quicker than the repo man. "So what the hell am I supposed to tell her?"

This question was working on her nerves. Couldn't these people think for themselves? Venus had long ago lost any patience for Craig. "I don't give a damn. Just get the chick out of here. Rojas is over at the door. He can handle it if you can't."

Yeah, maybe it would be best for Venus to do the dirty work. That's what Ty paid her to do, to take care of the petty task. Let her get rid of Dominique and save him the embarrassment of having to tell her he was a liar, a loser and his brother's flunky. Craig frowned. "You want her gone, you deal with it. I ain't doing nothing."

Venus looked up to find Dominique staring at her and Craig. She smiled, realizing Dominique remembered her as well. Craig's bad attitude didn't phase her. If Dominique didn't disappear, it would be her job and her writing opportunity that would go down the toilet. Craig was family and would have a job regardless of his low IQ. Even Rojas possessed more job security than she did, because he worked for an outside security company.

Venus threw Rojas a knowing look, then shifted her eyes identifying Dominique as she approached her. "Hey, girl. Dominique, right? You auditioned the other day."

Dominique gave an easy smile. "Yes. Of course. I remember you. Ty's assistant, right?"

Venus forced a phony Hollywood smile. "Riiight. Good to see you again. How you doing?"

"I'm good."

"Listen, you think I could tear you away from Craig? Ty would like to see you in his office."

A sly smile spread across Dominique's face. "Sure. But I'd thought he'd be here?"

"He has a feed in his office. He'll be watching from there for the first half hour or so. He tends to do that. People are always sweating him when he comes over here earlier. You know how it is."

Dominique waved her hand. "Yeah, I understand."

"I'm going to have Rojas from security walk you over. Keep you from getting lost." Venus pointed toward the door where

Rojas stood with his belly poking out, wiping salt from his lips. "I'd give you a cart, but all the PAs are using them right now, it being tape night and all."

Dominique shrugged. "Walking is fine. It'll be a good work-out." She didn't so much as glance in Craig's direction when she turned and followed Rojas out of the green room.

Venus glanced at her watch, her temples pulsating from the music blaring from the gigantic stage speakers and the urgency to complete the tasks delegated by Ty. She raced to the ward-robe room and demanded a white shirt for Ty. The designer didn't bite his tongue when conveying he had enough damn people to dress for one night and directed her to a rack of clothing filled with shirts and sweaters. She fished through them perturbed he'd ignored her order. When she climbed the ranks and became a producer he could forget about a job on her show. She yanked a white button-down shirt from the rack, hoping it would fit. She clocked her time as she trotted toward their covert meeting place. Every task had been completed in less then ten minutes. Surely, Ty would be impressed.

Venus was at the backstage entrance when Ty tramped down the dimly lit staircase. She was still huffing and puffing from running his emergency errands when he reached her.

Ty inspected the white shirt in her hand. He wasn't going to put on just any old shirt, even under duress. "Did you talk to Rojas?" he calmly asked.

She nodded, trying to catch her breath. "I pointed Domi-nique out to him. He said not to worry. He'd take care of it."

"Good." Ty made a mental note to cast Rojas in a small part. He rapidly pulled the pistol from his jacket pocket, his eyes panning back and forth as he handed it to Venus, instructing her to place it in his office drawer immediately. "Make sure you lock it." She trembled at the sight of it, but Ty gripped her shivering hands and reminded her she would be rewarded. She nodded, the lump in her throat making her speechless. The confidence she had ten minutes ago had evaporated. With the heavy metal item in her bag weighing her down, she ran like the dickens back to the production offices, scared to death. Now she was working for the mob.

Ty changed his shirt, splashed some water on his face in the bathroom and went down to the stage floor. He could feel the weight of worry in his feet, his size-twelve loafers feeling fifty pounds each. Now he knew how Frankenstein must have felt in his gigantic boots. He smiled faintly at Sasha, who sat in the front row, trying and failing to give her an assuring look. Sasha pointed at her watch as if to say, "When are you going to get started?" He motioned his lips," "Soon." She mouthed, "You okay?" He lifted his chin and lightly nodded in response. Hell, no. He wasn't remotely close to okay. He nervously scanned the crowded audience for Dominique's mysterious green eyes. People milled about the stage floor as the music boomed from every direction. He folded his arms across his chest to restrain his pounding heart. A few of the writers approached him making small talk, but Ty couldn't focus on anything other than his own terrifying thoughts.

Leede stood backstage with the other cast members, getting a quick touch-up on his makeup. He was tingling from his fingertips down to his toes. The warm-up comedian began his introduction to the audience, making Leede sound like the king of television. "You've seen him on *Def Comedy Jam*. You've seen him on *Comedy Central*. And you can see him every week on your favorite hit show. Please welcome the star of *Same Day Service*, Leeeeeeede Baaaanks." Leede stepped onto the dry cleaners set and walked right up to the bleachers so the audience could get a good look at him. Lily had worked her magic in making him look brand new again with makeup. He savored the sound of skin slapping skin as he drowned in the thunder of clapping. The applause induced his high and gave him an indescribable, euphoric feeling. A feeling he thought he'd kill to keep. Each clap was praise and attention. Here, at center stage, he was whole.

When Leede hit the stage, Ty felt some of the heaviness magically lift from his feet. He slowly paced the front of the stage floor, testing his legs, his arms still folded across his chest. He waved and offered a fake smile to Gary, who stood on the side of the stage. Ty silently prayed the show would run smoothly and on schedule with no glitches, obstacles or murderous surprises. From time to time, shit happened during tapings. Two weeks ago Censorship had halted taping because Naja's nipples were protruding from her tight shirt. Wardrobe scrambled for twenty minutes, placing another layer of band-aids over them. On another night, a light hanging from the ceiling popped and blew out. It had taken the lighting crew a half hour to replace it. On another show he'd previously worked on, a damn pigeon had apparently flown through the stage doors when equipment was loaded onto the stage. Taping was held up for forty-five minutes while some guy climbed the rafters in pursuit of the cooing bird. Ty glanced over the shooting schedule as the first scene started. He wanted no mishaps tonight. *Please, not tonight.*

24

Bernie was standing at the top of the stairwell as Maxwell made his way toward him.

"There's weed all in the hall. I'm damn near high. I can't deal with this. There are fifty extras worrying me. I can feel my blood pressure going up. I can't be high."

"I got it, Bernie. Relax. I'll take care of Cell Block. You go on down and handle your extras." Maxwell pulled a stick of incense from his pocket.

Bernie wiped his forehead. "Okay. As long as you got it."

Maxwell lit the incense stick he'd lifted from the prop master. "I got it," Maxwell reassured him.

Bernie descended the staircase leading to the left side of the stage.

Maxwell eased down the dimly lit hallway toward Cell Block's dressing room, the incense in his hand leaving a trail of smoke behind him. He rapped on Cell's dressing room at the end of the hall. One of Cell's cronies held the door ajar as Maxwell stepped in and cased the scene. There were maybe six or seven people gathered in the room engaged in friendly banter. A couple of bottles of Alize lined the coffee table.

"Max. What's happening, man? Is it showtime already?" Cell asked with a smile on his face, a big brown joint between his fingers.

As Maxwell moved across the room, he caught a glimpse of Zack with his peripheral vision, sitting in the corner like he was a part of Cell's entourage. Maxwell wanted to rip Zack a new asshole right then and there, but he forced himself to focus on the task at hand.

"Nah, man. We've got a situation. I hate to kill the party but the weed has to go. The head of the network is coming to the show tonight and he'll have our asses if he finds any contraband."

"Five-O on the premises?"

"Something like that."

"Say no more. My bad," said Cell. He addressed one of his boys. "Black Mel, spray some air freshener up in this piece and open a window," Cell commanded.

"There are no windows, Block."

"Then make one," Cell teased.

"Nah, you don't have to do all that. Here's some incense. This should help," said Maxwell as he handed it to Black Mel.

"A'ight man. Whatever you think will work," said Cell.

"You ready? You feeling good about tonight?" asked Maxwell.

"Mos' def. I'm ready to do this," said Cell.

The acting coach had helped Cell Block memorize his lines

by orally reciting them and saving Cell Block from having to read a word. In the process, his confidence had been restored.

"Cool. I gotta get back to the set." He slapped palms with Cell. "I'll check you later."

Maxwell turned to leave and called out, "Yo, Zack. Make a move, man. We've got work to do."

Zack slowly rose from his seat. "Later, Cell." He nodded and made an exit, with Maxwell on his heels.

Zack had gotten two steps into the hallway when Maxwell started in on him. "I know you weren't in there getting high with Cell. I told you not to try and sell him nothing. So what were you doing in there?" Maxwell hissed.

Both men stood still, searching each other's eyes.

"I came here to deliver the food he ordered for dinner. I was doing my job."

"It damn sure didn't look like you were in there working."

"You're always riding me. Like I said, it was nothing. You're too paranoid."

"Don't worry about me. You just keep doing what I need you to do. Now, go down to the craft services table and get me some gum."

Zack frowned. "Get you some gum? You must be trippin'. Maybe you should go back to rehab." Zack's words cut through Maxwell like a knife.

"Are you threatening me? Huh? Is that what you call yourself doing?"

Zack lifted his eyebrows. "Take it however you want. Ain't nobody scared."

"I get you a job, put myself on the line so you can keep

your job and this is how you thank me. Next time I'll let Ty fire you. Who'll be assed out then?"

"You will," Zack retorted.

"Excuse me?"

"Stop acting like you did me such a huge favor. You saved your own ass."

"Is that what you think? Please."

"I got you pegged, Buddha. You've got everybody around here fooled, but not me."

"I don't have to take this from you. You're nothing but a PA. You're fired."

"And risk me blowing the whistle on your little habit? Oh, my bad. Your addiction."

"And I will fuck you up."

Zack turned his baseball cap backwards. "I'd like to see you try. No, I'd like to see you explain it to your boy, Ty. What are you going to tell him? Huh, Buddha?"

Maxwell just starred at Zack, the agony of defeat paralyzing him.

Zack twisted his lips. "Yeah, that's what I thought. So, you do whatever you need to do to get me into the guild, and your secret's safe with me, Buddha." Zack stomped off, leaving Maxwell in shock.

Whatever game Maxwell was playing, Zack had beat him at it. From now on Zack would make the rules and Maxwell would abide by them, at least for now.

Russ Tobin's face looked as though an artist had taken a number-two pencil and carefully drawn in his wrinkles, making his aging features look like a fine piece of art. His layered haircut fell across his square head like feathers, right down to his gray temples. For all the long hours of work, stress and ulcers, Russ still managed to look good for his age. Wearing a navy Baroni suit, a pastel-blue shirt and striped tie, Russ was "the suit" of all suits.

He appeared on the stage and approached Ty with a wide grin that matched his broad shoulders, greeting Ty as if they were old friends from college.

Ty straightened his back and tugged at his jacket before extending his right hand to Russ, a network god.

"Hey. How are you, Ty?"

Ty gave an easy smile. "I'm doing good. And you?"

"I'm well. The show has gotten off to a good start."

"So far, so good. I'm glad you dropped by."

"I'm sorry I haven't come by before now. It's just that my schedule has been full." Guilt required him to make an excuse for his absence. As the studio head, it was customary for Russ to visit the set of all the highly rated shows at Rex. However, politics usually got in the way and some shows were neglected.

"I understand," Ty said.

The audience roared and whistled in response to Cell Block's entrance onto the stage. "Looks like you hit the jackpot with this kid. The audience loves him." Russ nodded approvingly.

"Cell Block is the biggest name in hip-hop right now. With a few promos, we should have our highest rating this season." It would be several weeks before this episode aired, but Ty was optimistic. Or at least wanted Russ to think he was.

"I've been talking with Gary and David about the ratings."

Ty stiffened, "Oh, yeah."

"I don't think there is anything wrong with the show, but I'm not sure it's enough to compete in your time slot," Russ said.

Ty listened, bracing himself for bad news. If only his heart would stop pounding, then he could hear Russ more clearly.

Russ chewed on *Tums* as he spoke, nursing his ulcer. "I want to work with you on this. I know you don't care for the idea of adding a white character to the show, but I think we need to do something or *American Icon* will eventually steamroll us."

Ty nodded.

Russ paused as the actors completed another scene. He surveyed the stage, appraising the actors, the set, his money. He shoved his hands into his pants pockets. "You're doing a good job over here. And I want you to keep on doing it. But I'm going to change your time slot to another night. That's one reason I came by here tonight. I wanted you to hear it from me."

Ty nodded, displaying no emotion. "To what night?" There was certainty in Russ's voice. Ty knew he'd already decided precisely when.

"Wednesdays. You'll have a strong lead in behind *Two and a Half Men*."

Ty thought swiftly. "There is always the chance we'll lose our base audience. How soon will this happen?"

"Next week," Russ said. "And I'll give you all the promo needed to make a successful transition. We'll buy some advertising on other networks as well."

What could Ty say? Russ was god at Rex TV. As an employee he had no choice, no voice in the matter. It was damn better than a cancellation. Intuitively, Ty knew this would be his last opportunity to make *Same Day Service* work. If the ratings came in lower than expected for any reason, the show would be cancelled without hesitation, without notice and without a wrap party. This much he knew for sure. So he pushed for more. "How about two encore episodes for good measure?"

Russ shrugged. "Okay." What the hell? Russ gambled from his gut and gave Ty the benefit of Gary's doubt. Under Ty's guidance the show had been a huge hit before. Maybe it could be one again.

Ty remained on the stage floor long after Russ Tobin had left the building, his eyes systematically scanning for Dominique every so often. He followed the cast carefully as they read the script, making their marks and hitting every comedic beat. It was like watching a beautiful orchestra, every musician playing her instrumental part to perfection. But Ty couldn't rest until Naja and Cell Block had kissed. Cell had been in his room smoking pot, for God's sake. There was no guessing what else that knucklehead would do.

After almost two hours and six scenes, Ty stood catatonic as Cell Block leaned over and pecked Naja on the lips as if he were a professional actor. She smiled into the camera. Ty quickly stepped across the stage so she could see him, hoping there wouldn't be a second take. He had to make eye contact with her and know that the kiss was okay, that Cell Block had not made the same mistake twice and that Naja would not have reason to sue. He nervously rubbed his goatee as the actors replayed the scene for a second time. He held his breath, his nerves dancing as Cell Block planted another kiss on Naja's cherry lips. It was as if they were moving in slow motion. It was taking so long. Finally, the director screamed, "Cut."

Ty quickly maneuvered his way closer to the set, stepping over a million electrical wires zigzagging the floor. He gazed at her, his pupils begging her to make eye contact with him. Her eyes seemed to land on everyone but him. Then she looked in his general direction with a blank face. Her eyeballs roamed a few seconds before connecting with his. She paused, and winked. Relief swept through his body and the sense of feeling was restored to his legs as if miraculously healed by an evangelist. He shifted his weight from one leg to the other as if trying them on for the first time. He wanted to do nothing more than run up and down the bleachers, giving everyone in the aisle high fives like Arsenio Hall. Instead, he ran his palm over his bald head and exhaled, playing it cool as always.

Ty wouldn't, couldn't allow himself to celebrate his victory and savor this achievement. Sure, he had triumphantly prevailed over a few battles this week, but the war had yet to be won. There were still fourteen more episodes to go, and when the show aired in its new time slot next week, he'd be competing against the only other black show on a major network. He knew with all his heart both shows would not survive and another ratings war would begin.

Venus gazed into the crowd, studying the nameless faces as they endlessly applauded. The cast ran out to the stage one by one taking their bows as if it were the end of a Broadway show.

Venus walked from the side of the stage, maneuvering

around stage equipment, and approached Ty, who was reclining in a director's chair at the far left of center stage.

"Where is she? Is she gone?" Ty asked the moment Venus was near.

"Yeah. Rojas took care of the situation."

Ty glanced at Sasha, who was sitting in the bleachers, and smiled.

"I know, but did he have any problems? Did she put up a fight?" He needed some reassurance that Dominique, who'd appeared out of nowhere like a ghost, was gone. He didn't care what Daisy said, come next week Craig would also do a disappearing act.

"None," she lied. Damned if she knew. She hadn't seen Rojas since the show started.

Ty readjusted himself in the canvas chair, only half satisfied with her answer. "On Monday we can sit down and talk about your writing. I'm willing to give you a shot at a freelance script, but you'll have to work for it. I want you to pitch at least four or five ideas and hand in an outline for approval."

Venus started grinning. A freelance script would net her almost twenty thousand dollars, which was like hitting the lottery to her.

Ty remained stern. "You'll have to work like everyone else."

Venus continued to nod, smiling from ear to ear as Ty spoke to her in a condescending manner. She'd learned to pay his tone no mind, provided she wasn't PMS-ing. He was forever the boss, and she, the young apprentice. But she still liked him in spite of his faults and his flaws. She still wanted to play on his team, knowing she had a lot to learn from him.

"There's only one stipulation," Ty added.

Her heart paused. She should have known there would be some kind of trap. These Hollywood people made her ass ache day and night.

"I want you to write in a part for Rojas."

Her shoulders dropped. She exhaled. "Why I gotta write in the fat dude?"

"You want the script or not?"

She shrugged. "Yeah."

"This is only the beginning. If you're lucky enough to have a career in this business, you will be asked to write in a lot of people and characters you don't want to. Remember that."

Ty walked to the front of the stage where the cast lingered, giving out autographs, posing for photos and mingling with fans and friends. One by one he received them, saving the needy for last. He lifted Naja's fingers and kissed the back of her hand. "That was an outstanding performance. You are a true professional and I will always have your back."

She pursed her lips. It was bullshit if she'd ever heard any. "Thanks," she halfheartedly replied, still sour over her feud with Sid.

Ty smirked. "Thanks for the shout-out on Leno. You gave Russ Tobin good reason to make an appearance tonight."

"Did he say that?" she asked with her eyebrows arched.

"No. I said it because I don't believe in coincidences."

She smiled and he winked at her.

Ty pounded Cell Block's fist and they leaned inward, touching each other's shoulders. "Thanks for doing the show. I think you might have a future in acting." Cell half smiled. Ty normally extended an invitation, out of courtesy, to the guest cast to reappear on the show. But Cell Block would not be welcome to return if there was a reunion show twenty years from now.

Leede tried to suppress the emotion stuck in his throat by clenching his jaws as Ty moved toward him. Leede locked eyes with Ty and pounded his chest with his fist to symbolize the depth of his feelings. It was as close as Leede would ever come to saying, "I'm sorry and I love you." Ty readily translated this sign language created in the street, where young men didn't dare display an ounce of sappy emotions. Ty gave an easy smile, but did not return the gesture. True forgiveness was at least a month away. Leede didn't want to think about what would have happened had Russ come to the set and found the flashing red lights of an ambulance and police vehicles or what the headlines would have read in Monday's trades and LA times. So he skipped the subject.

"What did the big man want?" Leede asked.

"To give his blessings. He thought you were great. No new characters. Only a new night."

"A new night? You feelin' that?"

"Either I take the new night or they'll get a new show."

Leede chuckled. "You know you are their favorite producer."

Ty flashed his white teeth. Me or Maxwell, he thought. "Your flattery has never worked on me," Ty quipped. "I'll see you later." Ty waved him good-bye.

What Leede needed was an old-fashioned, head-spinning, green-gook-pouring-from-his-mouth exorcism to kill the demons running rampant in his head. Even a lobotomy might suffice. But Ty would settle for professional counseling. It would be an excruciating conversation to tell a star he was a lunatic and needed a shrink and possibly medication. Leede frowned at the mere mention of the word "late." If rumors somehow got out about him having a gun and using it, Leede's career could be severely hampered, setting him back years. As Ty went on a thought tangent about Leede, he spotted Gary standing in his pathway. If he mildly disliked Gary previously for his politics, he absolutely loathed him now for mentally tormenting an insecure actor. Yet it would profit him nothing to kick Gary's ass in the middle of Stage Six like he wanted to. So, Ty forced a smile and kept his stride.

"Good show," Gary said.

"Russ thought so too. I'll see you next week. Have a good weekend." Ty dismissed Gary and David from his life and his mind, if only until Monday.

Sasha walked onto the stage, carefully studying Ty as he approached her. The anxiety held captive in his eyes the previous night had been replaced with hope. "What's going on? I saw you talking to Russ Tobin. What did he say?"

"I've still got a show."

She smiled. "I knew that. You worry too much."

"Easy for you to say. But I do appreciate your vote of confidence."

"It was a good show. Leede was fired up. There were a group of junior high school kids behind us, screaming out his name every chance they got. They were giving me a headache."

"Have you forgotten your days as a groupie?"

Sasha tilted her head and placed her hand on her hips. "I beg your pardon. I was never a groupie."

They shared a good laugh for the first time in three days.

She ran her palm over his cheek. "You look beat. Why don't

you come home and let me take care of you. A hot bath and a massage will make you feel brand new."

He exhaled. "You have no idea how good that sounds."

"Perfect. I'll even give you a ride home in my new Benz."

"I have to pass on the ride, but I'll take a rain check."

"Oh, come on. I'll wait for you."

"No, you go ahead. I need to take care of something, but I'm right behind you. I swear."

He pecked her on the lips, unconcerned about the pinkish lip gloss that transferred onto his.

"Okay," she reluctantly agreed. "But you'd better not be too long. You owe me some makeup sex." She winked at him. "Just me and you."

25

Ty entered the glass doors of the production building and jogged up the steps to his office. His footsteps echoed through the hollow building. It was a little after 9 P.M. and everyone had left to have drinks at Pinot's on Sunset Boulevard. Tonight he would savor the quiet solitude of his office.

He sat behind his desk and opened the top left desk drawer and gazed at the revolver. Only two hours had passed since Leede had acted like a gangster, but the emotions attached still lingered. His hands a bit shaky, his heart rate slightly higher than it should have been.

He went to his credenza, which doubled as a mini bar. On the bottom shelf was a bottle of Dom Perignon one of the writers had given him at the beginning of the season, bottles of Grey Goose vodka, Grand Marnier, Hennessy, and several glasses. Ty poured himself a shot of Hennessy and gulped it down in one swallow. As he poured a second helping he heard footsteps approaching. When he glanced up, he saw Maxwell's silhouette in the doorway.

"What's up?" Maxwell said.

Ty turned his attention back to his drink, holding his head back and gulping it down as quickly as he'd done the first.

Maxwell took this as a positive motion and sat down. With the bottle in one hand and his shot glass in the other, Ty took a seat across from him. He placed the bottle and a miniature glass on the table within Maxwell's reach. Maxwell examined the bottle, uncertain if the gesture was an invitation or a dare. He decided to ignore the bottle and the hefty energy that saturated the room. "I thought the show turned out well. Even Cell pulled through like a champ. The audience was digging the shit out of him. And I think the weed helped him relax."

"Yeah, I was checking that," Ty replied.

"He might have been worth the trouble."

"The ratings will determine whether he was worth it. But that stunt with Naja was a close call."

"Yeah, I guess so. I was surprised to see Russ Tobin. Did you know he was coming through?"

"Twenty minutes before he got here I did."

"They are sneaky bastards. I don't know if I trust the suits anymore." Maxwell was beginning to realize the suits would treat him no differently than they'd treated Ty.

"I never did."

"You never trust white people."

Ty looked Maxwell in the eye. "With the exception of about four people, I don't trust *anyone*. And that number is dwindling by the hour."

"So what did Russ say? Is he trying to force the white character on us?"

"Nah. No new characters."

"He came up here to say that?"

Ty propped his legs across the coffee table. Mentally and physically exhausted, he sighed. "Wednesday night. The show is being switched to a new night."

"That's the same night *The Bernie Mac Show* comes on."

"I'm hip." Ty ran the palm of his hand over his face. "Look, man. I'm tired. The suits have given me hell all week. Cell Block, Naja and Leede didn't spare me either. I'm all wiped out. So, you got something to say? Spit it out."

Maxwell picked up the bottle, poured a shot and swallowed it, thinking about what he *really* wanted. Forgiveness and a clear conscious, he thought, as he leaned back in his chair. "A truce. I want to go in peace with no animosity between us. I did what I had to do for me and I meant no harm to you. Believe that."

"Sounds like you're leaving?" Ty asked.

"I know how you roll. Isn't that how it goes down?"

"If you leave, it's on you. You're the one with all the big plans for yourself."

"You're not going to fire me?"

"Not unless you know something I don't. As far as I know you've been doing your job and I don't have reason to." In retrospect, Maxwell's betrayal was a petty crime and paled in comparison to the assault and attempted murder Leede had committed. He couldn't give Maxwell a life sentence and allow Leede to go free.

Besides, the suits would be all over him if he cut Maxwell loose in the middle of the season, since they'd still have to pay out his contract. Nor could Ty give them the tiniest notion that their petty antics had worked in dissembling his staff.

Ty continued. "I'm not mad at you over your meeting. Like you said, you had to do what you had to do for yourself. And as long as you are working on this show, I expect you to stay focused on what you have to do here. If your deal interrupts with what's going on here, then we'll have to talk about your leaving. There aren't many black people in this game to begin with. So, I don't think we can afford to fight amongst ourselves."

Ty gazed at Maxwell. Outwardly Maxwell resembled the same young man who'd worked by his side as a PA, making copies and coffee, delivering scripts and lunch. But Ty realized inwardly they'd changed as gradually as fall leaves turned from red to orange and then gold. They'd turned into the power-hungry, ego-driven, credit-taking, self-serving individuals they had vowed to never be, and their friendship would never be what it had been in the past.

Maxwell stood up and held out his fist toward Ty and Ty gave him a pound. "You've got yourself a deal. Man, we've come a long way and we've done a lot of miles together."

Ty smirked. "That's right, motherfucker. And I've put up with all your shit. You should give me a damn plaque or something."

Maxwell laughed. "Yeah, whatever. Are you going to Pinot's?"

"Nah, man. Not tonight. I'm going home to my woman."

"That's a good idea. You should rest up, take it easy, 'cause I'm shooting hoops on Sunday morning and I plan on kicking some ass."

Ty smiled. "Look, Tin Man. You better go see the Wizard of Oz and get some oil for them rusty knees of yours. I don't want to hear your bones crackin' while you're checking me."

"Don't worry about my bones. You just make sure your raggedy game is on point. White men ain't the only ones who can't jump."

"When you've got a three pointer like mine, you don't have to jump. Ask Larry Bird."

Maxwell headed toward the door. "We'll see what happens on Sunday. We're going to take this to the court and put an end to all this talking." He looked back at Ty, who was smiling, his feet still propped up on the coffee table. "If I get a green light on my deal, I'll be looking to you for advice."

Ty nodded. "After this week, I could write a book."

"I know that's right," Maxwell replied before walking out of the room.

Ty backed his truck out of his parking space and drove toward the gate, coasting at fifteen miles per hour, the speed limit he often violated. Tonight he had the good sense to take it slow since he'd had a drink and was carrying a weapon, registered in someone else's name, in his glove compartment. The sky was dark and the security booth was lit up with a guard on duty inside, the only sign of life on the deserted lot. The guard waved as Ty drove through the gate. As he was pulling off the lot, about to enter Barham Boulevard, he caught sight of a pedestrian in his headlights. Rojas tramped on the sidewalk, his slew feet pointing east and west at once. He carried a duffle bag with the Rex logo and wore his plain clothes.

Ty stopped and rolled down the passenger window. "You need a ride?"

"Hey, Ty. What's up man? Nah. I'm just picking up my car. You know they make us park in structure H, all the way around the corner."

The electronic door locks thumped. "Get in. I'll drop you off."

Rojas opened the door and hurled his massive body up and into the gray Range Rover. He twisted his butt into the seat and surveyed the dashboard. "This shit is *nice*." He glided the palm of his hand over the plush leather upholstery like he was feeling a woman's ass. "This feels like butter. What is this, Coach? Kenneth Cole?"

Ty chuckled, nodding his head as he pulled off. "I don't know, man." He paused. "I'm going to have you come in and read for a part."

"Really?"

"Yeah. You earned it. Thanks for taking care of my friend."

"Maaan, she was fine. The last thing I wanted her to do was leave my sight. It hurt me to get rid of her. I swear it did."

"Was she mad?" Ty asked with a guilty grin.

"Hell, yeah. She was pissed. I thought I was going to have to call for backup."

"For real?"

"Sort of. She was threatening to sue and then she refused to move. She kept asking why she was being put off the lot."

Ty drove slowly, listening like a hawk. "What did you say?"

"I didn't have to explain that to her. I saw it in her eyes and in the way she talked. She knew exactly why she was being asked to leave. I told her to tell me the answer to that question." Rojas hung his elbow out of the window as he spoke. "She eventually calmed down and we started talking about acting. Russ Tobin was leaving about this time. Once she saw him, that was all she wrote. She recognized him like that." Rojas snapped his fingers. "She didn't see me after that. Like my big ass was invisible. As I headed back to the stage, I turned around and she was walking with him, running game I suppose. He was listening to whatever she was saying."

"Russ Tobin?" Ty tried to picture Dominique under Russ Tobin's glass top desk, giving him a blow job.

"Yeah, man. The president. Can you believe that?"

Ty shrugged as he pulled over to the curb in front of the parking garage. "She's in the right place. Hollywood is the home of big dreamers."

After Rojas rolled out of the car, Ty drove off into the night feeling as heroic as a crime crusader who'd overthrown evil. He'd put out fires, negotiated with a gangster, dodged a bullet, saved his relationship and his show. Had his life been a movie, this is where the credits would roll. Him cruising in his midnight-blue SUV, the city lights sparkling like stars in the background and the title soundtrack playing as names and titles in fancy letters scrolled across the big screen. But his life was not a film and the season wasn't even close to an end. There were fourteen episodes left to tape and edit, about sixteen-plus more weeks to deal with the suits, ninety-eight more days to contend with the egos of Naja and Leede and who knows, maybe a couple of more hours of Dominique.

Every production week presented its own expected and unexpected dramas, challenges and mishaps. Who knew if Leede would act a fool again next week? Or what Naja would complain about next? The only thing Ty knew for sure was that the change in schedule would present his biggest challenge, his greatest worry. Starting Wednesday, *Same Day Service* would be up against the only other black show on a major network. This was just another evil plot, pitting one black show against another, knowing only one would own the night, only one would be allowed to stay on the air. At least that's how he saw it. Perhaps the ratings would drop on both shows due to a split audience and both would be cancelled. Either way, it would be a rate-high-or-die situation and once again, he'd be at risk of losing his show.

He'd spend very little time savoring this week's victory before plotting and planning his next strategic move to keep his show up and running, to ensure he'd win the Wednesday night crowd. As much as he would have liked for Gary and David to magically disappear from his life as they would in a film, they'd report to the Monday morning table read just as he would. They'd have new ammunition, and his battle with the network would pick up where it had left off this evening. Because, unlike in the movies, real-life wars are seldom won in seven days and issues are rarely resolved within ninety minutes. Ty's life, his dramas and *Same Day Service* were all to be continued.